The Ma

THE
SECRETS
OF
SAINT JOANNA

Steven Knapp

The Secrets of St. Joanna
The Mason Wright Series Book 2

Copyright 2020 by Steven Knapp
ISBN: 978-0-9994623-9-3

All rights reserved
Printed in the United States of America

No part of this book may be used or reproduced in any manner whatsoever without the written permission of the author except in the case of brief quotations embodied in critical articles and reviews.

This is a work of fiction. Names, characters, places, and incidents are either a product of the author's imagination or are used fictitiously. Any resemblance to actual events, or persons or locales, living or dead, is purely coincidental.

Published by
Can't Put It Down Books
An imprint of
Open Door Publications

www.CantPutItDownBooks.com
Cover Design by Eric Labacz
www.labaczdesign.com

Back cover photo and author photo by Lori Chapin

For:
The Men and Women who Refused to Bow to Tyranny and
Rose up to Resist.

"The only thing necessary for evil to triumph is for good men
to do nothing"

1
London, England
September 1940

BLOOD. THERE WAS A LOT OF BLOOD, some dried to a dark, reddish-brown tone, some still wet on the man's chest, dripping from the cotton sheets to the floor.

How could this happen, the detective thought to himself as he quietly stared at the body of his friend. He walked slowly around the room, his footsteps creaking on the old English floorboards. The slightly overweight, middle-aged man lying on the bed in the second-floor bedroom was naked, with a sheet covering the lower half of his body. A large gash across his neck was barely visible through all the blood. This man had died a violent death, with his throat slashed, his face bruised; this crime scene was not for the faint of heart. If the police assembled outside had quietly wondered to themselves if this was a random killing, a crime of passion, or something worse, they got their answer when an investigator from the constable's office pulled up and ordered everyone out of the house. Killings like these were not an everyday occurrence in London, especially during wartime.

The investigator was interrupted by Constable Bradley leaning in at the door. "Excuse me, sir. We checked with the neighbors," he said as he looked quickly at his notes. "A Mrs. Cartwright saw a man and a woman leave the house yesterday; the man was possibly a chimney sweep. She did not know about the woman. Both in their early- to mid-forties. A black truck with the label 'Thompson Chimney Sweeps' was parked here. She said the house is normally empty so, with all the activity, she became concerned and called our office. That is all I could get. We are currently working on a more detailed description. She did say the woman was quite glamorous, looking a bit like a movie star."

The investigator looked toward the doorway and nodded. "Well done, thank you," he replied. "Get me that description right away and thank Mrs. Cartwright."

Frank Sullivan, known to most as Sully, was a Special Assistant to the Constable Office of North London. He was only called in for Special Circumstance crimes with Wartime Security ramifications. The term Special Assistant encompassed a wide variety of duties. He ultimately reported to Winston Churchill, so his presence in the upstairs bedroom told everyone at the scene that this was something more than a random killing.

As Sully stared at the bed, he noticed something clasped in his friend's left hand. He leaned in and pried open his fingers. They cracked, as rigor mortis had begun setting in. He pulled out a crumpled piece of ripped, bloody, white paper. He unfolded it slowly, revealing the word *Totenkopf.* Under the word was a symbol of a skull with blood dripping from its mouth.

The investigator looked up from the note to the doorway, where Constable Bradley had remained, watching the scene. "What's your name, son?"

"Bradley, sir."

"What's your first name?"

"Charles, sir. The boys call me Charlie."

"Charlie, has anyone else been in this room?"

"No. We arrived fifteen minutes before you, secured the house, and then received the call to stop everything and wait for your arrival." Bradley paused. "May I ask why all the secrecy?"

"No, you may not," Sully replied without hesitation. "What you can do is clear the house and set up a perimeter outside and down the block. We need to secure this area immediately. No one comes in or out without my knowing about it, including Mrs. Cartwright."

"I only have access to a few men," Bradley replied unsteadily. "We are short because of the war effort. I will call in every available man, but it will take some time."

"I will make a call," Sully told Bradley without looking at him. "This man was a good friend of mine. Word of his condition does not leave this room. Understood?"

"Yes, sir."

"Now, go secure the area. I want to be left alone in here."

"Yes, sir, right away." Bradley turned and left the room. He gathered the other men in the hallway and disappeared down the steps, their heavy boots shuffling against the wood floor.

Sully stared at the note and then at the body. He had seen a few crimes like this. They often were perpetrated on women, usually prostitutes. To see a man beaten, his throat slashed, was rare, even in the worst neighborhoods in London. However, the nature of the crime was not the reason Sully was standing in the second-floor bedroom of 16B Hogsmeade Road. This address was a safehouse for the War Offices of Britain, and when word came through of a discovered body, the address immediately sparked a call to the man currently standing there. When Sully had entered the bedroom, he'd quickly recognized the body on the bed as John Cleary, one of his best men. Sully stood looking at Cleary, knowing his murder was not random because of the work they both did.

Sully was an American living in Britain. His parents had emigrated to America from Wales at the turn of the century. His father had served in the American intelligence office during World War I and established a reputation as a reliable information man, eventually joining the intelligence community.

Sully followed in his father's footsteps, relocating to London after World War I to join a special branch of service as a liaison to Britain. His reputation had earned him several promotions and his connections to the American government made him invaluable in these times. His service took him all over Europe, but he had settled in Britain when Adolf Hitler came to power. He worked in collaboration with the French and British governments to track the expansion of the German military over the years, as Germany had begun rebuilding its military might in March of 1935, in violation of the Treaty of Versailles. Sully's job was to track the movements of German military commanders, dignitaries, ambassadors, and spies. Still, Sully's pleas to both governments to crack down on Germany's expansion fell on deaf ears. Europe had let its guard down as Germany expanded, and now, most of western Europe was infiltrated with German agents posing as tourists. Many of them simply disappeared after arriving in Britain, and it fell on Sully to track and monitor them. He spent most of his time between London and Paris, the most fertile locations for German spies.

Sully had several contacts in both cities reporting to him about the movements of German agents under their surveillance. One of his best contacts had gone dark, and Sully had not heard from him in a few days. He was one of his most trusted men, cautious and brilliant at his job. Now, Sully realized why, as Cleary lay slain on the bed in front of him, covered in blood and holding a note with an indecipherable word and a picture of a skull. The note was a calling card left on purpose, stuffed into Cleary's dead left hand. Sully knew well enough to know this was an assassination; Cleary had been killed for what he knew.

Sully left the room and went to the other bedroom. He opened the closet door and began pulling things out. He moved several boxes and stacked them behind him against the wall. He removed some clothing and the shoe rack at the bottom of the closet, placed them next to the boxes, then grabbed the shelf with his right hand and banged underneath with the palm of his left. The shelf popped loose, exposing a gap in the paneling of the back wall. He tossed the shelf aside, placed his fingers in the opening, pulled the wooden paneling forward, and removed it from the closet.

He had known Cleary for some time, and therefore, most of his secrets. In this business, you needed a place where things could be stored out of the public eye. This safe house had a false back in the closet in the guest room upstairs, used to store and drop information. Inside was a small radio and two boxes, one marked "Foreign," the other, "Domestic." He opened the box marked "Domestic" and flipped through the names of his agents one by one. The files contained paperwork on each agent and a history of their work. Copies of most of these documents were kept in the safe in his office, but these secondary copies were stored as backup and updated once a month. If Cleary had other notes, they might be in here.

He pulled out the file marked "Cleary," stood up, walked over, and placed it on the bed. He opened it and started to quickly read the pages, looking for any mention of *Totenkopf.* Cleary had been surveilling several people, but which had gotten him killed? Sully continued reading the file, finding no mention of the word. As he reached the end, however, he found a few pages of handwritten notes. This was what he was looking for. At the top of the page, the word *"Totenkopf?"* was circled in red ink. Under that were some notes: *"Hashshashin,"* "Ancient order?" "Modern version?" "occult." At the bottom of the page was an address: 24 Holston Road. Underneath that, a name: "Mason Wright?"

Keeping the handwritten notes, Sully put the rest of the files in the covered box and placed it back in the wall. He popped the paneling back in place and returned the closet to its original state. The address on the paper would be his next move.

He closed his eyes for a second and slowly shook his head. Opening his eyes, he walked toward the entrance of the room and began down the steps. He stopped at the front door, yelling, "I need a map of London!"

A few men outside looked at each other before Bradley spoke up. "I believe I have one in my glovebox."

Moments later, Bradley was driving Sully in a 1938 Wolseley Series III police car across London toward Holston Road. As they drove through central London, several streets were blocked off due to debris from German bombings. The raids had become a nightly occurrence for nearly two weeks now, and the British people, though scared, regarded it as a new part of their daily life. Police and ordinary citizens would band together to search through the rubble and coordinate cleanup after the bombs fell. Fires raged across London at night, and the brigades were stretched so thin that they welcomed the extra help. Many of the more seasoned brigades' men had been called away to the war effort, so it was not uncommon to find women and children on the fire line.

Bradley turned the police car onto Oxford Street only three kilometers from Holston Road. Sully looked out the window at Londoners going about their daily routine. Parts of the city looked like peacetime rather than wartime. He enjoyed living in London and admired the British resiliency with the Third Reich knocking on their door. They still managed afternoon tea and a somewhat normal routine while constantly surrounded by talk of the war. Plus, the nightly bombings were terrifying. The sirens would wail while most Londoners gathered their families in the safety of The Underground, the city's subway system.

Bradley turned onto Holston Road and parked near the entrance to the street. They sat for a minute as Sully surveyed the area.

"What is it, sir?" Bradley said, breaking the silence.

"Not sure; an uneasy feeling," Sully said as he looked around. He reached down to his ankle and pulled a small caliber pistol from its holster.

"You better take this," he said, handing it to Bradley.

"I am not allowed to carry that, sir."

"You are today," Sully replied as Bradley took the weapon. "Only use it if you have to. Don't shoot yourself and definitely don't shoot me."

Policemen in London did not carry weapons, but Sully had received special permission to carry a gun. He would not do his job without one. For now, he kept his weapon holstered, but he was a quick draw if needed. He trusted Bradley would do the same.

Sully and Bradley walked slowly up Holston Road and carefully scanned the area, eventually arriving at the column marked 24. The two-story flat was non-descript; red brick, old and chipped, blended in with the rest of the block. There were no signs of disturbance and all the windows were obscured by curtains. As the two men waited at the entrance to the property, they noticed a man walking down the other side of the street with a case in hand. Sully walked toward him. "Excuse me," he said.

"Yes?" The man spoke warmly in a thick, British accent.

"Do you know who lives across the street in number 24?" Sully motioned to the flat across the way.

"I don't think anyone does," the man replied. "An older woman lived there a while, but she passed several years ago. She had a son, but I have not seen him around. Is there something I can help you with?"

"No, thank you," Sully replied. "I am from the Wartime Real Estate Office and we are trying to account for the number of civilians still in London. We were told there was someone living here, but I guess we were misinformed. Happens all the time, thank you, sir."

The man watched for a moment as Sully walked back across the street toward number 24.

Upon arrival, Bradley pointed Sully's attention to a black truck parked across the street at the other end of the block. Sully crossed again and approached it. "Thompson Chimney Sweeps" was written on the side, and it was empty and unlocked. Sully opened the side door and looked inside: nothing. He briefly checked the truck bed: empty.

He walked quickly back to number 24 and started down the path to the front door, Bradley following close behind. When Sully stepped on a stick, cracking it in half, Bradley nearly had a heart attack. Then, when they reached the front door, Sully checked for any wires; he was most worried about a bomb in the house. He took every precaution, as he did not plan on blowing up today. Satisfied there were no booby traps, he knocked loudly on the door and looked over at Bradley as silence emanated from the house. A visibly nervous Bradley tried his best to appear calm.

"Exciting, isn't it?" Sully said with a slight grin.

"Yes, sir," Bradley responded with a less than convincing nod. "What do you expect to find?'

"I don't know, but let's find out."

Sully reached for the front doorknob and turned it. The knob clicked, and as he glanced at Bradley with a slight look of surprise, he removed his pistol and slowly opened the door to look in. The house was empty, musty, and dirty. It looked and smelled as if no one had been there in a long time. He pushed the door open until it bumped against the wall and stepped inside, followed closely by Bradley.

The smell of "old" dominated the room, as the windows in this place had not been opened for a long time. The carpet was filthy, the curtains were dusty, and the plaster had cracked and faded.

"I guess the cleaning service was off this week," Sully said as he scanned the room.

"I don't think there ever was a cleaning service," Bradley said seriously, eliciting a slight nod and grin from Sully.

"Let's search the first floor, carefully," Sully said.

Bradley nodded and headed for the hallway to the left, holding his pistol. Sully moved straight ahead into the dining area, where an old glass light hung in the center of the room. He ducked around it and reached the kitchen, where he wiped his finger across the counter, picking up a thick layer of dust. Looking out the back door, he could see overgrown grass and an old, rusted bike leaning against the shed. He opened the kitchen cabinet above the sink, but the door hinge broke, leaving the cabinet door hanging awkwardly. Sully opened the other cabinets to find a few plates and a lone teacup.

Bradley entered the kitchen as Sully turned around. "Nothing. Completely empty," Bradley said.

Sully nodded. "Same here, it seems. Let's try upstairs." Sully glanced around the room, a look of curiosity on his face. Though there was nothing in the house, he did not like this feeling. He felt he was being watched, even though no one was there.

Bradley again followed Sully as they walked upstairs to the landing. A large crack in the plaster moved unevenly up the wall. A few pieces fell onto the stairs as Sully ran his fingers across it. They reached the first bedroom and stopped at the entrance for a moment. Bradley entered, walked around the small room, and came back to the doorway, shaking his head. "Nothing," he said as he looked at Sully.

They walked together toward the end of the hallway, where Sully walked inside the master bedroom. There was a small wooden box in the middle of the floor. He knelt to inspect it, admiring the old wood, and noticed two small hinges on its back. Some inlaid wood on the top was obscured by a layer of dust. It looked like an old jewelry box. Feeling somewhat certain it was safe, Sully picked it up and wiped the dust off the top, exposing an inlaid symbol of a skull dripping blood. Still crouched down, Sully opened the box and removed a folded piece of paper. He placed the box back on the floor and unfolded it. Written in the same text as the bloody paper from the other location, he recognized the calling card: *Totenkopf.*

Sully looked up at Bradley. "We need to get out of here, immediately," he said as he grabbed the box. Suddenly, the sound of glass shattering enveloped the room as a bullet raced right over Sully's head. He hit the ground, but a second bullet struck Bradley in the arm as he dove on the floor. Sully crawled over to the shattered window, cutting his hands on shards of glass, as Bradley rolled over and propped himself against a stone wall out of view. Sully glanced out the corner of the window and noticed a person on the terra cotta roof across the street packing up a rifle. He recognized him as the man he had just spoken to on the street.

"You okay?" Sully yelled to Bradley.

"I don't know, sir; I've never been shot," Bradley replied as he put pressure on the wound with his left hand.

Sully crawled over to him for a look. "You'll be fine. Just keep pressure on it."

Bradley watched as Sully darted from the room. He ran

down the hallway, down the stairs, and out the front door. He raced across the street and kicked in the door to the flat. The door jamb splintered with the force of Sully's boot as the door slammed against the wall, revealing a sparsely furnished flat.

Sully ran inside and up the stairs to the second floor, weapon drawn. The door to the attic stairs was open, so, after a quick glance, Sully climbed up and walked across the empty attic to an open window providing access to the roof. He stepped outside to see the gunman running across the adjoining roof, carrying a black leather case. Sully ran across the roof, stumbling on the uneven tiles. He fired a shot but missed as the gunman stumbled. Regaining his balance, the gunman ran toward the edge of the roof, tossed his case over the edge, and jumped. Sully fired again as the man disappeared over the roofline, his bullet ricocheting off and shattering the ceramic roof tiles in every direction.

Sully slowed down as he approached the end of the roof. Not knowing what was over the edge, he lay on his stomach and inched his way up to look over. When he raised his head, the tile in front of him exploded into pieces as a bullet blew it apart. Sully rolled over and grabbed his face. The jagged pieces of terra cotta had cut the skin under his right eye. Squinting, he wiped some blood from his face. "Dammit," he huffed, blindly firing two shots over the edge. The gunman had jumped onto a lower roof and was perched with his rifle aimed directly at Sully.

Sully rolled over and thought for a moment as he caught his breath. He exhaled and grabbed a piece of roof tile. Moving it side to side, he dislodged it and slid down the roof a bit to another spot farther down. He cocked his pistol, threw the tile far over the edge from where he was lying, and waited for the impact. The tile hit the lower roof and broke apart with the sound of several plates hitting a kitchen floor. Sully looked over the edge; the distraction had given him the opportunity he had hoped for. The gunman glanced over at the area where the tile exploded, so Sully fired two shots, one hitting the cement wall behind, the other striking the gunman. He fell over onto his back and grabbed his right side, clearly wincing. He tried to raise his rifle, but Sully fired first, striking the man in the chest. He crumpled over as blood pooled and ran down the roof tiles.

Sully jumped down and kicked the rifle away. He leaned over the bleeding gunman, now barely hanging on. Sully applied pressure to the wound; he did not want the man to die. He wanted to question him, but the blood was pooling everywhere. The man began to choke as saliva and blood began gathering at his mouth, his chest convulsing. The man briefly opened his eyes and, with a bloody smile, bit down on something with his teeth. Sully shook the man and yelled, "No! Dammit!"

He knew there was no use; he had seen this happen before. The man had broken the pill in his mouth to poison himself, rendering him brain dead within a few seconds. Sully had been briefed on these pills, which were sometimes obscured as false teeth.

He let go of the gunman and rolled over onto his back. His face and hands were bleeding and his knee hurt after jumping from rooftop to rooftop. The man lay motionless next to him, his eyes still open as saliva bubbled around his mouth and pooled down, mixing with blood on his chest. Pushing himself up, Sully stood over the body. He had to go check on Bradley.

After climbing back through the window, Sully found that Bradley had made his way downstairs, still bleeding, but in decent shape. Bradley had crossed the street and used the call box to phone for medical help; they were on their way.

The medical team arrived with a few more officers, who quickly cordoned off the house. This was clearly an ambush; they had been lured here by the notes in John Cleary's file. Neighbors reported a man and a woman at the previous address, but Sully had only encountered the man; the woman was still out there. He grabbed a few officers to help him continue searching the place while Bradley tended to his wound. They spread out and began rifling through drawers, under furniture, and under cushions.

Sully went back upstairs to search the bedrooms. The first bedroom had barely anything in it. He opened the closet to find a few pieces of clothing. Tossing them aside, he checked the walls and shelving for any abnormalities: nothing. He then ventured back up to the attic to find some old trunks filled with clothes and empty boxes.

Sully was startled by a voice from downstairs, belonging to one of the medical professionals. He summoned them upstairs to the attic. They wanted to collect the body from the roof, but Sully wanted the body brought to the living room so he could thoroughly examined it. They nodded in agreement as two men with a folding cloth stretcher carefully climbed out the window.

Convinced the attic was clear, Sully returned to the living room to join the other men; no one had found anything substantial. Bradley was to be taken to the hospital to have the bullet removed. Sully thanked him for his bravery and assured him they would figure this out.

"I'm sorry, sir, for getting shot," Bradley said.

Sully smiled slightly. "You did great, Charlie. Hopefully this will be the only time."

After Bradley left, Sully went through the kitchen, stopping at a latched door. He unlocked the latch and slowly opened it. A light switch on the wall to the right was barely visible in the dark, but the first thing he noticed was a staircase leading straight down and a stench wafting up from below.

Sully fetched a flashlight from one of the others and headed down to the basement. He removed a handkerchief and covered his nose as he reached the bottom. The light flickered as he turned to see a body tied to a wooden chair. The man was dead and beginning to rot, flies circling his corpse. The man was in his late-fifties, Sully guessed, and probably the homeowner. He had been killed by a single shot to the head, execution style. The man's head hung down as his chin rested on his chest. There was nothing else in the basement. Sully wondered what he had stumbled upon or, more accurately, what he had been lured to. A voice above called him, so Sully turned and quickly jogged up the stairs.

The body from the roof had been delivered to the living room and was lying on the stretcher on the floor. The rifle was next to the body along with its case. Sully crouched down and asked the medical personnel for a rag. He lifted the blood-soaked jacket lapel of the man and reached into his breast pocket, searching for anything that would identify him. Coming up empty, he felt around the man's pant pockets: nothing. He rolled the body over and checked for back pockets, or something in his waistband: still nothing. He told the medical personnel that they could take the body to the morgue and informed them of the second one in the basement. He ordered two officers to accompany the bodies.

"Do not stop for anyone," Sully told them. "If anyone asks, use my name. This is a wartime security issue and needs to be kept quiet." The men agreed as they removed the body and left.

Sully returned to the middle of the room and picked up the rifle. Familiar with all types of weapons, he recognized it right away as a Mauser Carbine 98, the standard-issue weapon of the German infantry. This model had been modified with a silencer and was easily dismantled to fit in the case. With a range of up to four hundred yards, Sully was lucky to be alive. He wondered how a German agent was running around London with this weapon without anyone having any idea. Sully also believed this was far from over; John Cleary was on to something, and he needed to find out what.

Sully put down the rifle and moved on to the case lying next to it. He popped the two latches to find a small booklet emblazoned with a skull on the cover. Sully picked it up, pulled off the elastic strap wrapped around, and opened it. There were several pages of notes and diagrams. He thumbed through the pages, eventually arriving at one page containing a list of names. "LONDON" was written above them. He recognized just three.

The name at the top with a line through it was John

Cleary's; the next name on the list was his. Though it had been close, no line would be drawn through "Frank Sullivan" yet. Sully assumed this was a list of people to be eliminated, but the only other name he recognized was one he had only seen twice. Two crime scenes, two murders, *Totenkopf,* and a familiar name; that's all Sully had to work from. Then he wondered to himself: *Who the hell is Mason Wright?*

2

MASON WRIGHT SAT AND WATCHED intently as Collette Moulié thumbed through recently intercepted documents detailing the ouster and imprisonment of thousands of German Jews. He would have helped, but Collette was adamant that she did not need him to. Mason knew not to argue. With everything Collette had been through lately, Mason understood why she alone would want to oversee the documents.

Mason had been in France just a few months prior, helping to smuggle out one of the world's greatest art treasures to the United States for safe keeping. He'd nearly lost his life, but it had been worth it for many reasons, including the woman now sitting across from him. Collette was the daughter of Jacques Moulié, a prominent figure in the French art world. Jacques had asked Mason, the son of his old friend Aldon Wright, to help him remove many of France's most valuable art treasures from various museums to safer locations before the German army arrived.

While Mason worked to help her father, Collette discovered and took in a 13-year-old German Jewish immigrant, Anna Dressler, who had been living on her own. Anna's family had sent her to France before the occupation to save her from being rounded up in her hometown of Saarbruken.

Then, without warning, Collette was taken by a German Lieutenant named Johan Kliest. After being forced to play cat-and-mouse with the man, Mason was able to find and rescue Collette, even though Kliest got away. Mason thought about Kliest every day, vowing one day to get revenge.

Mason, Anna, Collette and her parents then relocated to London to help in the war effort. Jacques, having been asked by the art minister of London to consult on the safety of London's art treasures, was put up with his family and friends in a flat near the center of London. Jacques believed in the preservation of paintings and sculpture for public consumption, but with war engulfing all of Europe, he was quickly becoming an expert in hiding them.

Meanwhile, every time new documents regarding Jewish immigrants arrived in London, Collette searched them for any trace of Anna's family. Collette had promised Anna to do everything in her power to locate them.

German Jews were disappearing by the thousands, with some sent to hard labor camps and others imprisoned or shot for their religious affiliation. If Collette could find where Anna's family had been taken, maybe she could find a way to reunite them. Collette knew this was a long shot, but she would do everything she could.

The newest documents had only been delivered to the London War Offices in the last few days. When Mason was informed of the new batch, he and Collette immediately responded.

"Would you like some water?" Mason asked as he glanced at Collette.

"No," she said without looking up.

"I am going to get some water," he said, standing up.

Collette gave him a slight wave of her hand, shooing him away. Mason stood motionless for a second before walking to the door of the old wooden office. When Collette was this focused, he could dance around in the nude without her noticing. Even if he were to tell her he was going to jump out the window, she would have given him the same wave. She was determined, and he loved that about her.

"Oh, look, a whole garrison of German soldiers are coming down the hallway; we better run," Mason said playfully as he looked outside the office.

Collette looked up at him with her eyebrows raised. "Please leave," she said.

Mason chuckled and left the room, closing the door as quietly as an old wooden door could be. He then walked down the hall to a small table draped with a lace tablecloth; some teacups, a ceramic teapot, and a glass pitcher were arranged on top. Mason grabbed a small cup and filled it with water. He had special clearance to be in the War Offices due to his recent endeavors in France. With Jacques' help and some phone calls from Paul Ganoux, a police officer who had helped him escape France, Mason was now allowed in these hallways.

Men and women passed busily by, as phones rang throughout the building. Many of the offices were just wooden frames with windows, so Mason could see into most of them. Maps hung on walls with push pins of all colors designating troop movements and other information. Several floors beneath the building were the War Rooms, where London's command met daily with Prime Minister Winston Churchill to discuss events and plan. Mason had not received clearance to go there, but he hoped one day to be granted entrance. For now, he was just a guy hanging around the tea station.

As he watched all the back and forth, Mason thought of all the men and women who had little choice in this war. So many people had enlisted to fight, but the men and women in these hallways were just as valuable as those on the front lines. Yes, people may have simply sat at their desks, rifling through papers or talking on the phone, but everyone here was doing the impossible, trying to keep up with the flow of information to get it into the hands of the men downstairs, ultimately deciding their fate. Mason hoped that one day these people would be remembered as the ones behind the scenes helping to win the war.

It was therefore imperative to keep out of the way. Mason sipped his water and watched the chaos around him. Germany occupied most of Europe, and everyone here fully believed Hitler was coming for them next. The Germans had launched an air offensive called *Adlertag,* or "Eagle Day," in early September, and bombings were now a nightly occurrence.

Still, Mason had a contact in the information department who tracked down German commanders. Roger Knightsbridge was in his early-forties, wore glasses, and had a thick English accent, which Mason often had difficulty deciphering. He would constantly laugh at his own jokes, which Mason barely understood, and always walked incredibly fast from desk to desk, office to office. It was hard to keep him still, seemingly existing only on coffee and speed walking, but the man was exceptionally good at his job.

Mason walked toward the end of the hall, where Roger was standing over his desk on the phone. He abruptly placed the receiver down and turned, nearly running into Mason.

"Ah, my Yankee friend, to what do I owe the pleasure?" Roger was out of the office before Mason could answer.

"Well, come on, follow," Roger said, waving Mason on.

Mason quickly followed Roger, who was halfway down the hallway in a split second. He disappeared into another office on the right, and when Mason reached the door, Roger was already exiting it.

"I am looking for a Lieutenant Kliest," Mason said, blocking Roger's way down the hallway.

Roger slipped by. "Kliest? I'm not familiar with that one, but I will look into it."

Roger disappeared down the stairs, leaving Mason standing there. Roger may have been a walking bundle of nerves, but he was as sharp as they come; if he said he would investigate it, he would. Mason was sure of that.

Mason returned to the office where Collette was and slowly opened the door. Collette was resting her head on the table, the pile of documents in front of her. She raised and shook her head as he entered. "Nothing," she said.

"I'm sorry," Mason said as he closed the door. Collette stood up as he walked over and embraced her. "We'll find them," he whispered.

As they stood together, a commotion erupted in the hallway, just before British soldiers came into the room. "Can we please see your identity cards?"

Mason backed up a few steps and reached into his pocket for his identification. He handed it to the soldier, who glanced at it. Satisfied, he returned it to Mason and turned to Collette.

"I am with him as his guest," she said.

"I still need some identification," the soldier said politely.

"What is this about?" Mason interjected.

"I am not at liberty to say, but I do need to see her identification," the soldier replied.

Collette handed over her identification. The soldier gave it to his partner, who checked it against a list of names on a clipboard. He reached the bottom of the first page and flipped to the next. He located her name as an authorized guest of Mason Wright and returned her identification.

"We apologize for any inconvenience," the man said.

Mason was amused at the politeness of these two men carrying out a profoundly serious task. He loved the British.

Mason and Collette left the office and headed down the hallway toward the stairwell. The normally chaotic scene was even more so than usual. Soldiers were stationed throughout the building, and security was heightened. As Mason and Collette reached the front door, two men entered the building. Mason and Collette stepped aside as one man quickly ushered the other toward the elevator.

"Sully, over here," Mason overheard him say as the elevator doors opened. The two men then disappeared inside. It was obvious something had happened, so Mason decided it best he and Collette leave for the day.

Mason and Collette stepped onto the London streets for their short walk to the flat. The cool autumn day was refreshing to Mason, as he was used to New York City weather. Collette was not as enamored with the gray skies and stiff breeze that made it feel colder than the temperature indicated. She pulled her scarf tight as they turned the corner near Parliament Square. Big Ben, the 315 foot clock tower completed in 1859, rang out, signaling 4 o'clock.

Mason stopped to look up. "One of the greatest landmarks in the world," he said.

"It is beautiful," Collette said as she moved in closer to keep warm.

"Did you know that Big Ben is actually the name of the bell and not the tower?" Mason said.

"Yes, I knew that," Collette said as they stared up.

"You did?" Mason said sarcastically.

"Yes, and did you know that it weighs thirteen and a half tons? Or, that it is named after Benjamin Shaw, who oversaw its installation?" Collette looked at him with a smile, raising her eyebrows.

"Of course, everyone knows that."

"You, Mason Wright, are a liar."

"Okay, you're right, I did not know that, but I am impressed you do."

"As you should be," she said as she glanced next to her at the plaque listing all the facts about the tower.

Neither one of them noticed the glamorous woman lurking behind them. She wore a long, grey, wool coat, a colorful scarf around her neck, and large sunglasses. When Mason and Collette stopped, she did as well, pretending to admire the sights.

"I am cold. Let's go," Collette said, grabbing Mason's arm.

They continued past Westminster Abbey, a young couple in love during wartime. Access to many landmarks had been restricted due to the war, but Westminster Abbey still held services and allowed people inside to pray.

"Do you really think we can find Anna's family?" Collette asked Mason as they walked.

"I don't know, but we will do everything we can," Mason said. "Also, finding them is one thing; getting them out of Europe would be another."

"Anna deserves to know what happened to them."

"I agree, but we can't tell her information we don't have. If I could find Kliest, I could make him find them for us."

"Oh yeah, how would you do that? With all your wit and charm? You need to forget about him; I am sure he has forgotten about you."

"I can't forget about him after what he did to you. And, yes, my wit and charm would go a long way, especially with a gun to his head."

They turned onto the century-old cobblestones of Saint James Street, a few blocks from their flat. The woman behind them looked around; there was no one else on the block. She walked more quickly to close in on them, unbuttoning her coat and raising a pistol toward the back of Mason's head. She failed to notice two men exiting the building she was passing.

A voice screamed out, "Gun!" One of the men grabbed for her arm just as she fired. The bullet hit the taillight of a car right next to Mason and Collette, startling both of them. The other man exiting the building grabbed his friend and the woman as she tried to fire again, tackling them both to the ground. Mason ushered Collette into the vestibule of a nearby building and removed his Colt from his waistband. He looked around the corner to see three people tussling on the ground. Another shot rang out as one of the men rolled off into the street, blood staining his shirt. The other man continued wrestling with the woman, who was surprisingly strong for her small stature. Mason ran over and put the barrel of his gun to the woman's temple. "Let go, or you will die."

She looked up at him and released her gun. The man grabbed it, quickly moved away, and slowly got to his feet. Mason kept his aim on the woman, who smiled a little at him.

"Mason Wright, you should be dead right now."

Mason looked back at her. "I guess it wasn't my time," he said coldly. "How do you know my name?"

"I know a lot about you."

"Who are you?" Mason said, losing patience.

"No one. I am just following orders."

"Whose?

She smiled at Mason.

"Whose orders?" Mason firmly pushed the gun barrel to her head.

"An old friend of yours. Johan Kliest. He wants you dead."

With that she smiled and bit down on the capsule. She started to shake, saliva pouring from her mouth. She slumped backwards on the pavement, dying instantly.

Collette came running over. "Oh my God. Who is she?"

"I don't know," Mason said as he took a deep breath, choosing not to tell Collette what the woman had said.

Mason's blood began to boil as sirens started to ring in the distance. He thanked the man who had helped him and tried to help the other, but he was in dire shape when the ambulance arrived, and probably would not make it.

Mason and Collette were not safe anymore. While they relayed most of their story to the constable, Mason left out the woman's final words. Kliest obviously had not forgotten about him.

ACROSS LONDON, WORD OF THE ATTEMPTED murder reached Frank Sullivan.

"We found Mason Wright and have his information," Gordon said.

"That was quick," Sully said to his assistant. "How did we find him?"

"Someone tried to put a bullet in his head as he walked down Saint James Street."

Sully dropped his pen and looked up from his desk. "Tried?"

"Yes, she was interrupted as she pulled the trigger."

"She? Let me guess: a rather glamorous woman?"

"I'm not sure about the glamorous part, but it could be the woman you are looking for."

"Do we have her?"

"No, she bit down on a pill."

Sully looked down. "I want you to keep this quiet, Gordon. I need to have a chat with Mason Wright."

Gordon nodded and left Sully to lean back in his chair. This day was getting more interesting and dangerous by the minute.

3

MASON SAT ON THE COUCH in the living room of their London flat as rain pattered against the window outside. He and Collette were back home after the attempt on his life, and she was peppering him with questions for which he had no answers. She was not buying his explanation but telling her what the woman had said to him would just upset her more. Collette's parents were also understandably concerned, with Jacques especially worried they were being targeted for their prior activities in France.

Collette looked out the rain-soaked window, her head resting on Mason's shoulder as he tried to read the newspaper. Anna entered the room and sat next to them. Collette reached out with her right arm and pulled her closer. She looked at Collette with a mischievous grin.

"What are you up to?" Collette said with a smile.

Mason leaned over and chimed in. "What's going on?"

"I think you two should get married," Anna said cheerfully.

"Excuse me?" Collette exclaimed.

"Then we could have a big wedding and get all dressed up," Anna said, beaming with excitement.

Collette looked to Mason and back at Anna. "That is a genuinely nice thought, sweetie, but I don't think I like him enough to spend every day with him. He's a lot of work," Collette said as she winked at Anna.

Mason stood up and looked at the two of them. "I am a great catch!" he shouted. "Smart, good looking, funny, charming, did I mention good looking?"

"Yes, and don't forget humble," Collette said as she looked up at him.

"Plenty of women would jump at the chance," Mason muttered.

"Is that right?" Collette furrowed her brows.

"Yep, plenty."

Collette shook her head and looked at Anna. "He has a rather large ego," she said.

Anna laughed as Mason and Collette continued their sarcastic jabs back and forth.

They were interrupted by a knock on the door. "I'll get it!" Jacques shouted from the kitchen.

Collette turned serious as she looked at Mason. He gestured calmly toward her and headed toward the front door. Jacques met him in the hallway. "A man dropped this note off for you," he said.

Mason looked up. "Who was it?"

"I don't know, he didn't say. I believe he was just a courier."

Mason opened the note:

Mason Wright,
My name is Joseph Collins. I would like to speak with you about your request for information from the personnel office. Kindly meet me at 23 Blanchard Street today at 4 p.m. to discuss further.

Regards,
Joseph

Mason looked up at Jacques and handed him the note.

"Do you know a Joseph Collins?" Jacques asked as he studied the note.

"No," Mason said, shaking his head. "With everything that has happened, let's not share this with Collette until we figure out who this is and what he wants."

Jacques agreed before they both returned to the living room.

"Who was at the door?" Collette asked the second Mason returned.

"A gentleman from the personnel office," Mason said. "They have a question about my request for information."

Mason sat down next to Collette and resumed reading *The*

Daily Mail. Collette looked at him. "I didn't know you applied for additional information," she said.

Mason locked eyes with Jacques, sitting silently nearby.

"It's part of the process," Mason said. "I'm sure it's nothing. I just thought it could benefit our search. I thought I told you?" Mason lied through his teeth. He, too, was curious about the note, since he had not requested any information from the personnel office.

"No, you did not," Collette said suspiciously.

Mason shifted uncomfortably as Collette looked at him.

"It's nothing. Just routine," Mason maintained.

"Nothing is routine these days."

"It's a formality. Nothing more."

"You sure?"

"I'm sure."

Mason retired shortly after their exchange to the bedroom to gather his thoughts. Collette was not far behind. Mason couldn't escape her.

"What is this really about?" Collette demanded.

Mason sighed. "I don't know. Someone named Joseph Collins. I never heard of him, but I am going to meet him today. He needs to talk to me about something. He claims to be from the personnel office."

"Do you think it has anything to do with Anna's family?"

"I don't think so. He wanted to speak only with me and said it was urgent." Mason handed Collette the note. "I think it has something to do with what happened earlier. Something was going on over at the offices when we left."

"You're going to be careful, right?" Collette raised her eyebrow.

"I'm always careful," Mason said, moving closer.

"That's what I'm afraid of. You, always being careful, always attracting trouble."

Mason leaned in, kissed her, and embraced her as she buried her head in his chest. "I'll be fine," he whispered before kissing the top of her head. He wondered if that was the truth.

A few hours later, Mason put on a hat, zipped his jacket, and grabbed an umbrella, not only for the light rain, but also because he liked the idea of being able to cover his face. Collette kissed him. "Be careful," she said softly. Mason nodded and left the apartment. Jacques was waiting in the hallway.

"Do you have your pistol?" he asked with a serious look.

"Yes, I do," Mason said. "Try to keep Collette busy with Anna so she doesn't worry."

"I'll try," Jacques said with a smirk. "Won't be easy. After everything you two have been through, she won't relax until you come back through that door."

They shook hands before Mason walked down the stairwell. When he reached the front door, he stepped out onto the front steps and opened his umbrella. After looking both directions, he descended the steps into the grey afternoon.

Mason had roughly twenty-five minutes to get to Suffolk Street, but his plan was to arrive a few minutes late. He also wanted to watch the building for ten minutes before entering, to see if anyone was hanging around. Mason therefore stopped on Hanover Place near the National Gallery, a fifteen-minute walk from the Blanchard building. He walked along Hanover until he reached Floral Street, turned right, and walked past the famous façade of the Royal Opera House. He briefly admired the six large stone columns out front before continuing past the glass front of Floral Hall next door. He then stopped for a moment to check his surroundings.

Mason had been tracked and followed so many times in the past few months that he was getting quite good at making sure he was walking alone. Crossing the street to the other side, he stopped at a bill post. He read some of the advertisements and propaganda posters, which reminded Londoners to always be on the lookout for suspicious activity. "Remember, Loose Talk Can Cost Lives," read one poster; a large red one next to it read, "Keep Calm and Carry On." *What a British sentiment,* thought Mason.

After a minute or two he crossed the street, walked to the

corner of Floral and Rose Streets, crossed over once more, and turned left on Garrick Street. He paused to tie his bootlace while glancing behind him. There were several Londoners walking about, but no one in particular caught Mason's eye. He then turned onto Saint Martin's Lane and approached its intersection with Trafalgar Square.

The square, commemorating the battle of Trafalgar during the Napoleonic wars, had been a gathering place in Central London since the late 1800's. Nelson's Column, its center stone monument, towered over the square at 169 feet tall, while four lions guarded its base. Mason approached from the west; the square was not as busy as usual. Soldiers and sandbags surrounded the lions at the column's base, some soldiers looking no older than sixteen. Mason passed through the square, constantly changing direction to watch his back.

Finally, Mason reached Suffolk Street and turned right. The Blanchard building was across the street. He found a tree to lean on for a few minutes while watching the entrance. A van was making a delivery just past the building and the courier could be seen unloading boxes. Still, Mason watched this delivery man with interest, slightly skeptical of his true intentions. Then, as Mason approached the building, another man appeared and bumped into him.

"Pardon me," the gentleman said before continuing on. Mason turned and watched the man walk away, briefly checking his person to make sure he had not been stabbed or injured. He shook his head, approached the buzzers, and pressed the one marked number 23. A voice responded. "Yes?"

"Mason Wright for Mr. Collins."

"Check your coat pocket," the voice replied.

"I'm sorry?" Mason was a bit confused, but his comment was met with silence.

Mason rifled around in his pocket to find a slip of paper. It read: *Blue Bridge, St. James Park, 4:30.*

Mason quickly looked up and down the street for the man who had bumped into him, but he was gone.

Saint James Park was a few blocks away, but having

never been to the famous park himself, Mason felt a bit more exposed than he was comfortable with as he walked toward it. Approaching the entrance on Horse Yards Road, he noticed a few men sitting on a bench. Mason felt it better to avoid any more contact with people, so he hopped a small fence and headed into the park across the lawn. He could see a lake ahead as he slowly walked behind some trees. The Blue Bridge, which crossed the lake at its midpoint, was in his mind the perfect spot to be ambushed, so he was going to be incredibly careful.

Mason noticed a man in a tan overcoat at one end of the bridge, standing and leaning while reading a newspaper. While slowly approaching the south end of the bridge, he watched as the man suddenly folded his paper, looked across the bridge at him, and walked briskly away. Sensing something was not right, Mason turned to walk away when a man grabbed him by the arm and whispered, "Keep walking, Mason. We're not safe here."

Mason, never one to take orders from strangers, pushed the man away with his arm until he felt the barrel of a gun in his side.

Once again, the man told Mason, "Keep walking."

Mason did not recognize the man's voice, but it was clear he was not British. He sounded American.

"Who are you?" Mason said coldly.

"I just want to talk, but we can't do it here. I need you to answer some questions."

Mason, glancing at the man who was looking straight ahead, thought of Collette's words: "Be careful." He had thought he was, but now he was being led by a stranger through a park with a gun pushed into his side. Still, to everyone else, they simply appeared to be silently walking together during a rainy London afternoon.

The man led Mason out of Saint James Park, toward Knightsbridge Road, and south along Hyde Park. There was something familiar about this man, but Mason could not place it. When they finally reached The Burning Kettle Pub, the man let go to open the wood and glass door beneath a sign depicting a large, wrought iron kettle in a stone fireplace. The few barely audible people at the bar paid no attention to the two men as they walked across the wooden planked floor to a table in the back, near the crackling fireplace. The smell of an open fire filled the air, mixing with that of a near empty pub. They found a small, round table, where Mason shook out his umbrella before sitting down. His chair wobbled, so he switched it with one from the next table, while his captor watched his every move. When the barkeep came over, the man ordered two ales that were promptly delivered moments later.

Mason took a sip and broke the ice. "Mr. Collins, do you always kidnap strangers and take them out for ale?"

The man quietly leaned in. "You're American?"

"Yes, New York. You?" Mason stared across the table.

"How long have you been in London?" the man asked.

"I relocated here during the Crusades in the eleventh century," Mason smirked. "I'm actually a Templar Knight."

The man was not amused; Mason relented. "A couple of months ago, I relocated here to help with the war effort."

"And what, exactly, do you do for the war effort?" The man sipped and stared at Mason with his eyebrows raised.

"Whatever I can," Mason answered coldly.

"Can you be a bit more specific?"

"No, I can't," Mason said. "Forgive me, Mr. Collins, or whoever you are, I received a note out of the blue requesting a meeting I know nothing about with someone I've never met. I followed directions to a park, where I was taken by gunpoint to a local pub for ale. I appreciate it, I do, but I need to tell you, it is a strange way to make friends. Either tell me what is going on or I am leaving. Shoot me if you must, but I have better things to do with my time."

"I don't think you do, Mason." The man's serious response held Mason's attention.

Mason sipped his ale and looked around before returning his gaze to the man. "Who are you?" he asked in a hushed tone.

The man stared at Mason a moment. "Do you know a man named John Cleary?"

"No," Mason said, shaking his head.

"Ever been to 24 Holston Road?"

"No." Mason was growing impatient again.

"Does this word mean anything to you?" The man slid a piece of paper over to Mason with the word *Totenkopf.*

Mason looked at it. "I don't speak German."

"What about the word *hashshashin?*"

"I believe they were an ancient order of assassins in Persia, but I'm not entirely sure."

"How would you know that?"

Mason shrugged. "Sometimes I think I know more about the ancient world than the modern one."

"Do you know someone named Frank Sullivan?"

Mason sipped his ale. "I'm leaving unless you tell me what the hell is going on."

The man took a deep breath. "My name is Frank Sullivan, but most people call me Sully. I consult with a special branch of the London police that deals with foreign affairs. As you can imagine, things are a bit busy right now, and secrecy is paramount. I am sorry for this crazy day, but I need some information for a case I'm working on. One of my most trusted men was found murdered yesterday in east London. He was badly bruised, and his throat was slit. He was lying naked in a pool of his own blood, and in his hand was a piece of paper with the word *Totenkopf* on it. Under the word was a symbol of a skull dripping blood. In his notes, I found an address which turned out to be an empty house, and an attempt was made on my life. There, I found a box inscribed with the symbol of the skull. I found a list inside, a kill list of sorts, and at the top was my friend's name. I was second on that list, and the next name was yours."

Mason sat back in his chair. The two men were briefly distracted by an older gentleman who entered and loudly ordered a drink. Mason and Sully were both clearly on edge after the events of the last two days but turned casually back toward each other.

Sully continued. "Why did your name also appear in a dead man's notes?"

Mason, clearly startled by this revelation, leaned forward. "I don't know. What happened to you at the address?"

"A man shot at us with a rifle as we were in the upstairs bedroom, from the roof across the street. They were the last shots he ever took; I hit him twice. As he lay on the roof, he bit down on a pill and killed himself. This was not some idiot; this was a professional. He had no identification, but he was using a German sniper rifle, a Mauser 98." Sully paused to look at Mason. "Can you shed any light on this? Anyone who might want you dead?"

"People generally like me, but I may have some idea why my name appears on this list," Mason said. "A few months ago in Paris, I had several run-ins with a German lieutenant who was stealing artwork from Europe to help the Fuhrer start his dream of the greatest museum in the world. He managed to escape and I have no idea where he is now, but I was almost killed today after leaving the War Offices. The assassin was a woman, and as I had her at gunpoint, she told me that same lieutenant, Johan Kliest, wants me dead and will stop at nothing. Maybe Kliest sent some assassins to eliminate you and your friend for reasons beyond me, and while they were here, were told to come after me as well."

Sully exhaled. "I am in the process of checking through my friend's notes to find out what exactly he was working on that may have gotten him killed," he said. "I wonder if it has something to do with this lieutenant."

"I would love to know as well, since I appear to be on his list," Mason said sarcastically.

Sully finished his ale, sat back in his chair, and wiped his lips with his fingers. He stared at Mason a moment. "What was the lieutenant's name again? Kliest?"

"Yes, Johan. A real asshole."

"I've found they all are, the more I learn about them."

Mason saw a potential opportunity. "Do you have access to files on Nazi commanders?"

Sully pondered Mason's request. "What are you thinking?"

"Maybe we can find out some more information on Kliest, his location, what he oversees, anything we can use. See if any of your men are in the vicinity, find out what the lowlife is doing. I know him, his weaknesses, and I also know he would love to get his hands on me. If he is behind this, maybe we can work together to eliminate him. It would be my pleasure to put a bullet in that man's brain." Mason thought it ironic how he was now volunteering to partner up with a man who had just taken him at gunpoint thirty minutes earlier.

"I will try to dig up some information on him, but in the meantime, be careful out there," Sully said. "We aren't being targeted; we are being hunted."

"It doesn't seem like Kliest's style to send someone to kill me; I would think he would want that pleasure himself," Mason said. "There must be more to it. I am sure with your work there are several reasons for you to be a target. Me, I just beat him at his own game. The fact that he is still thinking about me means he is still vulnerable to emotion. That is a major advantage."

"I'll be in touch," Sully said as he got up from the table. "Thank you for being patient. I'm sorry for all the secrecy, but you can imagine what I'm dealing with right now." He reached across the table to shake hands with Mason.

"How will you be in touch?" Mason asked.

"I'll find you; it's what I do," Sully said. "Please do not say a word about this to anyone. This stays between us until I can find out more, and meanwhile, watch your six."

"You do the same."

The barkeep returned to see if the men wanted another round, but Sully declined and paid instead.

"What do you think the chances are of this actually happening? Me and you going to France?" Mason asked Sully while grabbing his umbrella.

"I am not sure," Sully replied. "There is a lot going on. To get authorization to do this, we have to make a good case that Kliest is behind it all."

"The attempts on our lives and the murder of your man aren't reason enough?"

"Unfortunately, that is not up to me. I'll see what I can do."

Mason nodded and turned around to leave. This had been a far more interesting meeting than he had imagined.

4

Lien, France

MARIE CLEARED THE EMPTY GLASSES as she delivered three more cognacs to the group. Lieutenant Volmer and his two colleagues exchanged smiles with her as she quickly wiped the table and picked up the empty basket of bread.

"Enjoy, gentleman," she said, turning back.

"We would enjoy them more if you would join us," shouted the lieutenant, as the other men broke out into laughter.

"Fraternizing with the enemy is not allowed Lieutenant. You should know that," Marie said over her shoulder as she walked toward a large oak bar against the far wall.

"I shall alter the rules," Volmer yelled as they once again broke into laughter.

Marie Riberau, the owner of Café Saint Joanna in the center square, had settled in Lien several years ago to open what had since grown to become the primary establishment in town. Marie was in her late thirties and nearly 5' 8", but it was her dark hair and vibrant personality built on sarcasm and quick wit that attracted and endeared her to nearly every soldier who entered her place. Always smiling, she was particularly good at keeping her customers happy and making sure they spent their money. A free round from Marie meant at least two more bought, and while every soldier was convinced they would be staying late with her, they were only disappointed when she led them out the door.

Marie spent all of her days working the bar and helping Phillipe in the kitchen. Phillipe, an older man who did most of the cooking, was an uncle of sorts to Marie, and soon Marie developed regulars who would frequent the café not only for her smiling face but also for excellent meals.

To her customers, Marie was just a beautiful, young entrepreneur, but Marie had been through so much in her young life that she was guarded whenever conversation turned to her. She was, however, a master at small talk and an even better listener. Marie would quickly remember the important aspects of conversations with her customers and use them to endear herself to them when they returned. She considered her customers family and treated them accordingly.

When the war broke out and many of her regular customers fled, Marie briefly considered packing up and leaving, too; then, when she thought about Joanna, she knew she could not do it. Joanna had cared for Marie when her parents had been killed by German soldiers in World War I. Joanna would have never run and so neither would Marie. She therefore remained open during occupation to gather information on the enemy and pass it along to the recently formed resistance. Though it was small, it was beginning to take shape.

Phillipe also had begun to convince a small group of people from various walks of life to gather information regarding the German occupation. This information was then passed to trusted couriers for the allied forces by radio or in person. Phillipe had survived World War I and, through the teachings of his father, knew some of the intricacies of information gathering. An aging alchemist by trade, Phillipe's strength came not from his body, but his mind.

Together, Marie and Phillipe established a small network of trusted couriers to whom they fed information. Marie maintained a ledger under the floorboards of the storage room in the back, where she documented every soldier who came through her doors. She developed a list of the hierarchy and was slowly figuring out the main players, including who was most dangerous and most vulnerable.

Lieutenant Volmer was still laughing with his underlings while Marie cleaned behind the bar. She had already begun her profile of him in her head, having met him only once before. He was very cordial, but after a few drinks, he would become loud and forward with her when she visited the table. By the end of the night, he would grab her by the waist, trying to get her onto his lap. She would quickly move away, escaping his grasp, and with a quick smile tell him to be careful: she might have to remove him from her establishment if he could not keep his hands to himself. He would reply in typical fashion, "I might like that, Mademoiselle Riberau," before laughing it off. Marie envisioned snapping his neck like a twig, hoping one day she might get the chance.

Lieutenant Volmer was the top German in charge of the occupation of Lien. He was a Nazi through and through and would die for his Fuhrer if needed. His cushy assignment as head of an occupying force in a small French village was reward for his command and success on the front lines during the Polish invasion. He had risen through the ranks with a reputation as a career man who would do anything asked of him, even if that meant murdering thousands of innocent civilians without a shred of regret. He was settling into Lien away from the front lines and planned on treating himself to some well-deserved revelry. After enjoying his first few days in town, he also hoped to enjoy the nighttime company of Mademoiselle Riberau.

The hour was late and Marie was beginning to close when a young man entered through the front door. He sat at a small table in the front, away from the soldiers. Lieutenant Volmer noticed the man immediately and stood to approach him, followed by the two soldiers from his table. He stumbled toward the man and introduced himself.

"My name is Lieutenant Franz Volmer and I am the commandant of this town," he said. "Are you aware that you are in violation of the curfew I have established? I could have you shot right here on the spot, but I am in a forgiving mood and will give you the chance to explain yourself."

The young man stared at the lieutenant blankly. Volmer turned to his two men and smiled. "Apparently this young man needs to be told of the curfew; he clearly does not understand it," Volmer said. "Perhaps the two of you can take him outside and help him learn."

As Volmer turned back around to face the man sitting at the table, he was stunned to feel a sharp, piercing pain in his shoulder. He stared at the small revolver in the young man's hand, smoke still billowing from the barrel. As Volmer staggered backwards, the man kicked back his chair and ran for the door. He only managed a few steps before being cut down by Volmer's men.

Volmer was on his back, blood pooling at his right shoulder. He began to lose consciousness but not before feeling the pressure of a rag on his wound. He looked up to see Marie at his side. She had run over from the bar and was holding the rag while barking orders to Volmer's men to get help. One of the men ran out the door while the other made sure the young Frenchman was dead on the floor, shooting one bullet into his forehead.

Marie remained at the lieutenant's side until the medical team arrived. She had aided in saving the life of a most vile man, and while she wanted to let him die, that was not the plan. Lieutenant Volmer needed to survive; it was her job to make sure he did. The young man who gave his life for the resistance had volunteered to fire the shot, a mission he must have known would end in his death. He was an expert shot and had trained for a month on the precise location of a serious, but non-lethal, shoulder wound.

As Marie watched the medics remove Volmer from the café, she knew she had done her part. Once recovered, the lieutenant would come back to thank her and continue his advances. However, having now saved his life, she might also gain his trust. She would gather as much information as she could, waiting for the day when she would no longer save his life, but rather, take great pleasure in ending it.

As Phillipe locked the door and cleaned up the blood, Marie retired to the storage room to catalogue the day's events. For a split second, her thoughts turned to the man who owned her heart, a man nobody knew of, but a man who promised he would come back for her one day. She said a quick prayer for his well-being and hoped he was safe. She then opened a drawer and removed a small box with a black pen inside. Her love had given it to her as a gift, asking her to write him as often as she could with the information they needed to fight the Germans. Now, the pen needed to be mightier than the sword. One day they would fight, and tonight, they moved one step closer. She closed her eyes for a moment and pried up the floorboard, exposing a dusty leather-bound ledger. She pulled it up, placed it on a small table, and opened it to the words at the top of the first page: *The Secrets of Saint Joanna.* After thumbing a few pages in, she began to write.

Marie still had blood on her sleeve; she wiped it, but it did not make much difference. As she wrote, her thoughts again turned to her love, and she wondered when they would see each other again. She vowed if they both made it out of this horrible mess alive, they would spend the rest of their days together in peace.

5

MARIE AWOKE EARLY THE NEXT DAY in her small house near the edge of town. She wanted to get back to the café to clean the floor again, as the blood from last night was still evident in some spots. Phillipe, too, would meet her there to prepare the café for that day's business. She expected it to be busy; after all, a German lieutenant had been shot in her establishment. Someone from Volmer's command would surely come by and while Marie was prepared for whatever came her way, she hoped any visit would be short, given that she had saved the lieutenant from assassination. However, Marie also believed there would be retaliation, maybe not against her or her establishment, but against someone.

Marie walked to the café every morning and normally passed through the checkpoints with ease. She did not fear the Germans; she hated them, but they did not scare her. Marie's kind demeanor and beauty concealed a woman with complicated history, whose story dated back to World War I.

The only daughter of an American ambassador, Marie had been in an adjoining apartment with her friend, Joanna, when her parents were killed during a nighttime raid on their flat by German soldiers. Joanna was a widow in her fifties who would often entertain Marie while her parents attended or hosted state dinners. Marie would walk down the hallway to Joanna's apartment to spend hours reading or playing with Joanna's dog, Foxy. One night, Marie's parents were entertaining a French couple whom the Germans believed to be spies. Three German soldiers entered the apartment and demanded the Frenchman come with them. He resisted, as did Marie's father. The German soldiers shot and killed everyone in the apartment, leaving the bodies there to rot. Joanna took Marie from the building and out to the country that night to raise her as her own daughter.

Today, Marie noticed more soldiers than usual at the

checkpoints. At the first, the man interrogated her fully, asking several more questions than usual. He was particularly interested in who she had seen on her way through town. Marie calmly answered the questions truthfully; she had seen very few people, mostly farmers heading to their fields.

As Marie approached the main square, there were several German soldiers with two vehicles parked outside her café. She figured there would be a visit from the enemy but had hoped it might come later in the day. She then noticed the black sedan with Nazi flags attached to the hood. The 1939 Horch Type 930 was the preferred vehicle of the Third Reich; clearly, Volmer's people were waiting for her.

She paused as a half-track pulled into the square and came to a stop with a screech of its brakes. The metal gate at the back of the truck was unlatched and fell open with a large clanking sound. Three soldiers jumped out, leading ten bound men away from the truck. They were paraded around the square for a few minutes as the townspeople looked on. Most of the men stared at the cobblestone ground as they were marched slowly across the square. A few looked around, knowing this would be their last glimpse of their hometown.

A German commander spoke as the men were lined up, side by side. "People of Lien," he said loudly and firmly. "We took control of your village peacefully. We have allowed you to go on with your daily lives. Your businesses are open and your town has been spared destruction. However, any violence or attack on a German soldier will be met with swift and harsh punishment."

The commander raised his arm and motioned toward Café Saint Joanna. "Last night in this café, there was an attempted assassination of a German commander. I ask anyone with information to come forward. I promise you will not be harmed, and you will save many lives."

The man turned slowly in a circle as he looked for someone to step forward. When there were no takers, he walked over to the crowd and slowly paced, peering at them from under the cap pulled tightly down on his head. The clicking of his polished black boots hitting the cobblestone was the only audible sound. The crowd became more anxious with every passing moment. Marie recognized some of her own townspeople, including Madame Rosemary Louvier, who owned the vegetable and fruit stand across the way, and Thomas, who made deliveries to the hotels. Both stood stoically as the commander paced back and forth. Rosemary and Thomas had plenty of information concerning last night's event, as they were instrumental in planning it, but neither would step forward; they had all sworn an oath to fight against the Germans and would die before giving any information up. Marie continued watching the events in the square unfold with nervousness about what would happen next.

"I will ask one more time," the commander said. "Anyone with information on the assassination attempt last night, step forward." He stopped in front of an elderly man in the front. The man stood silently as the commander stared him down. The old man managed to raise his innocent eyes, staring into the man's hateful ones. The commander shouted an order, never leaving the old man's gaze. Two soldiers came over and yanked the old man out of the crowd. They pushed him to his knees as the commander removed his side revolver.

"I am giving you one more chance to save lives," the commander shouted to the crowd. "Come forward if you have any information, or I will be forced to shoot this man, a member of your community." He pointed the Luger semi-automatic at the back of the old man's head and waited a few moments.

Marie spoke up. "Please, this man knows nothing, don't do this," she pleaded. Marie walked slowly toward the German with her hands raised near her head. "Please, he is old! Whatever happened in my café, he knows nothing of it. The person who did this was a crazy man! None of us know who he is or why he did it. We are a peaceful town and have obeyed all the rules. Please don't punish this man for the sins of another."

The commander holstered his Luger and walked towards

Marie. "Ah, the guardian angel who saves the lives of her enemy," he said condescendingly as he walked over. "You believe this man knows nothing?"

"Yes, I am sure of it," Marie said, sounding exasperated.

"You believe I should spare his life?"

"I do."

"Since you saved the life of Lieutenant Volmer, I will spare his."

"Thank you," Marie replied.

The man again yelled out a command as troops shuffled around. The bound men were then led to a corner of the square in front of a cobblestone wall and lined up next to each other. Ten German soldiers lined up in front of them.

"What are you doing?" Marie asked, her voice shaking.

The commander turned to her. "Mademoiselle Riberau, did you really think a Frenchman could attempt to kill someone in the German command and we would not retaliate? You may have saved the lieutenant's life, but you do not get to dictate the rules. I spared your old man, that is all you get. If it were up to me, I would have shot you where you stand for operating the establishment where this happened. Now, go to your café before I change my mind." He looked over at a soldier nearby and nodded. The soldier barked out an order and raised his hand. With one more command, the ten soldiers fired. The bound men fell one by one, some forward, some backward against the wall, and some sideways, dropping on top of the men next to them. Gasps sounded across the square as the soldiers approached the pile of bodies and fired several more shots into their corpses. Marie covered her mouth as she closed her eyes.

The German commander spoke up. "Let this be a lesson to everyone here. Do not cause any more trouble, or next time, we will kill twenty people, including women, children, and old men." His boots clicked on the cobblestone as he walked back to the black sedan. Marie stood motionless for a few moments before a soldier approached her, removing his black leather gloves.

"Marie Riberau? I am Captain Hauptman. Please come with us," the man said as warmly as a block of ice.

Marie stared into the man's blue eyes, recognizing him from the night before. She searched for a soul, some emotion, or a note of humanity. The man only stared back calmly, never leaving her eyes, as several soldiers gathered behind her. Marie looked around and noticed Phillipe leaning against the front of the café, surrounded by two guards. A few soldiers leaning on the back gate of the half-track exchanged cigarettes, one man lighting them for the other two. The rains in the fall made for muddy fields in France, but the all-terrain efficiency of the Maultier half-track solved that issue.

Marie stared up at the sun peeking through the clouds. It was an awful morning so far, but she needed to gather herself for the day ahead. "I will come with you as soon as I open my café," she said. "Please allow us to prepare for customers and I will go with you willingly." She managed her best reassuring look even as her voice stammered. "Allow me that after what you have done," she added, gathering her strength. "Please?"

The soldier answered her. "You have fifteen minutes, no more."

"Thank you," Marie said as she nodded and walked past.

Fifteen minutes was fifteen more than she thought she would get. Volmer clearly wanted to see her and his men would successfully deliver her, but she would make it on her terms. Marie always managed to shift a conversation to her side. She was a master at manipulation of the human mind. Her beauty and her personality especially lent themselves to achieving success with men. Even the most hardened soldiers eventually warmed to her. At first, she was not quite sure she could handle living in a town run by enemy soldiers, her love of country torn apart by an invading force, but Marie never ran from anything. As much as she hated being kind to the enemy, it was necessary for her to stay alive. Strong-willed and stubborn, she knew which battles to fight. Small victories win a war, and in her mind, every day she was alive was a small victory.

Marie motioned to Phillipe to follow her, but as he moved, two soldiers stood and blocked his path with their rifles. "Let him go," said the man in charge. The two men moved away and put their rifles at their sides. Phillipe walked over to join Marie at the arched front door with a small glass pane at the top. A small sign hung next to it, written in beautiful, purple script: *Café Saint Joanna.* A basket containing some herbs and flowers hung below the sign. Marie usually filled this basket with handpicked items from the fields behind the café. Sometimes it was lavender and mint, other times wildflowers, but it was one of the first things she did every day. Flowers were sparse these days; somehow even the flowers knew to leave when the Germans showed up.

Marie unlocked the bolt as Phillipe stood waiting behind her. She entered her establishment, followed by Phillipe, but as she started to close the door, it was stopped with the boot of a German soldier. Marie felt the push on the door from the outside and pulled it towards her. Two soldiers entered, one shaking his head. He told her the door would remain open, without uttering a word. Marie brushed it off and released the door. It swung open, nearly hitting the wall. One soldier guarded the door as the other stood in the middle of the room. Neither said a word as they glanced around the café.

Marie went behind the bar, turned on the lights, and returned tying an apron around her waist. Phillipe went in the back to prepare the food. Marie busied herself behind the bar before wiping down tables. She then smiled at the soldier in the middle of the room as she walked by, but it was not returned. She managed to disappear for a moment into the back, but only returned with a mop and bucket. She slopped the cloth mop onto the floor, sudsy water puddling underneath it, and moved it back and forth along the floorboards where the bodies had lain the night before. After a few minutes, she grabbed towels from behind the bar and, on her hands and knees, dried the floor to her satisfaction. After throwing the damp towels in a heap behind the bar, a voice caught her attention. "Your fifteen minutes are up," Hauptman said.

Marie paused and began to untie her apron. "Very well," she said as she walked toward the door to the kitchen. "Phillipe, I'll return when I can." Phillipe nervously acknowledged her and Marie headed for the door.

Hauptman followed her out as another man opened the side door to the black sedan. Marie slid onto the leather seat in the back. The soldier slid in next to her, forcing her to move to the other side, the butt of his rifle hitting her ribs. *These men have no manners*, she thought, shaking her head. Even if she had saved their commandant's life, it mattered not. She was still the enemy.

The sedan drove toward the Hotel Lien. High on the hill overlooking the square, it had been seized by the German Wehrmacht when they entered Lien to set up their command. The hotel was a historic building dating back to the 16th century, but it had been renovated several times over the years.

As they pulled up to the main entrance, Marie noticed two guard towers adorning each side of the main staircase and Nazi flags hanging from the columns. A Flak 36 anti-aircraft gun was also set up on one end of the parking lot, with a few soldiers assigned to it.

A soldier stepped forward and opened the rear door. Once open, he stood at attention and extended his right arm. "Heil Hitler," he said as Captain Hauptman exited the vehicle. Marie's side door was also opened by a soldier as she slid out and walked behind the car. Hauptman motioned with his right hand to the stairs. "After you, Fraulein."

Marie started up the steps as the guard soldiers watched her every move. She looked up at the four-story hotel, with its grand columns and flower boxes adorning the windows. *Such a beautiful building*, she thought, *wasted on the dirt of humanity*. A few soldiers appeared at the main entrance and stepped aside to allow her to enter. They must have noticed Hauptman behind her.

"This way," Hauptman said as he motioned Marie into a hallway on the right. They proceeded past the front desk, where a few young soldiers voiced more vigorous "Heil

Hitlers." Hauptman and Marie reached the end of the hallway, where large double doors opened to a ballroom. "Please wait in here," he said.

Marie entered the rather sparsely decorated ballroom and took a seat at one of the tables. Chairs were stacked in one corner and the curtains were pulled tight, so no outside light was visible. A large crystal chandelier hung in the middle of the room, polished brightly. Marie recognized the sound of the locking door as they sealed her in the ballroom. She quickly started taking mental notes of the room's size and its window locations. She wandered around, checking the doors; one opened, but it was a closet filled with tablecloths and linens.

A few moments later, she heard the door unlock. She strode to the main entrance as it opened. Hauptman returned and apologized for keeping her waiting.

"What am I doing here?" Marie said, trying to act accommodating.

"The lieutenant wishes to thank you for your help last night. He is waiting for you in his room."

Pity, Marie thought. She had hoped Volmer was in severe pain and clinging to life, but that was clearly not the case. She followed the captain to a back staircase and up to the second floor. Once there, she encountered more enemy soldiers who stared coldly at her as she walked by. Marie took mental notes of how many she encountered.

Past the soldiers, she noticed a smaller man with spectacles behind a large desk covered with papers. Seeing the two of them coming, the man quickly picked up a black telephone, said a few words, and hung up. He muttered something as they approached. Hauptman acknowledged him and continued to lead Marie down the hallway. She noticed a lack of commotion on this floor compared to the main.

As they approached the last door, Hauptman stepped aside and motioned her to the doorway. "Please," he said as he reached down and opened the door for her. Marie entered the room to find Lieutenant Volmer lying in bed in a corner of the room. Heavily bandaged, he was reading some papers when she entered.

"Please come in, my dear," Volmer said, removing his glasses. She walked into the room and over to the bed. Volmer reached out with his good arm.

"My savior," he said as he grabbed and kissed her hand. She nearly vomited. Volmer had a large bandage over his shoulder and his right arm was in a sling. She also noticed several medicine bottles on the table next to him.

"Please sit down," he said, pointing to a chair near the bed.

Marie backed up a few steps toward the chair and sat down. She crossed her left leg over her right, straightened her skirt, and pulled her sweater tighter.

"I wanted to thank you for what you did last night; you saved my life," Volmer said.

"That is not necessary. All I did was help another human being in need," Marie answered.

"You did not have to, but you did, and I appreciate that. We are in your country against your will; I am sure not everyone would do the same."

"Oh, I don't know," Marie said innocently. "How are you doing?"

"The doctor tells me I will be sore for a while, but the bullet has been removed and I am assured a full recovery will occur."

"That is good," Marie said, trying to sound convincing.

"Thank you." Volmer winced as he tried to reposition himself. An awkward silence fell over the room as Marie looked around. She wondered how long she was expected to sit here and lie to this vile man.

Volmer broke the silence. "The man who shot me, did you know him?"

"No, I don't know him. Well, didn't know him," Marie said, shaking her head.

"Are you sure you have never seen him?"

"He may have come in once or twice, but I don't know who he is. Sometimes people stop in for a drink. I cannot remember every face. He did not look familiar to me."

Volmer stared at her for what seemed like an eternity, his eyes boring into her soul. Marie began to feel uneasy until Volmer spoke up again. "I asked you here."

"You summoned me here," Marie interjected, eliciting a stare from Volmer. "But go on."

"I *summoned* you here not only to thank you, but to ask you a favor. In a few weeks, I will be hosting a special night here at headquarters. My friend Johan Kliest will be visiting and I would very much like you to provide the food and drink for the evening. It will be held in a private cabin in the back of the hotel, overlooking the town. There will be eight guests. Would you do this for me? We will pay you handsomely."

"I am very busy at the café; I don't know if I would have the time."

"You'll find the time," Volmer said with a grin.

The hair stood up on Marie's neck as Volmer smiled at her. Another awkward silence ensued until the lieutenant picked up a phone receiver. He said a few words before Hauptman entered through the door.

"He will take you back to your café," Volmer said. "Thank you for coming by."

"I am not sure I had a choice," Marie said sweetly. Volmer smirked and slowly nodded his head.

Hauptman walked over and stood next to Marie, motioning toward the door. "Please, this way."

Marie stood and walked toward the door. As she reached the doorway, Volmer spoke again. "Mademoiselle Riberau, please do consider my offer."

Marie turned around to face him. "I will," she said as she left the room.

She began to breathe normally again once downstairs. She knew Volmer would want to see her again; it was the plan, but still, she wanted desperately to get out of this hotel and back to her café. As her car pulled away from the hotel, she took a deep breath and started to focus on all the details she had filed away. When she got back to the café, she would go to the back and document everything. Then, once that was finished, she would try to have as normal a day as possible in the middle of a war.

6

CAROLINA TURNED THE SKELETON KEY but was startled by the sound of the deadbolt. Each time she closed her family's bakery, she would pause and stare down at the lock, wondering how long its sound would define her. Her way of life had been stripped from her for months now, since the Nazi occupation of her country began. Life was decidedly different now in France: curfew was enforced at 7:00 p.m., with patrols rounding up violators in the streets. Many were never seen or heard from again. It was just after 4:00 p.m. when Carolina left the bakery with a slight headache, ignoring the dreariness of the day with thoughts of her lost country.

As the wind picked up, she pulled her scarf tight and put on gloves. She walked over to the bicycle leaned against the front of the building and prepared to ride back home. The farm, which had been in her family for generations, was located east of town in the hills. She used to enjoy bicycling home, as she would share pleasantries with the townspeople, admire the swaying trees lining the road, and smell the lilacs in the springtime. All that changed when the German army entered Lien. Her ride was now devoid of people, the trees were not as inviting, the lilacs were long gone, and there would be a checkpoint on the road out of town. Having grown accustomed to this daily scrutiny, Carolina checked her papers to make sure everything was intact before she left; she had come too far with the resistance to slip up now.

Carolina mourned the vibrancy of France, now stripped to the bone and soulless since the Nazis' arrival. Her father, an officer with the French foreign ministry, was constantly summoned to Britain for meetings, and as the situation worsened, her sister and parents relocated to England while she stayed behind to run the family farm. As the eldest daughter, Carolina's toughness belied her quiet demeanor.

Every day after closing, she would ride home to the farm,

feed the animals, and cook dinner before climbing the stairs to the attic where, exactly at 10:00 p.m., she would turn on her father's radio transmitter and recap the day's events with her father in code while wrapped in a large blanket. He was not interested in the bakery or the farm; he only wanted to know about the occupation, troop movements, weapons, checkpoints, and any other information Carolina deemed useful. Still, she looked forward to speaking with him.

Rain began to fall as Carolina approached the checkpoint, dismounted, and walked her bicycle up to the barrier. The guardhouse on the left was a wooden structure with a small desk, containing some papers and a radio. The road was blocked by a wooden gate painted black and white, where two guards with guns thanklessly inspected all papers. Though many of the same people passed through daily, the soldiers never made any attempt to converse. They simply asked one question: "Your papers?" If satisfied, the guards would then lift the gate and allow passage. If not, a further interrogation followed, often escalating to a beating or detainment.

Carolina reached under a red blanket into her basket as she approached. "Bonjour," she said to the soldiers.

The guard only moved his hand closer to the trigger of his Gewehr rifle; he relaxed once he saw the loaf of bread she had retrieved. She smiled softly as she handed it to him, and to the other guard, her papers. After passing inspection, Carolina swung back up on her bicycle and continued home. The wind had picked up and was howling across the fields through the trees, but she pedaled away, faster and faster, until the German soldiers were out of sight.

As she rode along, Carolina wondered about the two men at the checkpoint. Were they friends? Brothers? Did they know each other well at all? As they shared today's loaf, would they feel any empathy for the poor French girl on her bicycle, or were they as cold as their faces implied? She hoped they enjoyed their bread tonight; tomorrow, there would be none. Instead, she was to put a bullet in their foreheads, drag their bodies into a field, steal their uniforms and weapons, and quietly go on her way.

It all started when Carolina was informed that she was to meet a man she had only heard stories of at her bakery. He was there to help the resistance grow after helping to protect France's greatest art treasures. Having come back to his homeland after fleeing, he was rumored to have said, "If I am to die, it will be on French soil." He planned to wage war in the shadows with a small group of freedom fighters and was therefore seen as a symbol of hope. The idea of meeting this man tomorrow excited Carolina and renewed her sense of purpose.

As the wind gusts created an eerie sound across the valley, Carolina began to crave warm soup upon turning onto the gravel driveway leading to her farm. Gone was the sweet smell of evening air, the faint sounds of wildlife, and the distant lights of neighboring farms; all was replaced with cold, quiet darkness after the occupation.

Carolina stopped and began walking her bicycle up the driveway, the sound of gravel crunching under her feet. A gate banged against a fence in the distance as she propped her bicycle against the garage and gathered the bread and vegetables from its basket. The Nazi occupation, having moved into the main town square and government buildings, had severely limited supply, with a majority of the food from town being diverted to German troops. Carolina's bakery was forced to bake all the bread for the hotel without compensation, other than being allowed to remain open as a functioning business. Still, she was able to hide some essentials at the farm for her own consumption, though she rarely ever felt like eating anymore.

Carolina walked around a corner of the house toward the open gate. She scanned her property and listened for anything unusual, but she heard nothing but the wind and a few birds chirping in the trees above. She reached the gate and caught it as it swung open. The latch had broken off and was lying in the grass below. She inspected the rusted metal and mentally added "broken latch" to the growing list of things she needed fixed. Then she found a large log to prop against the gate and hold it closed.

She returned to the front of the house and unlocked the door. It was cold and quiet except for the creak of the floorboards as she walked. She entered the kitchen, gathered a few small candles for the evening, and boiled some water for tea. She lit a small lamp on the table, even though light was forbidden after curfew for French residents. She pulled the curtains tight and began unpacking her basket.

Her night continued as most did with tea and dinner, but as she sat at her kitchen table, she heard a creak in the ceiling above. She immediately put her tea down and listened intently. *Another creak* - something or someone was moving upstairs. Carolina walked quietly over to the kitchen cabinet and removed a small handgun. After checking the chamber to make sure it was loaded, she gingerly moved into the living room and wrapped around a doorway for a look. The stairs led up into darkness, with a rug serving as a runner up the middle of the treads. As she approached the bottom of the stairs, Carolina knocked into the table in the front hall; a vase rattled back and forth. She quickly grabbed and stabilized it, then stood motionless. She heard nothing but was not convinced. Carolina grabbed the bannister and began her ascent, her hand shaking slightly on the railing. With the last remaining bits of daylight just barely illuminating the hallway at the top of the stairs, nothing seemed out of place. Still, she walked as softly as possible as she reached the top, using the carpet for support. As Carolina glanced around the corner and down the hall, she saw that the door to the master bedroom was open. Carolina always kept the doors closed when rooms were not in use, as the little bit of heat generated from the fireplace was barely enough. With her gun pointed in the direction of the open door, she gently walked the upstairs hall. As she reached the master bedroom, a man emerged and grabbed her gun with his left hand while holding her with his right. He spun her and threw her to the ground as the gun flew down the hallway. Carolina tried to claw her way back toward the weapon until something hit her hard in the head.

A small woman with the same height and weight as Carolina appeared with the man in the doorway. She even dressed and styled her hair like Carolina, whose limp body was now being carried by the man down to the kitchen. He tied her to a chair and splashed cold water on her face. Carolina awoke to splitting pain in her head, a strange man, and the feeling that she was looking in a mirror. The woman approached and leaned in. "Hello, Carolina. Please don't be afraid. We will not harm you as long as you behave," the woman said softly as she ran her hand down Carolina's face.

Carolina pulled her head back from the woman's hand. The woman smiled and abruptly slapped her across the face. "Do cooperate Carolina. It would be a shame to ruin that pretty face of yours."

7

CAROLINA WOKE TIED TO A CHAIR in the basement of her house. She had no idea what time it was, but the light shining through the small basement window told her it was the next day. Her captor came down early to check on her. Without saying a word, he checked the knots on her wrists and disappeared back upstairs.

Sometime later, the sound of two sets of footsteps coming down the centuries-old staircase stopped her from struggling to free herself. The woman appeared first, followed closely by the man responsible for Carolina's throbbing headache.

"Good morning," the woman said. "I would like to tell you what is going to happen today. I will be meeting Ganoux at the bakery. That's him, right? Your leader?" She leaned in and stared directly into Carolina's eyes. "Your uprising will be over before it even begins. You could have adjusted under occupation, but you chose not to and will now pay with your life."

Carolina looked at her and wondered, *how do they know his name? We never exchanged names.* She shifted in the chair and maneuvered her wrists against the ropes.

"Paul Ganoux will unfortunately die today as well," the woman continued.

Carolina spoke through dried lips. "Whoever you are, I haven't a clue what you're talking about."

"You know exactly what I am talking about," laughed the woman. "But since you ask, I'll tell you who I am; you won't be around long enough to tell anyone. Have you ever heard of *Totenkopf*? I suspect not. We are a society built on thousands of years of organizations dating back to the eleventh century, beginning with the *Hashshashin*. We are killers, but what makes us more dangerous is we are ordinary people – men, women, old, young - willing to die for the cause. I guess you noticed how you and I look similar. I was handpicked for this job because I could transform myself into you rather easily. We are many, and we will slowly infiltrate every society as we wait to be called upon. I am one of the lucky ones, having been called upon so early. Now, I get to prove myself." The woman looked at her watch. "I have to go, I have a bakery to open."

She said something in German to her partner as he nodded in approval. She then reached down and gently slapped Carolina's cheek. "It's a shame you're so pretty," she said as Carolina pushed back in her chair and turned her cheek away.

When they left, Carolina was once again plunged into darkness.

THE WOMAN LEFT CAROLINA'S HOUSE and stole her bicycle to ride to the bakery. She passed through the first checkpoint using Carolina's papers with ease. Her training had focused on assuming another's identity, so she felt natural taking on the life of someone else. She was told her life was no longer her own when she was recruited and had since forgotten her own existence. Her loyalty was to *Totenkopf,* and total secrecy was essential. She was sure most of the Third Reich did not even know they existed.

As she rode along the muddy road, she thought about the day ahead. Paul Ganoux was due to arrive at 3:30 p.m. with information on a resistance movement designed to covertly sabotage German activities. The woman made the final turn and arrived at Carolina's bakery. After she leaned the bike against the wall, she removed her things from the basket and found the key to the front door.

A small bell attached to the door jingled as she entered the bakery. After turning on the lights, she went to the back and gathered wood for the brick oven. She needed to keep up the appearance of a working bakery until Ganoux arrived. As the oven reached the right temperature, she kneaded some dough into small loaves of bread and slid them inside.

Though she was ready for business by midday, her sign still read "Ferme," as she would not open until later. At 2:30

p.m., she emerged from the back and unlocked the door. She removed the sign from inside the window and turned it over to read "Ouvrir." Since most of the bakery's bread was taken for German consumption, the woman did not expect many customers. In fact, she did not expect anyone until Ganoux arrived. So, she waited patiently in the back, checking and rechecking her pistol. It fit nicely under her apron as she secured it one last time. Then, at 3:25 p.m., she began to sweep out in front of the store.

Her job was to extract as much information from someone as possible before eliminating them. While the German information department could intercept communications in clear weather, her people wanted to squash any uprising before it even took root. The thought of everyday townspeople waging a secret war was taken seriously, even if few believed they had any possibility of doing harm. Most in her office believed they were merely pests, and so far, they were right. She had encountered little resistance from Carolina, and she expected the same from Ganoux. He was a has-been, a relic from World War I.

As she finished sweeping, she noticed a middle-aged man approaching down the road. He was walking briskly toward her store with a slight limp in his right leg; it was him. She went inside and busied herself behind the counter. Ganoux had never met Carolina, so the woman was confident he would not know the difference. The woman went over their conversation one more time in her head. He was to enter her shop and ask her if she had any bread left. She would answer yes and ask, how many loaves would he like? He would answer two. That was the code the Germans had intercepted from Carolina's communications with London; that is what would convince Ganoux she was his contact.

The bell rang as Ganoux entered. He was in good shape and looked young for his age. He was nearly six feet tall with salt-and-pepper hair and was wearing a long coat and gloves. He entered and wished the woman a good afternoon as he rubbed his hands together, shaking off the chill from outside.

"Do you have any bread left for sale?" he asked in a friendly voice.

"Yes," replied the woman. "How many would you like?"

"Two, please." Ganoux replied while intensely studying the woman behind the counter.

The woman invited him into the back. She walked by him and locked the door, turning the sign to "Ferme" again before Ganoux followed her through the curtain into the kitchen.

"How was your journey?" the woman asked. "We are awfully glad to have you here."

"It was fine," Ganoux replied. "Do you have the supplies I requested?"

"Yes, they are in the basement. Follow me."

They took the stairs down to the stone basement. Bags of flour were piled against the wall and a shelf unit on the opposite wall was filled with pots. She turned on the single light bulb; it flickered twice before lighting.

"Everything is in here," she said, approaching a large wooden trunk in the corner. In one motion, she unlocked it, pulled the top open, and rested it against the wall. She removed two sacks and placed them on the table in front of him. He opened both and slid the contents out: a map of Lien, false papers for him, and a revolver. The other sack contained some ammunition, a compass, and dynamite.

"You were able to get everything," he said as he looked up.

"Yes, everything you requested," she said.

"Very good. How far do we need to travel to your farm?"

"It is a 15-minute bicycle ride," she replied, watching his every move.

"How many checkpoints?"

"Only one just past the grist mill, heading out of town."

"Good, we will go now and talk more once we have arrived. Thank you for this," he said, motioning to all the items on the table.

She nodded and smiled. "Thank you, Monsieur Ganoux, you have given me hope."

He stared back at her and nodded slightly while putting everything back into the two sacks. "Yes, we will do great things," he said.

She walked over to the chest and reached for the top. Ganoux followed her across the room and, as she reached down, grabbed her by the neck with his left arm. With his right, he removed a knife and quickly sliced her throat. The sound of her gulping for breath was her last. She fell to the dirt floor as blood leaked from her neck. Ganoux stood over her as he contemplated his next move. He looked around to find a large canvas cloth, which he used to cover and dump the woman's body into the chest with a large thud. He closed the top and locked it.

The orders Carolina had received were all followed exactly, except for one: she was never told his name. When the woman thanked him personally, he knew instantly that she was not Carolina. He had no idea who she was, but Ganoux knew they had already been compromised.

As darkness descended, he grabbed his packs, turned off the light, and proceeded up the stairs. The brick oven was dying down, so he left it with a few embers still glowing. He stopped as he exited the kitchen, backed up two steps, and grabbed a loaf of bread off the blue-and-white tiled counter. He had not eaten all day. Suddenly, he stopped, shook his head and tossed the loaf behind the counter. *This bread was not made by a woman from France,* he thought to himself as he reached the front door. He would eat some other time.

In need of access to a radio, Ganoux decided to go to Carolina's farm. Not sure of what he would find, he chose the long way over hills and through fields, to approach from the back. He walked slowly, but he no longer had a limp. The path led him to the outskirts of town, where he could enter the field well before the last checkpoint and walk through the shadows until he reached the cover of trees. The lack of light slowed him a bit as he walked over rocks and through low-lying branches, but just twenty minutes later, he arrived at Carolina's farmhouse.

He noticed a dimly lit room through pulled curtains, though the rest of the house was shrouded in darkness. After removing and loading his gun, Ganoux walked down the hill toward the rear of the house. He reached a gate and pushed over a large log that was keeping it closed to proceed through. He quietly approached the back door. No activity was evident in the house or around it. He tried the handle: it clicked, but would not open, bolted from the inside. Making his way around the side of the house, he found two flat wooden doors leading down to a basement. He tried the right handle and lifted it up to reveal stone steps leading downward. Ganoux leaned the door against the house and slipped inside, closing it behind him. The basement was completely dark and quiet. He entered from the stairs and found himself standing on a dirt floor. He accidently kicked something and nearly fell to the ground, but once he caught his balance, he could hear heavy breathing to his left. He froze and raised his gun. He also retrieved his flashlight and held it parallel, pressing the switch. He was startled to see a woman staring back at him with wide eyes. She was tied to a chair and had cloth wrapped around her mouth. She looked very much like the woman whose throat he had just slit; he had found Carolina.

He stepped toward her when he heard footsteps upstairs on the wooden floorboards. He shut the flashlight off, raced over, and crouched underneath the stairs. As he waited, a light was turned on and feet began to walk down the stairs. He held his breath and waited as a man appeared and looked around the basement. Ganoux watched through an opening between the stair treads. Carolina stared at the man as he approached her. Ganoux dropped his packs and removed his knife, still covered in blood from earlier. He slowly walked up behind the man, who turned and stumbled backwards with surprise. The man tried reaching for a gun in his waistband, but Ganoux quickly put his foot directly into the man's chest. The man fell backward and hit the floor as Ganoux punched him in the jaw. The man's lip started dripping blood as Ganoux elbowed his ribs. The man winced and looked up just in time to see a hand come down with a knife, plunging deep into his rib cage. He grabbed the arm but quickly lost strength as Ganoux twisted the blade, removed it, and plunged it back in. The man fell limply to the floor, his head coming to rest on its side.

Ganoux fell onto his back. He had been in Lien for four hours and already killed two people. This was not his plan. He stood up after a moment and walked towards Carolina, whose eyes were wide with fear. He untied the rag from her mouth as she gasped and spit on the ground. Ganoux cut the ropes squeezing her wrists and stood over her. She looked at him, still gathering her breath.

"Carolina?" Ganoux wiped his bloody hands on the rag.

She nodded with fear, unable to get any words out.

"I'm Paul Ganoux. We have a lot to talk about."

Carolina stared up at the man standing over her, amazed at how calm he was. "How did you know I was here?"

"I didn't. I went to your bakery and a woman who looked remarkably like you met me there. We talked for a few minutes when she called me by my name. Those were her last words." He looked at the man on the floor. "Do you have any idea who he is, or the woman?"

"She mentioned a secret association of assassins called *Totenkopf*. I came home yesterday, and they attacked me upstairs. I have been extremely cautious, but somehow, they knew who I was and where I live. The woman seemed to be a leader; this guy just watched over me the whole time."

Ganoux paused for a moment and glanced around the basement. "*Totenkopf?*" he repeated.

"She said they knew about you. "

"We need to be more careful going forward. Whoever sent them will be awaiting information. When they don't get any, someone else may come looking around." Ganoux looked at the man he had just killed. "I need to get rid of this body. Is there a barn on your property?"

"Yes, it's across the pasture, but it's falling apart."

"Even better. I'll drag him to the barn and bury him. We will also have to get rid of the woman at the bakery, she is rotting in a chest there."

Carolina massaged her aching wrists, red with rope burn, and breathed deeply. "Thank you," she said, looking at the body on the floor. Ganoux gave her a slight nod.

"Let's get to work," he said. "I'll take care of the body; then, I will need you to show me the radio. I don't think we should use it anymore. We can assume it is being monitored. Tomorrow we will meet the others, and once we are all together, I will lay out the plan."

With that, Ganoux grabbed a tarp, wrapped the body, and slung it over his shoulder. He left the basement through the same doors in which he arrived. Carolina said and felt nothing but calm. She had been waiting for this man to show up and, now that he was here, she had no doubt he was the perfect man for the job. For the first time since Germany invaded, a small glimmer of hope seemed to crack through her thoughts.

8
LONDON

MASON ARRIVED BACK AT THE FLAT. As he was taking off his coat, Collette appeared in the foyer. "So, who was this man?" Collette always got straight to the point.

He closed the closet door. "Hi, nice to see you, too."

She was not amused.

"It was nothing, just a man who had additional information on the possible whereabouts of Kliest."

"Mason, forget about him. He is long gone. What are you going to do? Go to France and find him?"

"If I have to," he said as he walked by her into the living room, where Jacques was sitting and reading a newspaper. He put it down and looked at Mason over his glasses. "Everything all right?"

Mason nodded as he sat down. "It was nothing."

Collette came and sat next to him. She leaned into him and put her feet up on the couch. She said nothing as he kissed the top of her head.

They were back at the War Offices the next morning, searching through more information. In trying to find Anna's family among millions of displaced families, they were essentially looking for a needle in a stack of needles. The amount of people who had fled Europe amounted to half the population, and the fact that her family was Jewish made the situation even more difficult. Rumors were circulating around Europe everyday about the atrocities committed against Jews by the Nazis. Mason was not optimistic they would locate Anna's family alive, but he hoped any information they could find might one day give her some closure.

As Collette continued poring over documents, Mason left to visit Roger. When he reached Roger's office, however, it was empty. Mason slowly wandered in and stood over Roger's desk, trying his best to look casual. He rifled through some papers with one eye on the doorway, listening to the sounds of the office outside. *Can't hurt to look,* he told himself. He went over to the filing cabinet and pulled out a metal drawer as quietly as he could. Roger's files were meticulous and in alphabetical order, with last names prominently displayed. He used his two fingers to quickly move through the files. "Rogers," "Sanders," "Stonewall," "Sullivan" – Frank R. Sullivan. He pulled the file and opened it on top of the cabinet, quickly scanning through it. He looked up when he heard Roger's voice and the quick shuffling of his feet coming down the hall. Mason closed the drawer and shoved the file down the back of his pants, covering it with his shirt. The metal edge of the file scratched against his skin. He sat down in front of the desk as Roger entered. Roger stopped suddenly, caught off guard and displeased with his uninvited guest.

"Hey buddy," Mason said as he stood and extended his hand toward Roger.

"Mr. Wright, must you always show up here at the most inopportune times? Can't you make an appointment like the rest of the world?" Roger put some papers down on his desk.

"I am sorry about that; I didn't know I would be here today." Mason glanced at the papers on the desk. "Since I am, can you give me the information on Kliest?"

Roger quickly turned the papers over and gave Mason a disapproving look. "How did you know I had information on him? Who told you that? It is classified intel."

"You just told me," Mason said with a smile

Roger exhaled and shook his head. "You Yanks are a tricky bunch. I did receive some information on his command post, Mason, but it is confidential." Roger's voice turned to a whisper. "I could be sacked and doing porridge."

Mason looked at him quizzically. "Porridge?"

"Jail time, I believe you would say."

"Roger, you can trust me. I just want to know where he is. There is a war going on; do you think I am going to jump right into the middle of it to go after him? Just tell me where he is, and you will never have to tell me anything ever again."

Roger stared at Mason a moment before shakily walking over to his file cabinet. As he opened the top drawer, Mason hoped he had shuffled the files back into place. Roger pulled out a file and came back to the desk. He pulled out one sheet of paper, handing it to Mason.

Mason glanced over the page, recognizing Kliest's name and rank, as well as some family information and background. Then, listed at the bottom was his current posting: Paris.

Mason handed the document back to Roger, who quickly returned it to the cabinet. Roger returned behind his desk. "Mr. Wright, please let me get back to work."

Mason thanked him and left his office. He happily walked back toward where Collette was sitting but stopped to pour himself a cup of water. Mason smiled slightly as he drank; the newly promoted Major Kliest was closer than he thought.

As Mason walked back into the document room, Collette looked up. "Where have you been? I think I found something," she said.

Mason pulled over a chair and placed the water down. Collette slid a piece of paper across the table that had several names listed on one side. Next to the names were a series of numbers and, on the right side, a list of destinations. Mason followed Collette's finger as she slid it down the page. She stopped at the name "Dressler." Next to it was the number 3 and, on the right side, "DRANCY."

Collette surmised that Anna's mother and her two sisters may have been separated from her father, symbolizing the number 3, but neither of them recognized "DRANCY." Collette was excited, but Mason had no idea how to verify who "Dressler" was, given that it was a common last name. Still, he let Collette be happy with her finding.

"I may know someone who knows what "DRANCY" is," Mason said as he stood up and walked toward the door. "Wait here."

Mason walked back down the hallway toward Roger's

office. He stopped and turned around; Collette was right behind him, raising her brow. Mason opened his mouth, then thought better of it. "Okay, let's go."

When Roger saw Mason back at his door with a woman he did not recognize, his displeasure was evident. To make matters worse, Roger was on the phone as Mason knocked lightly on the outer frame.

"I will get to it right away. Yes, thank you," Roger said before hanging up the receiver. "Mr. Wright, what is it now? Last time I checked, I do not work for you!" Roger then stood and introduced himself politely to Collette. "Roger Knightsbridge, a pleasure to meet you."

"Collette Moulié. Thank you for seeing us, Mr. Knightsbridge," she responded.

"I never seem to have much choice, do I?" Roger said, looking Mason up and down. "This one is quickly becoming a thorn in my side. Every time I turn around, he's in my office wanting information, classified information."

"Oh, come…" Mason tried to interject.

"I understand," Collette said with a slight smile, cutting him off. "He can be rather pushy."

Collette and Roger continued their conversation without further acknowledging Mason, but he listened as Collette told Anna's story and the documentation they had found. Roger seemed more interested than ever. After a few minutes, Collette asked about "DRANCY."

"I have come across that term several times," Roger said. "We are in the process of trying to decipher what exactly it means. As far as we can tell, it is a stopover camp where refugees are registered before being sent to work camps. It is located outside Paris. But Miss Moulié, this is extremely sensitive information."

"I can't thank you enough, Roger," Collette said kindly. "If there is anything I can do for you, please don't hesitate to ask."

Roger glared at Mason. "If you could keep him out of my office so I could work, that would be greatly appreciated.

Maybe he'll take you to Paris with him."

Collette glared at Mason. She stood and thanked Roger before ushering him out of the office.

Halfway down the hallway, she grabbed Mason by the arm. "What is this about Paris?"

"It's nothing."

"It's something."

Mason moved in closer to her and whispered angrily. "I can't forget about Kliest, okay? He took you from me, he nearly killed you, and as long as he is alive, I will always remember."

He turned and stormed away from her. The mere thought of Kliest had soured his mood.

9
LIEN

CAROLINA WOKE THE NEXT MORNING still feeling sore. She found Ganoux in the kitchen cleaning a pistol. After exchanging pleasantries, they sipped coffee as Ganoux laid out the day's plans, beginning with finding the tomb of the Touleau family in the Cemetery of Lien.

It was another grey day as they headed into town, with rain possible at any moment. Ganoux had successfully altered his papers to show he was a resident of Lien and blended in with a group of produce farmers at the first checkpoint. He walked casually behind the wagon of one, the wooden wheels shaking with every rotation. The entire cart nearly toppled when it hit a ditch in the road, but the old horse pulling it was entirely unfazed by the soldiers.

When they reached the town square, Carolina led them up the hill to Saint John's Church; its cemetery housed nearly all those who had died in Lien. The sixteenth century church looked down upon the square and the countryside from the highest point in Lien. Its small, gothic-style steeple held two bells that were forged in Italy and donated to the town after a fire devastated Saint John's in 1863.

Carolina was the first to climb the steps to the front doors. The large, wooden doors were open, allowing the smell of burning candles to escape. Ganoux followed and glanced inside, noticing a few parishioners praying in the pews.

"The entrance to the cemetery is just around this corner," Carolina said, leading Ganoux around the outside of the church and down a small path to a wrought iron gate. The German army had suppressed many things, but they still allowed the Catholic people of Lien to worship and visit with their deceased. Ganoux and Carolina entered the graveyard and ventured toward the aboveground tombs. These family tombs housed up to six bodies in rather ornate, stone burial chambers, many with large iron and glass doors. Inside, each stone floor contained an altar and wooden prayer boxes, with candles, bibles, and mementos of the interred dead. During an internment, the coffin would be carried from the church by family and friends to the tomb and laid to rest on the stone shelf, while the prayer box remained outside for anyone to drop in a note or a memory.

The Touleau family, having lived in Lien for hundreds of years, had a massive tomb in a secluded section of the cemetery that stood out from the rest. A gravel walkway wrapped around several large trees, leading to three stone steps at the front of the tomb. A large stone urn sat on each side, with columns adorning the entrance like an old Roman structure. Carolina, having only been in this portion of the cemetery once, was taken aback by the size of the tomb. She followed Ganoux up the steps, where he produced a key, unlocked the door, and pulled it open. The heavy door creaked as he pulled it aside. They slipped inside and closed the door.

The twelve-foot by twelve-foot main area housed four coffins, two on each side. A small altar was directly across from the front doors. Ganoux set his pack down on a stone bench in the middle of the room and turned to lock the door. The only light streamed in through a decorative, iron rose lattice.

Ganoux again produced a key and opened the prayer box closest to him. He retrieved an oil lantern, lit it, and placed it on the top shelf.

"How do you know about this place?" Carolina asked him while looking around.

"My family has known the Touleau family for generations. Mr. Touleau fled to America when the war broke out, but I told him I would remain. He asked me to look after their mausoleum."

Ganoux unloaded his bag and placed two guns, a knife, and some papers in the prayer box. He then turned to Carolina, holding another key. "I need you to hold onto this. We will use this place as a gathering spot for weapons and information. I will not always be able to be here, so you need to have access in my absence." Carolina took the key and placed it in her front pocket. Ganoux continued. "You will need to start coming here during the day and be seen entering and exiting the cemetery. The more you are seen around the church, the less suspicious you will be. I suggest you also start attending services and make yourself known to the pastor."

"I have been to this church several times and know Father Lassiter well," Carolina responded. "He will be happy to see me back."

"Good. Now, I want you to exit and stop into the church to pray. I will meet you at the café at 6:00 p.m. Sit at a table against the wall in the back, keep to yourself, and bring a book to read. When I enter, if I am not wearing this scarf, you are to leave immediately, go to your house, and wait for me. Understand?" Ganoux held out the scarf for her to see.

Carolina nodded, unlocked the door, and left. Ganoux stayed behind on the bench for a few minutes. He retrieved a small map of Lien and flattened it on top of one of the coffins. He followed the area on the outskirts with his finger until he located the train tracks. He then followed the route along the tracks and stopped over the name of his next destination: the Rouge Bridge. He tapped the map twice and exhaled.

Ganoux left the cemetery and passed by the front of the church. He briefly caught a glimpse of Carolina with her head bowed in silent prayer, sitting in a pew near the back. The bells of the church rang in 11:00 a.m. as Ganoux walked briskly out of town.

THE RAILROAD TRACKS WERE approximately one-quarter mile from the road. Beneath the cover of trees in the forest on the south side of town, Ganoux walked with purpose as branches cracked under his boots and leaves blew across the ground. When a steam train whistle was audible in the distance, he knew he was close. He reached a clearing at the top of the hill and paused for a moment, taking out the map.

Just over the next hill would be another clearing, where he would have a clear view of the bridge and the tracks.

Though the wind picked up as he reached higher ground, some hawks still glided effortlessly above. Ganoux reached the second hill, dropped his bag, and took out a pair of binoculars. He lay on his stomach at the edge of the clearing and brought them to his face. The tracks immediately came to life in front of him. Two Wehrmacht soldiers with rifles stood outside a guard house before the bridge, talking and smoking. A path for access had been cut through the field leading to a road in the distance. A heavy-duty BMW Zundapp 750 CC motorcycle with a sidecar was parked nearby. Smoke billowed from a steam pipe on the roof. It was exactly as Ganoux had envisioned, including the several hundred foot drop in terrain as the bridge extended across the Lien River valley.

The Rouge Bridge, which connected Lien to southern France, was used as the primary mode of transportation by the German army when moving goods, troops, weapons, and supplies from Paris to the south. A single train leaving Paris at 7:45 a.m. would stop at Lien forty-five minutes later. Troops returning from leave in Paris frequently rode this 700BR 44 eight-car steam train, as it was the quickest way to Paris and back. Other trains were reserved for the French residents coming and going from the capital city.

Ganoux focused on the bridge, taking mental notes as he scanned every inch. The single-track bridge was rusted with faded red paint, but he paid particularly close attention to the supports on each side of the bridge, rising from the rock of the mountain's edge. Ganoux's plan was to destabilize it just enough to collapse under the weight of the train. Such an "accident" would take several enemy lives without retribution. He would return to this spot the next morning to watch the train arrive.

Ganoux gathered his things and traveled back down the mountain toward the town. He reached a farm and went straight to the barn, meeting a man who would help him with his next task.

"Phillipe, it is good to see you."

"You as well, my friend."

Phillipe, an avid hunter, had a stone pit in his barn used to coat unused animal parts in a mixture of fertilizer and chemicals that slowly disintegrated flesh and bone. Ganoux was particularly interested in this aspect of Phillipe's expertise.

"We have two bodies, one in the farmhouse, the other in the bakery," he said. "I will retrieve both and dispose of them here. We can do one tonight and one tomorrow."

Phillipe nodded. "You can put the body in the pit and cover it with a layer of hay from over there," he said, pointing to some bales sitting near a wooden chest in the corner. "And you can take my truck; she is not much, but she should do the job. I've filled the back with hay and cow manure, thinking the smell might deter the soldiers at the checkpoint from conducting a thorough search. Be careful, my friend." Phillipe shook Ganoux's hand.

Ganoux nodded slightly and left the barn. The old truck started quickly, though smoke poured from its exhaust. He drove down the path to the road and turned right towards Carolina's farm, leaving a trail of smoke behind him. At the checkpoint, two soldiers approached the driver's side window. One took Ganoux's papers while the other walked to the back of the truck. He barely searched the bed as he covered his nose.

"What is the nature of your trip?" the soldier at the driver's side window asked with curiosity.

"A delivery," Ganoux said flatly.

The soldier glanced past him at the front seat. The other soldier then said something to him in German, waving his hand in front of his face as he walked by. The soldier waved him on.

Ganoux reached the farm and parked near the barn doors. The body of the man, wrapped in a large canvas cloth, needed to be buried in the manure to return to Phillipe's farm. Ganoux climbed onto the back of the truck and removed two bales of hay. He then grabbed a pitchfork and spread the manure to two sides. He dropped the body in the middle, covered it, and went back on his way.

The same soldier stopped Ganoux at the checkpoint, but the other never even left the warmth of the fire burning in a metal drum outside the guardhouse. As Ganoux drove away, he smirked as he thought of how powerful a weapon cow dung was in times of war.

Once back at Phillipe's barn, he removed the manure-covered body and dumped it into the stone pit, where both he and Phillipe covered it with Phillipe's liquid mixture. Ganoux covered his mouth and nose as the smell rose from the pit: one body down, one to go.

10
LONDON

MASON LEFT THE FLAT EARLY the next day to clear his head; Kliest had been clouding his mind since they left the War Offices. He walked down to the corner and over to a small café for some coffee and a pastry when a car pulled up next to him.

"Get in," Sully said as it came to a stop.

Mason looked around before hopping in the front seat.

"I have some interesting information," Sully said. "I just received word that the Germans are planning celebrations throughout occupied Europe as a reward for their troops. Several large cities will be hosting high commanders, Paris being one of them. I have a contact outside of Paris who runs a café in Lien. She told me the Hotel Lien will also be hosting a visitor: your old friend Johan Kliest."

Mason's eyes widened as he heard the name. "Are you sure?"

"You can never be sure in times of war, but I trust my people," Sully said. "Apparently, he is coming in for a private celebration away from the glitz of Paris. The town of Lien is small enough to disappear for a few hours."

"Seems odd that someone of his stature would shun the spotlight. Is anyone else going with him?"

"That I don't know, but the town will be hosting the celebration at the main hotel, which has now become headquarters for the command of Lien."

"Can you get me there?" Mason suddenly felt a rush of excitement building inside.

"I don't think that is a good idea." Sully shook his head. "No offense Mason, but you're just a civilian. You think you are going to just show up and kill a German commander? You will never make it out of there. Once word got out that a Nazi commander was murdered, the city would be shut down and you would be hunted like an animal. In fact, you would never even get close to him, given the high levels of security."

Mason stared at Sully. "What is happening to us right now? Why must we sit around and wait to be killed on the streets of London? This is a good chance to get to him outside of Paris. We may get the answers we are looking for! I may be just a civilian, but I made my way from New York to Paris and all around France while eluding Kliest and his people, and I had the last laugh as he fled. This is pretty damn personal for me."

Sully stared at him a moment. "Look, Mason, I get it. I don't disagree with you, but it is a complicated mission to pull off. If we kill him, the town will suffer far too much retaliation."

"Then we make it look like an accident."

"How would we do that?'

"You said it's a celebration. Lots of people would provide us cover. Food and drink could both make a man sick, possibly even deathly ill."

"We would still need to get in there."

"You have someone in Lien that can get us into town. We can figure it out from there."

Sully thought for a minute. "My contact in Lien is working to gain the trust of the Germans. It's a long shot, but I suppose we could try it. She will also be working with an old friend of yours."

"Who's that?"

"Paul Ganoux."

Mason's jaw dropped at the sound of Ganoux's name. Sully proceeded to tell Mason about the growing resistance in the French countryside. "He is gathering information on the rail station. Seems there is something very secretive going on there. He wants to disable the bridge and is looking for competent people to help him pull it off."

"If they could use the help, we need to go. This sounds

too good to be true. Killing Kliest would be great, but blowing a bridge and supply route up, that sounds like fun."

Sully looked at Mason. "You're serious?"

"Absolutely. Ganoux is a top man and a friend. If we can get there, we can help. That would be a small victory which, let's face it, we could all use right now."

Sully agreed to seek the authorization needed for Mason and him to travel into France as part of a highly covert operation. Mason left the car and started walking back to the flat. He had promised Collette he would never keep anything from her again, but he knew her reaction to this would not be good. He took a few breaths as he hopped up the front steps to the building.

Collette was sitting in the kitchen with Anna when he entered. He sat and exchanged small talk for a bit until Collette's mother, Angeline, brought in a puzzle and asked Anna if she would like to help her with it. Anna nodded as they both went to the dining room table.

Mason looked at Collette. "I need to talk to you about something very important."

Collette said nothing as she sipped her tea and looked at Mason.

"I told you Kliest was in Paris," he said.

Collette nodded, anxiously awaiting his next words.

"I met with a man named Frank Sullivan," Mason continued. "He is an American working here in London for a specialized branch of the police. Someone is targeting him and his people here in occupied Europe. There was an attempt on his life the other day and, after killing the assassin, he found a list with names on it. His name was on it – and so was mine."

Collette slammed down her tea. "Mason, this list – what kind of list?"

"He thinks it may be a kill list. The other names are men who work clandestinely under him. One man was murdered here in downtown London a few days ago. Sully asked me why I would be on the list, but I told him I had no idea. Then I told him about what had happened with Kliest and suggested maybe he had something to do with it."

"Does Sully know Kliest?"

"No, but he asked what this list might have to do with me and Kliest was all I could think…"

Collette interrupted him. "Mason, the world is at war. Why would a German commander remain obsessed with you right now? I think he may have other things to worry about."

Mason was undeterred. "I know Kliest; I beat him at his game. That sticks with someone like him. I know he would love to get his hands on me again."

"Mason, this is dangerous. If he got to one of Sully's men, he could get to you again. You lived through the events of the other day, but if he wants you dead, people will keep coming after you. We need to tell the British police."

"Absolutely not. This information is highly classified; Sully basically kidnapped me before he told me. The fact that he trusts me is the only reason I know this."

"What then, what are you going to do?"

"Kliest is stationed in Paris but will be traveling to the suburb of Lien for a private celebration. I can get to him there and we will never have to worry about this again."

"You want to go to France and confront him? Mason, that is ludicrous."

Mason shifted in his chair. "Our old friend Paul Ganoux is growing a resistance there, a small band of fighters working quietly against the Germans. I can meet up with him and ask for his help."

"You can't do this alone; it's too dangerous. Mason, he will notice you a mile away. You're out of your mind!"

"I can't just sit here and do nothing. I know we are helping with the war effort, but I need to be involved to a greater extent. I'm no good to anyone sitting at a table going over documents, and besides, I won't be going alone: Sully is coming with me. The plan is to meet up with Ganoux and find a way to infiltrate the party. Sully knows a woman who owns a café in town, who may be able to help us gain entry."

"You're right. You won't be alone."

Mason felt a lump grow in his throat. "What do you mean?" he said, knowing the answer.

"I'm coming with you," Collette said as she stood and walked to the sink with her teacup.

Mason stared straight ahead at her empty chair until she returned and raised her brow.

"Mason, I am not letting you out of my sight after what happened. If Sully is as good as you say, we should be fine. You two are Americans, I am French; you will need someone to navigate the language and the country. You need me there."

She makes a good point, he thought. *She always does.*

After a lengthy pause, Mason rubbed his face in exasperation. "I guess I can talk to Sully and gather more information before we make a final decision."

Collette agreed; she, too, felt helpless. Here she was, tucked safely away with her family in London while her country was overrun by Nazis. The pictures of Hitler touring Paris and posing in front of its famed monuments had shocked the world, just one day after France signed the Armistice of 22 June 1940. If Collette wanted to do more, this would be her chance.

As Mason continued to passionately discuss the details, Collette was reminded why she loved this man. Last time they were in her homeland together, they were always in danger. That was before the Nazi army took over; this time would be even more treacherous. Still, she, too, relished the thought of watching Kliest die. He deserved it after what he did to her. She hoped they could get close enough to kill him.

MASON CONTACTED SULLY and they agreed to meet. Collette joined them, as Mason explained his thought process as diplomatically as he could. He waited for Sully to respond, secretly hoping he would decide against it.

"I think it's a great idea," Sully said.

"You do?" Mason felt Collette's eyes boring into the side of his head.

"Yes, as a French citizen, she can go places we cannot.

Marie could use some help."

"Good, yes, I was thinking the same thing." Mason tried to sound convincing. He knew they were both right. Since Collette did not require fake papers, she would be able to travel and gather information with greater ease.

Sully, knowing Ganoux would be with them, felt they could pull this off. If Kliest was indeed behind the list of names, he would kill him himself. He just hoped Mason was not simply leading them into the belly of the beast for revenge.

There were still several questions to be answered and details to be planned, but Sully was quite persuasive when he needed something. First, Sully needed to request permission and a small plane from his superiors to drop into Spain. Sully would find a pilot willing to fly them into the Spanish border town of San Sebastian and subsequent transport to occupied territory. The Zone Libre, established following the Armistice of Compiegne, encompassed the southern half of France and its borders with Spain and Italy. It was run by a puppet Vichy government with limited power. Once there, they would need to rely on resistance sympathizers to get them closer to Paris. While confident they could get into France, figuring out how to get back home would prove more difficult.

When Mason and Collette told Jacques of their plan, he was visibly shaken, but understood why. He felt more comfortable once he learned they would be meeting up with Ganoux. Jacques agreed to tell Angeline, but Collette would need to tell Anna.

Mason hadn't felt such nervous excitement for an adventure in quite some time.

11

COLLETTE JOINED MASON ON HIS early morning walks, the extra security Sully had provided not far behind. Mason explained to her that Sully would contact them at some point.

"We just walk every day until he finds us?" she asked incredulously.

"Yes, we walk every day until he finds us," Mason answered, slightly annoyed.

A few days went by and finally one morning a car pulled up next to them. Sully motioned to them and they got in his car and drove away. They rode a few blocks to an abandoned warehouse where Sully stopped and the three of them ventured inside.

Mason sat next to Collette and the three began ironing out details for their mission.

"I had to cash in some favors but was able to get us a plane which will take us to San Sebastian, Spain. From there we will pose as workers at a vineyard. I have a contact who will meet us and transport us to the wine region which borders the occupied zone.

"I assume you can travel under your own papers?" he asked Collette.

"Yes, I still have active citizenship. My papers are current, I can freely travel in and out of France."

"Mason and I will be scrutinized upon entry, so we need to be very convincing or we are never making it out of Spain."

Mason nodded. "I'll be on my best behavior. Don't worry about me."

"Good. But Mason, this is a different level of security, the checkpoints are looking for any reason to detain someone; don't give them one. Try to be as cooperative as possible; it is the only way we will pull this off," Sully said as he glanced back and forth between the two of them. "Any questions?"

Collette spoke up, "Do you really think Kliest is behind all of this or is it something bigger?"

Sully looked at her. "Honestly, I don't know. I do not think we will know until we get there. Kliest's name has been linked to the killing of John Cleary and the attempts on both of us. I am sure he is targeting my contacts in Europe but so far I have heard nothing. We are researching the word Totenkopf but, again, we have not been able to decipher exactly what it is or how Kliest is involved. We have picked up some chatter about railway shipments going south but not much more than that. What is being shipped, we do not know. If he is still in the stolen art trade, it could very well be that. I will say that if he is not behind the list of names on the kill list, I am still sure he is doing horrific things to a lot of people. For that alone, he deserves what is coming to him. Britain is on board with any mission targeting military commanders. Cut off the head and the body dies. They have made it very clear; we are on our own once we get there. I have arranged for us to get there but it is up to us to get out. You both understand that?"

They both nodded as a noise outside distracted all three. Sully removed a pistol from his waistband. He headed to the window for a look, glanced outside, and then walked over to the main door. He opened it and a man entered carrying a brown case. The older gentleman wore glasses and walked unsteadily. He had the look of an old scholar with grey beard, and spectacles.

"This is Mr. Dowd; he will do our papers." Sully said as he followed the man to the table.

Dowd put his case down and opened it, removing a camera and some folders. He motioned Mason to the wall. "You, stand against the wall, please stand still."

Mason did as he was told and turned to face the old man. The man backed up a few paces. He held the camera at his chest and pressed the button. The sound of the clicking lens filled the air. The man turned the handle and took another shot. "One more," he said.

"Now you." he looked at Sully who repeated Mason's

steps. After a few pictures of Sully, the man opened his folder and produced two sets of blank papers. "I need you both to fill out the information in this section and then sign the bottom."

Both men did as they were asked, and then slid the papers back over to him. He scooped them up, put them in his case and closed it. "Good day, you will have them tomorrow," he said as he left.

Sully looked at Mason and Collette. "He is a man of few words but his papers speak for themselves; they're the best."

The three agreed to meet every day to iron out their plans. Sully would work on securing the transport, Mason would gather their gear and Collette would perfect their route. The warehouse would serve as their base of operations. Sully gave Mason a second key as they left.

The next day, Mason and Sully drove to a warehouse in south London. As they passed through the streets, Mason was amazed at the resiliency of the British people. They went about their daily lives knowing full well Germany would eventually come for them. They walked past anti-aircraft guns in their squares, sandbags in front of their buildings, and soldiers posted throughout the city. The Underground stations had been turned into bomb shelters in anticipation of nighttime raids. In June, the evacuation of Dunkirk had raised the morale of the English people. A whole country had held its breath as 200,000 young British men were stranded on a French beach awaiting ships to bring them home. With the Channel on one side and the German Wehrmacht on the other, the soldiers could do nothing but wait. Eventually enough ships, military and civilian, were able to evacuate everyone. It was a bitter defeat for Britain, but they basked in the glory of having their "boys" home in hopes of one day fighting again.

Sully pulled up to a military checkpoint outside a large warehouse. A British private approached the window with his Enfield Rifle on his shoulder. He motioned for Sully to stop.

"Identity cards please," he said in a thick accent.

Sully handed him his ID along with a requisition order signed by the office of the Prime Minister. The soldier looked

briefly at the ID and the papers before handing them back.
"Proceed," he said, waving them on. The gate opened, and
they drove around the back of the warehouse to a loading bay.
Sully parked and the two of them went inside and down a
flight of steps to a wall of fencing extending from the floor to
the ceiling. A man sat at a desk near an entry door. Sully slid
his papers through the opening to the man. He handed them
back with a quizzical look.

"It is not every day a couple of Yanks show up here to
pick up supplies."

"I guess it is your lucky day," Sully said as he grabbed the
papers.

"I don't like it. I don't like it at all," the young Brit said as
he stood and walked over to the door.

"I don't care what you like, I have orders which originate
far above you."

"You Yanks, so smug, you think you're so tough but when
we ask for help, you're too scared to enter the war. You sit
across the pond and pretend nothing is happening. A bunch of
cowards if you ask me."

Another soldier walked over. "Tommy, take it easy, it's
not worth it."

"No, it's ok," Sully said. "How about you open the door,
and we will see who the real coward is."

"With pleasure." the Brit said.

"Ah, Sully there you are, I have been waiting for you
two." The voice came across the room as a man approached.
The two British soldiers turned and snapped to attention, their
right hands in a salute.

"At ease boys," the man said.

The cocksure soldier stood at attention as his
commanding officer approached.

"Everything ok, boys?" the man asked, looking at his
suddenly uneasy two privates.

"Yes sir," they replied in unison.

Sully spoke up as the officer looked his way. "I have the
list of supplies I spoke to you about."

The officer looked back at his two soldiers. "Well boys, let them through."

One soldier fumbled for his keys and quickly unlocked the door. Sully and Mason walked into the large warehouse.

"How are you Jack?" Sully said to his old friend.

"I would be better if the Germans were not twenty miles away."

"I hear you." Sully replied. "This is Mason Wright."

"Jack Childers. A pleasure."

Mason shook his hand firmly.

Sully handed the list to Jack who gazed at it for a moment. "I believe we should have everything. Ok boys, let's get these gentlemen everything they need."

"Yes sir," the two said again as they grabbed the list. Sully shot the arrogant one a look as they scurried away.

The three remained behind and waited patiently.

"Sully, I am sorry about John Cleary; he was a good man."

"He was. We have some leads we are chasing down, but nothing yet."

"That's good. Well, I am happy you managed to escape harm. These days are getting more dangerous by the hour. You better watch your back, Sully."

Always…you too Jack."

The two soldiers returned with a handful of gear on a cart, a field radio, some flashlights, soldier's knives, two rifles, ammunition, some rope, canteens and two field medic kits." They packed everything into a gear bag and handed the rifles to Mason and Sully.

"Anything else you boys need, let me know."

"Thanks Jack." Sully shook his hand and Mason followed suit with a nod.

"Thanks boys," Sully said to the two privates.

Both Brits nodded and then the arrogant one spoke up. "I'm sorry, sir."

"It's ok, son, we are all on edge. What do you say we save all that aggression for the real enemy across your channel, who's close and getting closer. I hope you'll be as tough when they come knocking on your door."

"Yes sir," the private said sheepishly.

With that, Sully and Mason left the warehouse with their supplies and headed to meet Collette.

When they arrived, Collette was inside with some maps of Spain and France. She had laid them out on the table with some weights on the corners. There was a wine barrel in the middle of the room.

"Did you bring some wine for the warehouse?" Mason said with a grin.

"Not exactly," Collette answered, her eyes never leaving the maps. They gathered around the table and Collette shared her thoughts.

"I have studied these maps and think I can get us all the way to the line of the occupied zone. It may take us two days, but it should be straight forward."

Sully spoke up. "We will be traveling as workers from a vineyard, with a truck and a driver. Collette, you will ride in the cab with our driver, and we..." Sully looked at Mason "need to ride in the back with the wine barrels and the gear. We can switch out at various points but should only have two up-front at any given time. At the checkpoints, they will be inspecting the barrels, we have to hope they don't check every one of them."

"Why is that?" Mason asked with a glance. Collette looked at Sully.

"Mason, how limber are you?"

"What do you mean?"

Sully looked at Mason. "You and I will be in two of those barrels. The gear will be in a third. We need to be sealed in while we are moving and hope we do not run into trouble. That is why I had a wine barrel brought here—to practice."

Mason looked at the barrel "You serious? That looks pretty tight."

"Yes, it is, but it is the only way we can move undetected through France. The three barrels will be toward the front of the truck, the rest will have wine in them. Those will be the most accessible in case they get opened. Don't worry, our barrels will have holes in them so we have ventilation."

Mason continued to look at the barrel as he walked over to it. He crouched next to it and sized it up. He removed the top of the barrel and looked inside. The smell of French oak filled the air. Sully joined him at the barrel. Both men were similar in build so if one fit the other should as well.

"Want to give it a try?" Sully asked as he glanced in the barrel.

"Sure. I'm feeling pretty good."

Sully nodded and grabbed a chair from the table for Mason to stand on. Mason stepped up on the chair and with Sully's help slid into the barrel until he was standing inside, his bottom half obscured by the oak. He bent his knees and shimmied himself down into the barrel until only his head was showing.

"Wow...this is not comfortable." he said, moving around to try to get a better position. He managed to slide into a space where his legs were bent and folded underneath his rear end, and he still had access to his arms to pull the top over the barrel. Mason lowered his head as Sully covered the barrel.

"You shouldn't have had that second pastry this morning," Collette chimed in from across the room with a smirk.

"You're hysterical," Mason said from inside the barrel.

"You ok?" Sully asked after he rested the barrel lid over the opening.

"This is the most uncomfortable position I have ever been in," came the muted voice form inside the barrel.

"You have some time until we leave, I suggest you do some stretching, I don't need you pulling a muscle on our way into a war zone."

Sully removed the lid and Mason pulled himself up by the top of the barrel. He arched his back when he stood, and Sully helped him out back onto the chair. They switched positions and Sully wiggled his way into the barrel. He seemed to be more successful than Mason but neither one was very comfortable once inside. It was the best they could do so they would make it work.

"Hopefully, we won't need to be sealed for too long at any point, maybe only once or twice. Once we get into France we can relax a bit as we travel across the free zone. The hard part will be travelling in occupied France. We could be subject to emergency checkpoints at any time."

"I'll be fine," Mason said convincingly.

"Good, you don't really have a choice," Sully said with a slight grin.

"I told you to get in better shape but you didn't listen," Collette put in as she approached.

"Nothing wrong with my shape," Mason said looking at her.

"We leave soon. We will meet here that night and travel to the airstrip. Once airborne, there will be no turning back. Spain is hardly a neutral country; they have cozied up to Hitler to try to avoid being invaded. We cannot let our guard down at any point.

Collette joined Mason at his side. They stood there staring at the barrel, and Mason's thoughts again turned to Kliest. *One step closer* he thought. A plane, to a truck, to a barrel, to occupied territory, and then to Kliest.

Mason held Collette as he tried to separate the mission from revenge. He had to remain focused for everyone involved. Revenge was his motive, but he needed his perspective.

12
Lien

AT 6:32 P.M. GANOUX walked in the front door of Café Saint. Joanna to a half empty room. Marie Riberau was behind the bar to the left pouring some local Sancerre into two glasses. She delivered them to a local couple seated nearby. At a table to his right sat some Wehrmacht soldiers talking in German and behaving loudly; they were clearly comfortable as an occupying force. A petite French woman sat at a table in the back reading a book just as he had suggested. Philippe was clearing some dishes off a table near the kitchen. Marie looked up, and in French told the gentleman he could sit anywhere but the kitchen was closed. Curfew was 7 p.m., and the cafe would be closing soon.

Ganoux acknowledged the woman behind the bar and took a seat near the window. She came over. "Good evening. Would you like something to drink?"

"Tea, please."

She nodded and disappeared in the back. The German soldiers barely noticed Ganoux walk in as they were well on their way to forgetting most of the night.

He sat silently as his tea showed up. He sipped it as he studied the area. The stone walls were tastefully decorated with paintings of the countryside, and over the bar was a black and white picture of a woman and her dog. Above the frame written in black script paint were the words "Café Saint Joanna Est. 1932." A few minutes passed and the petite French woman stood and walked to the door. She waved to Marie behind the bar, "Au revoir," she said, pulled her coat tight, and left. She was soon followed by the young local couple who finished their Sancerre and rushed home before curfew.

Marie announced last call, much to the dismay of the drunken soldiers. They each ordered one more beer and proceeded to have a chugging contest, drinking little and spilling most on their uniforms and the floor. They slammed down their mugs and one man almost fell off his chair in laughter. Eventually they gathered what was left of themselves and staggered out the door. They left a soaking mess on the table and floor. Marie cursed them in French under her breath as she collected their glasses.

She stopped at Ganoux's table and left a pay slip. Ganoux collected it along with the key underneath. He left some money and departed through the front door. The drunken soldiers were outside attempting unsuccessfully to light some cigarettes. Between the wind and the booze, they were failing miserably and laughing as they stumbled away. Ganoux walked to the right on his way home. He gazed around the square—there was little activity. Curfew was any minute now and most townspeople were home already. He reached the end of the building, looked around, then slipped into the bushes on the side of the café. Slowly walking through the dark and briefly losing his balance on the uneven ground, he arrived at the back of the building. A figure stood by the back steps. He walked toward the person and as he closed in, Carolina's face came into view. Saying nothing, he walked down the stone steps to a door. Reaching in his pants pocket he retrieved the key he had received from Marie, using it to unlock the door. They both stepped inside and locked the door behind them. They waited for a moment and then Ganoux found his way to the light. He pulled the chain, and a bulb flickered on offering some light to the basement room.

"We will wait here until they are finished. How did it go in the church? Have you regained your faith?"

"Yes, it went well. Father Lassiter was happy to see me. I promised him I would be back on a regular basis. He was pleased to hear that. He told me his congregation was dwindling as more German soldiers began attending services. He asked me if I would be unsettled by this. I told him that my relationship with God was more important and I would continue to view it as such, so I would not be bothered by their presence."

"Good, the more regular, the better. You will not raise suspicion if you are always around. I did some poking around today, went through a few checkpoints so hopefully it will be easier from here on in. The Germans appear pretty content here. They don't seem concerned with the locals."

As he finished speaking, the sound of someone on the stairs took their attention. Ganoux grabbed his pistol and put his finger to his mouth, telling Carolina quiet. He inched toward the door and leaned against the wall on the hinge side of the door. The door slowly opened, and he readied his gun. He relaxed as Marie entered the room followed by Phillipe.

"Paul, it is good to see you."

"You as well, Marie."

Phillipe nodded toward Ganoux.

Marie looked around and then spoke up "Please tell me there is more than just the two of you?"

"Not tonight," Ganoux answered. "But soon there will be more. Tell me what has transpired so far. Have you been able to develop some trust?"

Marie retrieved her journal which bore the Cross of Lorraine on the cover, the adopted symbol of Vichy France and the Resistance. She recapped the night of the shooting and her subsequent trip to see Volmer. She told him about the retaliation and the firing squad; Ganoux nodded along.

"Do you think anyone suspects you or this place?"

"No." Marie replied "There is an air of cockiness around the Germans; they feel a sense of invincibility. The townspeople do not seem to provide a threat to them, so they pay little attention to us. Since the executions in the square soldiers have been in and out as if on holiday. And Volmer— he views this as his gift for all his war service. He is going to enjoy himself and indulge. I can feel his guard coming down every time I see him. His ego far outweighs his intelligence."

Ganoux explained his day and Carolina's ordeal with her captors. He mentioned Phillipe was helping him dispose of the bodies. They all agreed to be extra careful. Someone knew about them. Ganoux figured the two bodies would be missed by someone, and eventually, someone would come looking for them.

"Ok, let us get down to business. I went to the train bridge today and watched the guards for a bit. There is little more than a guardhouse and two or three guards by the bridge. A larger regiment is stationed on the other side of the ravine. That is what we hope to cut off. We would like this to look as much like an accident as we can—an old bridge that structurally gave out. The less reason we give the Germans to retaliate against the town and its people, the longer we can continue to do this. I think if we focus on the tracks on this side of the ravine we should be able to destabilize the whole bridge and then the weight of the train should take it down, a tragic accident, an old bridge that failed."

"How do we make the bridge vulnerable?" Marie asked.

"That is my department." Phillipe answered. "As you know, I have been a farmer for many years, and I have always experimented with alchemy. I have created a lethal mix of fertilizer, lye, and battery acid which is corrosive to steel. Applied directly to the metal, it will deteriorate over time. How long? I do not know; it depends on many factors. I believe along with a small explosive device, we can damage the supports, and hope the weight of the train brings it down."

"Phillipe and I will continue to watch the bridge and document the soldiers' movements. Once we have their exact schedule we will begin with the plan. Until then, business as usual. Marie, continue to gather information, Carolina, you go to church, and we will do our part. Oh…one more thing. We will be hiding supplies in an above ground tomb in the Cemetery of Lien. If you need anything held there, let me know. Right now, we have plenty of room but it will start to fill up fast."

"When will we see the others?" Marie asked as she secured her precious pen in her journal.

"I am not sure. They will be here when they get here."

She hoped it would be soon, it had been too long.

13
London

SULLY PICKED UP MASON IN front of his flat. They drove across town to Saint James Park and right into a large military presence on the southwestern edge of the park directly across the street from the Ministry of Defense. Sully parked on the street a few blocks away. As they walked toward the Ministry building, Mason wondered why they were there.

"Where are we headed?" he asked as they walked across the wet cobblestone street.

"We have a meeting. I need to explain the details of what has happened, and I decided since you will be risking your life, that you are entitled to be there," Sully replied as they reached the corner of Saint James Park.

The Ministry of Defense, which housed the War Offices of the British Empire, was located across the street from the park. Mason and Collette had been to the building several times over the last few months. Mason was authorized for entry due to an extensive background check and was listed on the official list of persons allowed limited access. He always entered through the front doors and would immediately have to register with the front desk before being allowed to proceed. The process was time consuming but he understood. In times of war, corners could not be cut. He would check in with the same men manning the desk every time. No pleasantries were exchanged; it was all business.

"We need to enter through the side entrance, so I need you to have your identification out at all times. Even though you are with me, they will scrutinize every aspect of you upon entry. Understood?"

"Yes," Mason replied looking at Sully. "I didn't know there was a side entrance. I always go in the front."

"All the regular folks go in the front; our meeting is

through the side door."

"I guess if people are trying to kill you, you get side door access?" Mason asked with a slight smirk.

"Yeah, something like that. Let's go."

Sully started across the street and up to the wrought iron gate. The street was closed to traffic and two sets of anti-aircraft guns bookended the street. Sandbags were piled near the main entrance and several British home front soldiers were standing throughout the street in groups of various numbers. Most were having casual conversations in between puffs of cigarettes. A few glanced at them. Two Yanks in street clothes were an odd sight at the Ministry these days but most of the soldiers knew Sully as someone who was frequently seen there, so they kept their distance. Sully was well known and respected to most people around here. They did not know his official title, just that he was important. The man he was walking with was not as recognizable, so a few soldiers kept their eye on Mason as they approached the gate.

"Morning," Sully said as they advanced to the gate. Two British soldiers emerged from the guardhouse at the entrance.

"Morning, Sully," one of them replied.

Sully passed his credentials through the opening and the soldier gave them to his partner who disappeared back into the guardhouse. They waited a minute and then he returned with Sully's papers. Mason handed his through and the same process was repeated. Sully confirmed their meeting, and both men were allowed entry. Mason was given a credential with a large V on it in red; he attached it to his shirt. Sully was given his credential pass which clearly showed he was more important. Mason's credential told everyone who looked at him that he was just a visitor. Sully's credentials showed a more permanent presence. It had his picture, his name, and a description with height and weight.

Sully and his Visitor friend entered the side entrance and approached the table. A man sitting behind the table stood as they approached. Sully raised his credentials as the man inspected it. Sully removed his pistol and laid it on the table in front of him.

"Thank you, Sully." The man turned his attention to Mason. "Morning. I need to see your identification, and you will need to sign the logbook. Please leave all weapons here."

Mason removed his Colt and laid it down, then handed over his ID and grabbed the pen. He wrote his name and time of entry in the column on the left and signed his name on the right. The man compared his ID signature to the one in the book. Satisfied, he handed it back to him. "This is Private Hollins. He will accompany you." Mason looked over to Sully with a quizzical look.

"They don't know you, so you get a chaperone."

"Ah." Mason said. "Private Hollins, Nice to meet you."

"Sir." Hollins replied at attention.

"Thank you, gentlemen," the man said, nodding. He grabbed the phone receiver on his desk, waited a moment and then spoke, "Frank Sullivan and Visitor on their way."

He hung up the receiver. "You can go ahead."

The men proceeded down the hallway to the doorway on the right. Sully opened the door marked "15" and they entered, Hollins following behind. Once they reached the stairwell, Mason started to gain a sense of where they were. The famous staircase 15 led down to the underground bunker where the war was being monitored. The beige paint on the stone walls was only two years old. Commissioned by the British government, the bunker was deemed operational on Sunday August 27, 1939, one week before Germany invaded Poland starting World War II.

As Mason and Sully headed down the stairs, Mason looked at the massive, red iron ceiling supports riveted together. Sully talked as he walked in front of Mason, who barely paid attention as he looked around, captivated by what he saw. Two men came around the corner and jogged past them up the stairs. They reached the ground floor and arrived in the main hallway entrance to the bunker. A man met them at the entrance and shook Sully's hand.

"Sully."

"How you doing John?"

"Doing quite well, you?"

"Still above ground, so doing pretty well."

"Not technically down here though," John said with a grin.

"Good point," Sully responded with a smile.

Sully introduced Mason and John nodded, "Pleasure, sir," with his thick British accent. "Follow me."

Mason followed behind as they passed through the bunker. They continued through the hallway past the large red Fire Protection tanks mounted on the walls, "To Be Used in Case of FIRE, Asbestos Cloths" was written in large black print on them.

On the left was a large open room where several men in uniform pored over information at their wooden desks. Telephones of three different colors, red, white, and green, sat on the desks as their wires went up the walls and across the ceiling. As the phones rang, women would enter the room and leave papers on the various desks. The next room on the right was the switchboard. A woman sat there connecting the calls coming in. Mason soaked it all in as they reached another doorway.

John stopped the group. "Please wait here." He motioned with his left hand as the two men entered the room. Hollins stood behind Mason like his shadow. A large desk with two chairs sat in the middle of the room. A black phone was mounted on the wall to the left, and a map of Britain hung on the opposite wall. A wooden tea cart on the right wall contained several cups, plates, a kettle, and some scotch.

Mason and Sully sat in the chairs. "This is impressive," Mason said.

"This is where they run the war. The British were smart seeing what was coming so they built this bunker, and it's a good thing they did because the war started a week later."

They waited for a few minutes and then a booming voice broke the silence, "Sully, who is killing my best men?" Sully and Mason both stood as in walked the Prime Minister of

Britain, Winston Churchill. He shuffled his feet as he passed them and stood behind his desk.

"We're not sure, sir," Sully replied.

"But you have an idea, don't you?"

"We have a theory though it is far from concrete. This is the gentleman I told you about, Mason Wright."

Mason nodded his head. "It's a pleasure Mr. Prime Minister."

"Son, nothing about this God forsaken war is a pleasure. So, tell me what I am doing here with two Yanks in my office? This better be good, Sully."

Sully recounted what had happened over the past few days and how Mason was involved. Churchill listened intently as he puffed on his cigar. The smoke quickly filled the room, causing Mason to cough. Churchill looked at him with a searing stare. Mason had never felt smaller. Sully continued and when he was done the Prime Minister turned to Mason.

"So, you have made a German major mad, and because of this, he is killing my men to get to you?"

Mason spoke up feeling slightly intimidated, "I think it is a possibility, sir. I do think Kliest is an extremely dangerous man and would be anxious to get to me. I cannot be one hundred percent sure but I think he is capable of anything. He oversaw securing stolen art for the Fuhrer Museum, and I managed to interrupt his plans. He was very unhappy. I do not think this whole situation is about me by any stretch, but I believe I am a part of it. I think he wants revenge and will stop at nothing to get it."

The Prime Minister grunted as he pondered the story. He turned to Sully, "You are sure about this mission to France? It is not exactly a safe haven at the moment."

"We have a plan, and we have contacts there. I have instructed the rest of my men to lay low for a while. The other names on the list have been notified and have gone into hiding. The only way to know for sure is to go into France and gather more information."

Sully briefly elaborated on their plan. They would fly to

San Sebastian, Spain, and then board a train to the Free French Zone where they would meet up with a man who would transport them by truck into occupied France. Churchill listened intently and nodded along. He stared at the wall behind them as he absorbed the information.

As Sully finished with his briefing, the Prime Minister stood quietly staring at his desk. Phones rang in the background and voices could be heard outside the room. Churchill raised his head and turned to Mason, staring at him for what seemed like an eternity causing Mason to shift in his seat, "If this man is indeed sending people to kill my best agents, you need to find him and eliminate him. Mr. Wright, I was briefed on what you did for the people of France; it was very admirable. If this does involve everything you say, I am asking you to help the British Empire now. I wish you could convince Roosevelt to come join our little party here but I will settle for any help I can get. Be careful, both of you, if anything happens to the two of you, I cannot help you. You do understand, you are on your own with this little trip you are taking? I do not want that on my conscience. Do not go getting yourselves killed. Sully, you have been a trusted man to me and to us here, I expect to see you back in one piece."

Churchill puffed again on his cigar and then waved his hand in front of his face dispelling the smoke. Mason held his breath as both men stood to exit the office.

A woman appeared at the door and he waved her in. "Elizabeth come in, these two are just leaving." She walked by Mason and Sully with a stack of folders and placed them on his desk.

"Sometimes I believe this war is being fought with paperwork," Churchill grunted as Mason and Sully started to leave the room.

"One more thing," Churchill said, stopping them both in their tracks. "John Cleary was a friend of mine as well, I knew him a long time, he was an exceptionally good man. I know there has been a small resistance forming in France. If you are unable to get to this Major Kliest, do not risk your lives doing something stupid but try to cause some disruption. John was a fine man who liked a little disruption himself, do not let his death be in vain. Make sure someone pays for it. Understand?"

"You can count on it, sir." Sully said as The Prime Minister looked back and forth between them.

"I'm particularly good at disrupting things." Mason added as they turned and left.

14

MASON, COLLETTE, AND SULLY DROVE through the streets of London on their way out of town. Mason had his bag at his feet and his treasured Colt in his waistband. Collette had her things with her, a pistol in her bag. She was reading through some last-minute documents delivered to them from the War Office. She sat in the back seat, Mason in the front, and Sully behind the wheel. A light rain fell outside on a gray, chilly day in London.

Sully turned onto Prince Albert Road as they passed Regent's Park. They were headed to a remote airfield outside of London where they would meet their pilot for the flight into Spain. From there, a train ride through Canfranc Station at the base of the Pyrenees Mountains, and then a ride in a wine truck across the border and into Occupied France. The trip would take over a day and involve several people who Mason did not know. This made him slightly uncomfortable considering his life was in their hands. He had only known Sully a few days. He trusted him even though he knew nothing about him. The trip was beginning to resemble his last journey to France. He had a sense that Sully was a good man. He was feeling better every day about having Collette with him. Initially he had been hesitant but he knew there would be situations which would require her calm demeanor, as opposed to his hasty decision making.

They reached the outskirts of London and as the city slowly disappeared, the rolling hills south of town started to litter the landscape. The headlights of their car barely lit the road due to the blackout restrictions imposed in September of 1939. Stop lights and car headlights were fitted with screens intended to deflect their light downward. The blackout had already caused an increase in civilian fatalities as people were hit by vehicles driving through the darkness. Not all casualties of war were inflicted by the enemy.

The airfield was located outside of Guildford and was a former shipping airfield for farming supplies which served the British Isles.

"When we get to the airfield we will meet up with Andy Lipscomb, the pilot who will take us to San Sebastian. I was put in touch with him through a contact who operates an off the books transportation business. They do not ask about my business, and I do not ask about theirs. Since our little excursion is strictly off the books, we could not log a flight out of a military base. Andy has been flying for many years, and I have been assured that we are in good hands. As long as he gets us to Spain, that's all that matters."

"What kind of plane are we flying over in?" Mason asked as he looked out the rain-soaked window at the passing fields.

"I don't know, but I do know we are landing outside of San Sebastian at an abandoned Spanish farm. I wouldn't expect luxury travel if that is what you're asking."

"No beverage service?"

Sully chuckled and looked at Mason shaking his head, "No, no beverage service."

Collette chimed in from the back seat, "Mason gets a little antsy when he flies. The last flight we took together, he threatened to throw Paul Ganoux out of the plane. I was able to talk him out of it."

"I was never going to throw him out of the plane, and I am glad I didn't because he turned out to be a good friend."

Sully interjected, "You told me he saved your life a couple times. Well, hopefully there will be no reason to throw anyone out of the plane this trip. I am hoping for an uneventful flight."

They arrived at the airstrip and pulled down the dirt road leading to a trio of old barns. They passed several rusted tractors and some farming equipment which was being swallowed up by the overgrown grass. A rooster wind vane spun on top of the middle barn. The rain let up a bit as they pulled in. Sully parked and the three sat quietly looking out the windows for any signs of a pilot or plane.

"Wait here." Sully said as he pivoted his head and looked in every direction. "I will see if I can find Andy and our plane." He pulled out his Walther Semi-Automatic pistol.

He opened the door and the chill of the English countryside filled the car. Mason and Collette sat quietly scanning the countryside for anything out of the ordinary.

Sully walked over to the old barn and peeked inside the large open doors. He saw nothing so he entered the barn. It was quiet, too quiet for Sully, so he readied his Walther. The barn was filled with an old plough and several tools lying near a pile of logs stacked in the corner. The floor was littered with pieces of hay; leaves blew in through the open doors as the wind picked up. He walked through quietly and reached the far end door. He looked out through the wrought iron bars and the back fields of tall grass swayed in unison. Seeing no signs of life, he slid open the large wooden door. The door opened halfway and then one of the door rollers got stuck. Sully could not pull it all the way open, so he slid sideways inside. He saw a light on in the second barn and walked over to the windows. He looked in and saw the plane in the barn but no signs of Andy. The second barn was twice the size of the first and served as the main hanger of the airfield. Sully walked through the doorway and looked around.

"Andy, its Frank Sullivan," he said, cocking his pistol.

The sound of the wind blowing the trees outside was all he heard. He glanced over at the dirty windows and could barely see much through the cracked panes. He walked toward the plane and looked inside. Some maps were on the pilot's seat and a brown leather bag lay on the co-pilot's seat. Sully turned around and was momentarily startled by a man standing in the barn looking at him. He started to raise his Walther when the man spoke up in a thick British accent, "You must be Frank." He stepped toward him with his arms raised, smiling. "You've got me."

"Yes, you must be Andy." Sully stepped forward and shook his hand.

"Pleasure to meet you," Andy replied. "We can leave as

soon as you're ready. I understand there are three of you?"

"Yes, I will go get the others and our gear. We are anxious to get off the ground."

Mason watched from the car in the direction Sully had disappeared. "He's coming back," he said as Collette collected her things in the back seat.

Sully opened the door and leaned in, "Let's go, the plane is ready."

Mason and Collette got out of the car, grabbed their bags and followed Sully through the first barn and into the second one. Andy was standing next to the plane. They exchanged pleasantries and loaded into the small English twin propeller Bristol Type 156 Beau fighter. The plane was originally designed for a crew of two, but this one was a test model by the British government and allowed room for two more people in a second row. When it was deemed to be too heavy for four people during wartime bombing flights, the prototypes were scrapped and auctioned off to the highest bidder. Perfect for a small transportation/smuggling business, although a fully functioning aircraft, it had minimal space, so it would be a tight squeeze getting everyone on board. Most of the equipment had been removed so a third and fourth person could fit behind the pilot. With a range of almost fifteen hundred miles, the plane had plenty of fuel for a one-way flight.

The four of them climbed into the small plane, Andy and Sully in the front, Collette, and Mason in the back. Mason shuffled around trying to get comfortable behind the pilot's seat. His right leg already ached from the angle in which it was bent. With his Colt stuck between his ribs and his leg, Mason envisioned a bullet discharging mid-flight and ending his trip before it began. He removed it and secured it in his bag, then shuffled his way back into some semblance of a comfortable position.

"Just try to relax," Collette said as she touched his arm. He looked over at her spot in the plane and noticed her legs crossed at the ankles as she sat back in her seat.

"Relax? Look at me. Look at my leg. I am not sure how long before it completely loses all blood flow. Check on me every hour to make sure I haven't passed out. Hope you're comfortable?" he said not meaning one word of it.

Collette smiled a sympathetic smile, "My poor baby. I am comfortable, thank you," she said sarcastically.

"Why did I agree to have you come along?" Mason returned the sarcasm.

"You had no choice." Collette turned away smiling and looked out the small window.

The propeller engines started; the noise was overwhelming. Sully and Andy had headsets to communicate during the flight; Mason and Collette in the second row had nothing to drown out the propeller noise. There would be no small talk, that was for sure.

Andy gave everyone the thumbs up for takeoff as they pulled away. The wind generated by the propellers blew the dusty barn floor into a frenzy, the pile of hay in the corner of the barn flew in every direction. Nobody noticed a pair of legs suddenly exposed as the plane left the barn.—The legs belonged to a pilot by the name of Andy Lipscomb who had agreed to take three passengers on a secret flight to San Sebastian but instead lay dead with a bullet in his head in a rural barn in southern England.

The plane reached the end of the field and turned for takeoff. The man piloting gave a nod to Sully. The Bristol Beau Fighter picked up speed and ricocheted as it sped across the field. Gaining speed, it lifted off into the English evening on a flight to Spain, an unknown man at the controls.

15

San Sebastian, Spain

THE FLIGHT LASTED FIVE GRUELING hours, and Mason was convinced his lower torso was no longer functioning as he had no feeling in his legs for the last two. He was afraid they would need to carry him the rest of the way to France. Not much was said during the flight. Mason held Collette's hand as the plane shook several times, not sure if it was for his comfort or hers.

The small plane rattled continuously and felt as though it was in danger of disintegrating at any second. Mason understood why it was not mass produced. Sully and the man piloting the plane were discussing the approach as the coast of Spain came into view. The plan was to land in a field outside of the city and then hike the rest of the way to town. As Sully motioned with his hands, Mason noticed that the pilot was seemingly disinterested in what Sully was saying. As Sully pointed out landmarks in the distance the pilot nodded but never turned his head to look, just stared straight ahead. Mason thought this strange as Sully was more familiar with the flight plan than the pilot. As they reached the mainland, Mason could feel the plane beginning to descend as an expanse of fields appeared in the distance.

Sully leaned back and yelled to Mason, "We are going to put her down over there."

Mason acknowledged with a thumbs up as he grabbed Collette's hand. She stared at him with a mixed look of appreciation and fear.

The wings of the plane moved up and down as they came in for a landing to a narrow strip of grass on the Spanish mainland. The wheels hit the ground, the plane bouncing up and down a few times before settling in. The pilot applied the brakes and they rumbled down the grassy landing strip, passing some trees and a long wooden fence. A house was visible along with some barns and a silo which towered over the farm. As the plane slowed to a reasonable speed, they turned toward the house and slowly approached.

The pilot stopped the plane near the house, out of sight from the road, and everyone lurched forward one final time. Sully and the pilot removed their headgear and opened the hatch behind the seats. The pilot climbed down first, followed by Sully. Mason was still trying to untangle his limbs, so Collette approached the hatch next, climbing down the seven rungs on the metal ladder until she reached the ground. Ducking under the plane, she walked over and joined the pilot and Sully. Eventually Mason emerged bent over, looking a foot shorter than he did when they took off. The look on his face said everything. He was never doing that again.

Sully pulled out some maps as Mason and the pilot gathered their gear. They would hike to town to secure the car for the ride to Canfranc. As Mason returned with some of the gear, a truck rumbled toward them. Sully stared at the approaching vehicle as it stopped to pull into the farm road.

"What is this?" Sully said, visibly annoyed.

"Some friends of mine," the pilot said as he pulled a gun from his bag.

Mason and Sully stared at the man holding the gun, Mason's weird feeling about this guy was proving to be right. Collette stood motionless, her bag in her right hand.

"Just take it easy," Sully said, slowly raising his hands.

Mason followed suit. "I thought you said this guy was trustworthy," he said looking at Sully.

"They said reliable, not trustworthy."

"Oh, great."

Collette slowly inched backwards as the pilot held both men at gunpoint. The truck approached down the dirt road leaving a cloud of brown dust behind it. The pilot focused on Mason and Sully as the truck pulled up and came to a stop with a squeak from the brakes. The doors opened and two men hopped out with pistols in their waistbands. Both men were older than Mason. One wore faded overalls and work boots; he looked like a factory worker. The other was shorter than Mason and smoked a cigarette; his brown crooked teeth—what was left of them, were all Mason noticed.

The pilot spoke to them in Spanish, and the taller one disappeared behind the truck as the shorter one approached Mason. He looked up at Mason and motioned for him to raise his arms higher. Mason blankly stared back at him and his bad teeth and did nothing. The man raised his pistol and pointed it at him, so Mason slowly raised his arms a bit higher. Through puffs of his cigarette, he frisked him on both legs and was satisfied Mason was not armed. He then waved his finger signaling for Mason to turn around.

"Can I ask you something?" Mason said as the cigarette smoke floated around his head, "Do they not have dentists in Spain? I'm just curious."

The man smiled. "That is very funny. Turn around," he replied in accented English.

Mason slowly turned, briefly feeling the butt of the gun hit his neck before he crumpled to the ground. The pilot yelled in their direction, the short man looked at the pilot and they had a heated conversation. It was clear the pilot did not want Mason in a heap on the ground. He yelled toward the back of the plane and the factory worker reappeared. Together, they picked up Mason's limp body, dragged him over to the truck, and left him on the ground next to it.

As the pilot and his two friends focused on Mason, Collette dropped her bag, turned, and sprinted toward the barn. By the time they noticed, she was disappearing through the open barn door. The shorter man standing over Mason exhaled in annoyance, dropped his cigarette, and ran after her. Sully moved to the left and knocked the man to the ground as he ran by. He stood over him as the pilot walked over and pointed the gun at Sully. "Don't move."

Sully once again raised his hands and with a slight smirk backed up a few paces. Feeling the effects of Sully's shoulder into his chest, the man picked himself up off the ground and slowly headed in the direction of the barn.

As Collette entered the barn near the stable area, she looked for anything she could use as a weapon, realizing the second she dropped her bag she had dropped her pistol. The pickings were slim. Some lead ropes hung next to an old broom in the corner, a few metal buckets stood on the floor next to some bulk bedding. On the opposite wall she found her only choice, a pitchfork. She grabbed it off the hook and disappeared into a corner of the barn behind the large rear wheels of an old tractor. She crouched down, silently listening to her heart beating out of her chest as the man reached the entrance to the barn. He had his pistol out in front of him as he entered out of breath, the cigarettes clearly taking their toll. The old barn was two levels, with three stalls and room for the tractor. The expansive second floor was the hayloft.

He slowed and started checking every direction for any sign of her. As he passed the first stall on his right he noticed the faded metal nameplate on the far wall as he peered in through the padlocked door: Juju "Let's see if you are hiding in Juju's stall," he said aloud as he looked in. Nothing. "Come out my dear, there is nowhere for you to go."

He leaned into the next stall and looked around, again nothing but some tack hanging on the wall, a few leather straps, and some ties. Walking across the hay strewn floor toward the next stall, he found some items piled against the wall covered by a tarp. Grabbing the edge of the tarp with his left hand, his gun in his right, he ripped the tarp away. Dust filled the air as he threw the tarp aside, exposing a pile of oat bags stacked on the floor. The sound of coughing filled the air as he inhaled the barn dust. Collette heard the man gagging and knew it was the shorter of the two men who had arrived; she could tell he was getting closer.

She moved to the front of the tractor to try to get a look at him. She heard him throw something aside and could see his silhouette through the barn wood, he was in the third stall. She moved back to the safety of the large tires of the tractor and found an old horseshoe hanging next to the opening going upstairs. She slid it off the hook and tossed it against the back wall breaking the silence, then ran up the stairs. Hearing the noise, the man turned around and slowly emerged from the stall, walking carefully toward the sound.

He listened carefully and heard the footsteps above him. The staircase was at the rear of the barn and led to the hayloft.

Collette was perched behind a stack of hay by the front pulley access doors. Still regaining his breath, her target reached the top of the stairs and listened intently as he walked across the smooth floorboards. Collette was breathing heavily as she saw the man approach. He turned his back. Seeing her opportunity, she stood and charged him. She swung her rusty pitchfork and connected with the back of his head. He lurched forward and fell face first to the ground, his body limp. Collette dropped the pitchfork, picked up his gun, looked around and noticed a handle on the floor. She pulled the handle and opened an access door to the first stall below. Grabbing the man's legs, she dragged him toward the open hatch, rolled him over, and pushed his legs through the opening. With all her strength, she grabbed his shoulders, picked him up and pushed. His body slid smoothly against the hay strewn floor as gravity took over, and like dropping hay from the loft above, the man fell through the access door feet first and landed on the floor of Juju's stall. She sat back and gathered her breath, exhaling. One down.

OUTSIDE, MASON ROLLED over on the ground as he came to. He looked up, dazed, and saw the tall man standing over him, pistol in hand. He stretched his eyes and squinted, slowly looking around, and saw Sully standing a few paces away in a similar situation, hands up and guarded by the pilot. What he did not see was Collette. And the cigarette smoking man was missing. He suddenly gained his faculties, "Where is she?"

"Your little girlfriend has run off but don't worry, she will be brought back soon enough," the pilot said with a slight smile.

Mason looked at Sully who gave him a slight nod. After a

few moments, the pilot was visibly annoyed, and said to the other man, "Go check on him." The tall man acknowledged and walked cautiously toward the barn.

INSIDE, COLLETTE HAD FOUND a rear entrance to the barn and was peering around the corner; she saw the second man heading toward the front. Heading back in, she found her spot behind the tractor. The taller man came in, gun drawn. He stopped at the first stall and saw the crumpled body of his friend. He whispered something to him but no reply. Collette stood up and approached him from the side.

"Drop it," she said, aiming at him before he noticed anything. He turned, obliged, and raised his hands, smiling as he stared at the petite woman in front of him. He dropped his gun to the floor.

"You going to shoot me? No, I do not think so. A pretty girl like you? You're too scared."

He lunged at her and she fired. The bullet struck his right shoulder sending him to the ground. He grabbed a fistful of hay and threw it in Collette's face, leaving her momentarily blinded as he got to his feet. He jumped toward her, she stumbled and fell backwards, her head hit the floor. She lost her grip on the gun, and it slid back near the other stall doors. Collette wiped her eyes quickly as the man came at her again. She rolled out of the way as he landed on the floor. She dug her feet into the floor and propelled herself toward the stalls. The man grabbed her foot with his left hand. She kicked at his arm, finally getting loose, and picked up the gun. She turned and fired again, striking the man in the stomach, sending him backwards awkwardly.

Outside the sound of two gunshots echoed through the property as the three men stood there. They all looked at the barn wondering who had shot whom. Inside, as the man lay on the ground bleeding to death, Collette stared up at the wall and the framed pictures hanging off the rusted nails. Above the pictures of the horses whose barn floor she was lying on, she read some of their names, Po, Rose, Juju, Louie. She closed her eyes and envisioned all of them running free in their paddock, and hoped they were in a safer situation than she was.

MASON PICKED HIMSELF UP and stood next to Sully as the shots rang out. The pilot was switching glances between them and the barn, getting more upset with every second. He yelled something in the direction of the barn; no sound returned. Collette heard the man as she waited by the back door. She could see Mason and Sully standing together as the pilot contemplated his next move. Finally, he ordered Mason and Sully to walk toward the barn. He followed with his gun pointed at their backs. They walked across the dirt and grass and reached the opening at the front of the barn. The sliding front door was pulled open a few feet.

"Both of you, inside," the pilot ordered. Mason and Sully entered the open door. They turned around as the pilot pulled the door closed, locking it from the outside. He looked around and turned back toward the plane. He jogged past the end of the barn and was met by Collette, gun drawn. He stopped in his tracks and looked at her with shock. He was caught off guard, Collette noticed. She fired a shot past his right ear, and he stumbled backwards, startled by the noise. He threw his gun away and raised his hands. She fired another shot between his legs, and he continued backing up, tripped on the rough terrain, and fell to the ground. She walked calmly over to him and pointed the gun in his face. He raised his hands even higher, "No, No Please?" She looked at him for a moment. "Get up."

Once on his feet, she pointed toward the barn. They reached the front sliding door, and he unlocked the latch. He pulled the door open and Sully and Mason emerged. They saw Collette standing behind the pilot with a gun. Mason walked up to him and knocked him to the ground with a punch to the jaw. The pilot fell easily and rolled onto his stomach grabbing his face as Mason shook his right hand in pain. Sully grabbed Mason by the arm, "Don't...we need him. Information."

Mason ripped his arm away from Sully's grasp and walked toward Collette.

"I heard the shots. Thank God you're okay." Mason was clearly shaken.

"Yes, I'm ok." She looked up at him with a slight smirk, "And thanks to me, so are you."

"I owe you one."

16

MASON, COLLETTE, AND SULLY SURVEYED the scene in the barn: One man bleeding to death on the floor, another unconscious on the hay in the stall. Sully pulled the pilot aside as Mason hid the dead body in the corner of the barn under a tarp.

Sully pulled out his pistol and held it to the pilot's forehead, "Start talking. Everything I was told about Andy Lipscomb paints a decidedly different picture than you. What did you do to him?

"I don't know who that is." The visibly traumatized pilot responded.

Sully said nothing as he cocked the pistol.

"All right," the pilot said, starting to shake. "Andy and I have known each other for some time. We're in the same business, so we run into each other a lot. We became friends— well, as friendly as two smugglers can get; we share an occasional beer. He told me about a good job he landed, and it would be a good payday which have been hard to come by since war began. He didn't know the people but he knew there would be three and a quick flight to Spain leaving today from the farm outside of London. Like I said, paydays have been hard to come by. I like Andy but I needed the money just as bad as he did, so I took his place."

"Where is he?"

"Under a hay pile back in England. He talked too much at the pub. You never share the details of a job but he was feeling rather good and had one too many beers."

A frustrated Sully rubbed his eyes as he exhaled. He cursed under his breath and walked back over to Mason. "These guys are nobodies. Just thieves looking for a payday. We have to get to the station; we can't take them with us."

Sully dragged the pilot up to the hayloft and made him jump through the door into the stall with his friend. He landed on top of him as his legs buckled, and both men lay on the floor, one wincing in pain and one still unconscious.

Sully moved the plane between the barn and the silo, obscuring it from view. They loaded in the truck and drove out, turning onto the country road leading away from the farm and toward the city of Canfranc, a municipality located in the Aragon Valley in Northeastern Spain. At the International Canfranc rail station, they would board their train for the ride through the Pyrenees mountains and into France.

Mason drove as they turned toward the town, the Pyrenees mountains in the distance. He noticed a pack of cigarettes on the dash and thought of the smoking man lying in the barn.

The traffic heading out of town was heavier than that traveling in. Canfranc was now a major rail stop for anyone trying to escape occupied Europe. The busy station was a daily stop for refugees, spies, and resistance fighters smuggling information in and out of France. Mason and Collette were posing as a couple heading to visit family in Vichy France, the southern part of the country not under German control. The territory south of the Loire river in France was ruled by a Marshall named Phillipe Petain.

A former World War I hero known as the Lion of Verdun, Petain was named Chief Marshall of Vichy France but was widely considered a puppet for the German government. Nobody was naïve enough to think that he could make any decisions without German consent.

The truck rumbled along the E-7 highway as the three made their way into Canfranc. The Pyrenees mountains bookended the town as they ascended from the banks of the Rio De Aragon on the right side and the outskirts of the town on the left. They passed the Hotel de Aragon, which looked every bit the luxury hotel that it was. Perched on a hill with views in all directions of the mountains, this hotel was a favorite among skiers in the wintertime with daily trips to the lodges in the mountains. They passed a signpost with several white arrows pointing in different directions, each with a destination written in black and a kilometer distance next to it: "Railway Station straight ahead 1 kilometer."

Sully spoke up, "Let's get as close as we can and find a place to leave the truck."

"Our train is due to leave in about one hour, so we have some time."

Mason signaled to turn left into a dirt lot down the road from the main entrance to the station. They would walk across the bridge and then into the main entrance to the station lot. Several people crossed the street in front of him, most carrying luggage from a trip. Every time Mason would inch forward someone else would walk in front of the truck. He was losing his patience, so he pulled forward enough for a man and woman to hustle out of the way. The man gave him a glare as Mason muttered, "Get out of my way."

They parked the truck, grabbed their bags, and locked everything up. Depending on how their plan went they might or might not come back through. They crossed the street and took the road across the river and onto the main terrace of the station. The towering, snow-covered peaks in the distance provided a nice backdrop to a station which bustled with people.

"Don't trust anyone here. It looks like a beautiful station but there are people listening everywhere for information on spies and smugglers. A lot of people and information are going through this station every day, and Franco is a friend to the Nazis, so he has his people looking out for anything suspicious."

Francisco Franco was the dictator of Spain. He enlisted Hitler's help in winning the Spanish civil war which ended in 1939, and for that he was indebted to Germany. He was put in power after his victory and ruled under the title of Caudillo, a man with military and political power. Though technically neutral, the country was aligned with the Axis powers and provided valuable material for the German and Italian war machine, so Sully considered Spain occupied territory.

After crossing the river, they entered the main square of

Canfranc Station and the massive station finally came into full view. At first sight it reminded Mason of the Louvre in Paris, a three-story building extending as far as could be seen, with arched windows and doors. The station measured 240 meters long and had a total of 365 windows and 156 doors. The copper roof was clearly French inspired as it rounded up to the top in classic Renaissance architectural style.

People were coming and going in every direction. To Mason's left he could see *policia* gathered in a group talking. A man on his right was selling the daily paper from a stack on the ground at his feet. Straight ahead across a small stone bridge was the main entrance to the station. Mason looked to his right and he could see some of the tracks as they disappeared between the mountains on their way to France. A train whistle signaled a leaving train and the steam engine started to chug away as it started down the tracks. Collette stood next to him, also looking around for anything suspicious. They were just another couple traveling during wartime.

"I will secure our tickets and meet the two of you in the main waiting area. Sit on one of the wooden pews and I will come sit down next to you with a folded newspaper in my hand. After a few moments I will get up and leave the paper. You pick it up; your tickets will be inside. Keep your eyes open for anyone following us. I have a bad feeling about this." Sully turned to them with a concerned look on his face.

"I know the feeling," Mason said as he looked around.

Sully walked away toward the man selling newspapers, he reached in his pocket for some change, gave it to the man, and walked away with the paper under his right arm.

"All right honey, shall we go to France? I know a great little war zone we can visit." Mason tried to break up the somber mood with some humor.

"I would love to," Collette said as she grabbed his hand.

"Can I ask you something?" she said as they began walking. "Why don't I feel awful about killing that man today in the barn? I was scared when I entered the barn and did not know what to do. And then, it all happened so quickly but I felt no remorse. Mason, that is not who I am, and I hope that is not who I am becoming. This past year I know we have both done things we regret, but I do not want to lose my humanity or I will become just as terrible as the people we are going after." She stopped him by the arm. "Do you understand what I am saying?"

Mason looked at her, "You did what you had to do. When Kliest took you from the warehouse, I did many things that I don't believe are a true indication of the person I really am, but I did what I had to do to get you back. I do not regret it for a second. You are the best person I have met in this world, and the world is a better place with you in it...Anna's world is better simply because of you. With how terrible her situation has become, you give her hope—hope of finding her family, hope of surviving, hope that love still exists in this world." He kissed her forehead.

"I mean, I am not saying that shooting a man and throwing another one into a horse stall—which was very impressive by the way, will not affect you at some point, but because of that we were able to get out of a sticky situation. All because of you."

She smiled. "You make me laugh."

He smiled and they continued into the station.

They walked in the main entrance and into a large waiting area. The huge windows provided light and formed shadows on the yellow and white painted wall. A large stone railing surrounded a downward staircase on three sides next to them, leading down to the tracks. On the wall to their right was a row of telephone booths made of stained wood and glass. A man sat in the front one with the receiver to his ear as he talked a mile a minute in Spanish. Collette pointed to an area where there were several wooden pews lined up. People sat with their luggage and several people stood against the back wall, many reading the newspaper. A child played with a doll on the black and white tiled floor in front of her mother and father.

Mason and Collette approached as a couple got up to leave. They sat down toward the end of the second pew and put down their bags on the floor. They waited silently for several minutes when Sully finally appeared walking quickly toward them. He sat down without making eye contact, leaving a space between them and opened his newspaper for a moment. He closed it and folded it, leaving it on the pew next to Mason. Sully got up and walked toward the main entrance when some *policia* entered through the front door followed by a short, disheveled man with bad teeth, and the pilot. Sully immediately turned and walked the other direction at a brisk pace which slowly turned into a jog. The *policia* looked all around until they spotted him. The pilot pointed him out, a whistle blew from one of the men and they ran after him.

How did they get out of their cell? Mason wondered as he quickly opened the paper and saw the tickets with a note on top of them.

"Track 7…RUN!" he read.

Mason grabbed Collette's hand and they ran toward the stone staircase. The *policia* had run in the other direction after Sully. They reached the top of the staircase and Mason almost knocked over a woman who had just reached the top. He squeezed by her with Collette in tow and they raced down the stairs to the track level. At the bottom of the stairs, Mason looked around for signs designating track numbers. Collette pointed to Track 7 and they took off. People moved out of the way as the young couple raced through the station. They approached Track 7 and noticed some *policia* standing at the door leading to the track. Mason stopped and they moved over toward the wall behind a group of women standing outside the bathroom. They waited for a minute as Mason thought of their next move.

"I have an idea," Collette said.

She walked over to a gentleman smoking a cigarette and asked for one. The man perked up at the sight of this beautiful woman, and immediately obliged. She smiled as he lit it for her. He asked her name and she just said, "Gracias."

As she turned to walk away, Mason wondered what she was doing. Either that was part of her plan or the stress was getting to her and she decided to start smoking. Collette walked over to a trash can which was filled with several newspapers and held the cigarette to the paper. It started to smolder, and she blew lightly until it began to flame. She dropped the paper in the bin and smoke started to come out the top. She backed up and yelled, *"Fuego, Fuego!"*

Immediately people began yelling and running away from the smoke. The two *policia* at the door ran over and one grabbed for the extinguisher which was mounted on the wall several feet away. The commotion of Collette's minor arson cleared the way for the two of them to calmly walk through the door onto Track 7.

Mason held the tickets as they approached the conductor. Some *policia* were waiting at the far end of the tracks so Mason stopped at the first entrance. He handed the tickets and their papers to the conductor, who glanced at them briefly and in Spanish said, *"Bienvenido a bordo."*

Mason and Collette climbed aboard and found their seats. They wondered about Sully—would he be able to make it on? They sat quietly waiting for the whistle to blow signaling departure. Mason looked out the window and noticed several *policia* come out the door onto the track side. They were pointing and raising their hands, palms up in a questioning manner. After a few moments they disappeared back inside, and the train started to slowly move. Mason grabbed Collette's hand and looked at her silently, concerned. He wondered about Sully, but they had agreed that should they be separated, the others would continue. *I guess our group of three has just become two.* He closed his eyes as the train picked up speed. Suddenly a man in an overcoat and hat bumped into his shoulder jolting him. He looked up at the man annoyingly. Sully looked down at him from under his hat, *"Pardome,"* he said and continued down the aisle.

17
Chateauroux, France

THE TRAIN PULLED INTO THE Chateauroux Station after a six-hour train ride. As the train horn signaled the arrival on Track 2, Collette woke suddenly and looked at Mason. He smiled at her. "We're here. Welcome to France."

Located in the Free Zone of France, the station was small enough to go largely unnoticed and got them as close to the Occupied Zone as they wanted to be. Mason started to feel the excitement of the adventure ahead. From here they would meet their contact and travel by truck to their destination. Though the train was only half full, when it stopped, everyone got up at the same time to fetch their bags. Mason and Collette sat in their seats and let the craziness subside before they finally stood up and made their way off the train. Mason stretched his arms up over his head after standing up and twisted back and forth trying to remove all the kinks he had acquired over the last day of planes and trains.

"What are you so excited about?" Collette said as she watched him stretching.

"It's good to be back. I like your country," Mason said smiling.

"I liked it better when it was free." Collette said with a blank look on her face.

The two stood track side as the train pulled away. Most people had dispersed. Mason noticed an older man sitting on a bench across the way. He was staring at the two of them and Mason began to feel uneasy. They waited a few more minutes wondering what had happened to Sully. Mason kept glancing back at the man on the bench.

"Where is Sully?" Collette asked as she looked around.

"I don't know," Mason said. He checked on the man at the bench again. He was gone. He turned back around and noticed a figure approaching from the darkness to their right, a man dressed in a hat and a wool coat. Mason nodded over toward the man and Collette glanced over.

"That's Sully, right?"

"Yup...Let's go." Mason gathered their bags and they headed off in Sully's direction. He entered the small station first with Collette and Mason behind him. They followed him out front onto the cobblestone street. One streetlight hung over the front of the station providing little, if any, light. Sully stopped at the side of the road as a taxi rumbled by.

"We are meeting my contact down the road at the Café Chateauroux. It's this way." The three walked down the dimly lit street toward town. Mason glanced back in the direction of the station and noticed the man from the bench heading in their direction. Sully and Collette walked in front and Mason a few feet behind them. He was so distracted by the old man he tripped on a raised cobblestone and almost fell flat on his face. Collette and Sully turned around, "You okay?" Sully said as Mason regained his balance.

"Yeah, I'm fine. Except there seems to be a man following us. He has been staring at us since we got off the train." Mason turned around and looked, but no one was there. "Oh, forget it, he's gone."

The wind began to pick up as they passed boarded-up homes. The flowerboxes were empty, the windows shuttered. One shutter hung loose, banging against the stone house in the wind. The town seemed deserted, which was expected but made for an eerie feeling. The German forces were only a few miles away. Though they were technically in the Free Zone, it very much looked like an occupied territory. The desolate town had few people and the ones they saw were a defeated lot.

They reached the door to the café and stopped for a moment as the wind howled.

"I'm going in to see if my guy is here. Come in a few moments after me and sit at a table. I'll wave you over when everything is clear." Mason nodded and Sully disappeared through the front door. Collette raised her shoulders as she rubbed her hands together trying to keep warm. Mason grabbed her and gave her a hug trying to warm her up. A woman walked by and Mason gave her a smile and a nod. The woman looked at him blankly as she passed.

"Have a good evening." Mason said under his breath.

After a few moments Mason opened the front door and he and Collette entered the café. The small, faintly lit café had several tables to the left, a bar on the right and a few booths beyond the bar. A man behind the bar was talking to an elderly woman who sat at the wooden counter stirring some sugar into her coffee. The man briefly looked up as the couple entered, gave a brief nod to Mason, and then focused back on the woman and her coffee. Two gentlemen sat at one table having a heated conversation in French. One man using his hands wildly as they argued back and forth about something Mason could not understand. A fireplace crackled at the end of the room and Collette pointed it out. "Let's sit by the fire."

Mason walked over to the table by the fire, pulled out a chair for Collette, and one for himself. A young woman came over with some water and bread. They sat and ordered coffee. Mason looked around and found Sully in the back booth talking to someone he could not make out. He could see Sully but the man was obscured by the booth.

The coffee arrived and Collette immediately wrapped her hands around the mug. Other than the two men arguing, the woman at the bar, and Sully and his contact, there was no one else in the café. Mason finally relaxed; they had arrived. Though their journey was just beginning, he was happy to have made it this far. He was happy Collette was with him, he was not sure he could have left her to do this. London was safe to a point but during wartime, truly no place was. Mason glanced at Sully every few moments until he received eye contact and a nod from him. Collette and Mason grabbed their coffee and joined Sully in the booth. As Mason approached, the man came into view, he recognized him immediately: the man from the bench at the train station. They sat down and Sully introduced them to Luc, a man in his fifties who was employed by one of the local wineries. Luc had lines on his face far exceeding his years, as if he had worked hard and lived hard. He reached out and shook Mason's hand. Mason obliged and Collette the same.

"Thank you for coming," Luc said to them. "My country greatly appreciates you."

Mason nodded and turned to Sully, "Where do we go from here."

"Luc will drive us in his vineyard truck to the winery. In the morning he will transport us across the demarcation line to the town of Lien where we will meet the others. The truck only has room for two up front. Collette, you will ride with Luc. Mason and I will ride in the back with the barrels."

Luc lit a cigarette as Sully talked. He blew the smoke up above the table and nodded along. Sully talked of the checkpoints in the occupied territory and how they would navigate them.

Mason spoke up, "Isn't it easier to travel under darkness rather than at first light?"

Luc shook his head, exhaled some smoke and tapped his cigarette on the ashtray, "I must stay on my daily schedule. Every day I make a delivery to the German side; they have allowed us to stay in business but we must give them sixty percent of the wine we make. We bring them our worst vintages because they do not really know the difference. Thank God, we were taken over by beer drinkers and not wine connoisseurs. With our supply, they keep some here, send some to Paris and the rest to Germany. I make my scheduled delivery every morning and they check me less and less. They expect me at a certain time so we will go at daybreak and hopefully they won't check too closely or else they will find you instead of wine, and that would not be good for you or me." He smiled at Mason through his tobacco-stained teeth.

"Yeah, I imagine that would not be good." Mason said blankly.

"The winery is about twenty minutes from here so use the *toilette* if you need but we should be going." Luc wrapped his scarf around his neck and tied it in a knot. Mason went off to the bathroom as Collette and Sully stayed back with Luc.

Around the corner of the building they saw the truck parked, a 1934 Renault AGC 48. The two-seat cab was painted red and on the door was some faded writing which said Sylvain Wine Company. The back of the truck had wooden siderails with a green heavy tarpaulin covering the entire bed. The back had a liftgate which opened down and allowed access to the bed of the truck. Collette walked around to the passenger side and opened the metal door which creaked as she pulled on it. Luc went around to the back and unlatched the tail gate. It fell open with a bang as it hit the bumper below. Mason and Sully hopped in and found themselves amongst several wooden barrels.

"Enjoy the ride, I am sorry to say it will not be smooth. I left you a bottle to open and enjoy; it will make the ride easier." Luc laughed as he closed the gate. He walked back to the driver side and hopped in the front.

"Mademoiselle, please hold on, this old truck can throw you around when you least expect it. I am only used to driving wine barrels, not people so I will keep that in mind."

"Merci," she said as she braced herself .

"Ahhh...*Parlez vous Francais*?"

"Oui," Collette replied as she told Luc of her family's farm and growing up in the country. Luc nodded as he started the truck.

In the back of the truck, smoke blew out the exhaust pipe and right into Mason's face. He waved his hands in front of his face and coughed, the smell of diesel exhaust filling the air. Mason had thought if he were not to make it out of France this time, it would be because of a German bullet. Now he wondered if he was going to suffocate on exhaust fumes before they even made it into occupied France.

The truck pulled onto the main road and shook back and forth as it moved off the grass and hit the pavement. The gears made a grinding noise as they headed up the road. Mason and Sully looked out the back as the town slowly disappeared.

They were one step closer to finding out who was behind the killing of John Cleary. Mason thought of Kliest and wondered where he was. Was he sipping some of the bad wine the French sent him, or was he simply running the war from his command post? Mason smiled to himself at the thought of Kliest's face as he looked up and saw Mason standing in front of him. Mason would make sure that he was the last person Kliest would ever see. Sully handed him the bottle of *Gamay Noir* and they passed the bottle back and forth as the town disappeared, and the truck navigated the country roads of the Loire Valley.

Roughly twenty minutes later they pulled into a small village and turned down the main road. Virtually no light from the houses shown on the road. They bounced back and forth in the back as Luc slowly drove the dark streets. Mason and Sully sipped the last of the wine as they turned onto a dirt road, passing under a metal sign which read Sylvain. They stood in the back and watched as they passed rows of vineyards on both sides. The truck pulled up to the main house and turned toward the four stone buildings on the left. The buildings stood side by side, connected by stone covered archways and gravel paths. Ivy engulfed each one, except for the doorways and windows. The doors and windows were painted red, making for a beautiful contrast with the fall-colored ivy. Above the doorway of each building "Sylvain Wine Company" was painted in arched, red letters on the stone; the ivy framed the arching letters. Luc stopped in front of the first building and turned the truck off. Mason and Sully hopped out of the back onto the dirt. Collette emerged from the passenger side and closed the metal door with a bang. Luc summoned them to the large, red double doors, where he pulled the left side open. He motioned the three of them inside and followed, closing the door behind him. All four stood in darkness for a moment until Luc turned on the lights, which flickered and then came on brightly.

They were in a large room filled with wine presses and other winemaking equipment. On the right side against the wall, was a stack of wooden crates used to carry the grapes from the fields to the warehouse. Luc walked forward toward a doorway and turned the lights on in the next room where cots and blankets waited for them.

"It is not much but it will have to do for tonight. I will bring you some bread, meat, cheese, and some wine. I imagine you must all be very tired so I will let you get settled."

"Thank you," Sully said as he shook Luc's hand.

Luc nodded. "I will get some food." He turned to walk away and then stopped. "Oh, stupid me, the *toilette* is down this hallway to the right. Ok?"

Collette grabbed her bag and headed for the bathroom, Mason began making up the cots as Sully surveyed the room and the warehouse. A few moments later Luc returned with a plate of bread and a charcuterie, a small knife, and some glasses. He grabbed a bottle off the shelf and the sound of the cork popping filled the room. He poured four glasses as Collette entered the room. He handed the glasses out and then raised his. "Thank you for helping my country."

They all raised their glasses and sipped the wine, a light Cabernet Franc from the 1935 harvest, a beautiful wine.

"Don't thank us, we haven't done anything yet." Sully remarked to Luc

"You have done more than you know; you have given me hope." With that, Luc turned and bid everyone goodnight. "I will see you bright and early for your ride into the war."

The three stood there solemnly as Luc left the room. They enjoyed the rest of the bottle and the food. Mason finished the last of the meat as he usually did. They were about to embark on an exceedingly difficult journey. Mason thought of Kliest, Collette thought of Anna and hoped she was safe, and Sully thought of John Cleary. Someone had gone to great lengths to attract their attention. Either they were going to surprise the Germans in France or someone was waiting for them and they were walking right into a trap.

18

LUC ENTERED THE ROOM EARLY the next morning bringing some eggs, bread, and cheese for breakfast. Mason rolled over and his back cracked as he stretched; he rubbed his eyes as they adjusted to the light. As they gathered at a small table in the next room, Mason and Collette sat, Sully stood, as Luc scrambled around finding a third chair for him. Mason cut bread as Collette made up some plates. Sully reached in over Mason's shoulder and grabbed some bread. Luc returned from the other room with a wooden chair and placed it in front of Sully. They sat and ate as they pondered the day ahead. Collette made a pot of coffee, welcoming on this cold and damp morning.

Once they finished, Luc removed the plates and produced a large map which he placed on the table in front of them. He leaned between Mason and Collette and ran his finger across the map, stopping on a spot and tapping it.

"I hope you two didn't eat too much because today you travel in barrels." He smiled as he glanced at Mason and Sully.

He turned back to the map, "We are here, Chanteauroux. We are three kilometers from the border with the occupied zone. We will follow this main road which will turn and take us to the border."

He ran his finger towards the center of the map where a red line ran diagonally across the map.

"This is the line between us and them. We will reach the border checkpoint at 8 a.m. It is my regular run. Collette will be with me in the front of the truck. I normally travel with one other person, that person differs from time to time, but the one constant is I am always traveling with a French citizen."

He looked at Collette as he continued, "You will be scrutinized by the German soldiers so be ready. They will ask you about where you live and how long you have been there. These are low level soldiers, but they are thorough. They still ask me things to make sure I do not slip up. Are you up to this?" he said with a stern look in Collette's direction.

"I am. I have lived in France all my life and I am angered by the occupation of my country. I am prepared to do anything to help end it as soon as possible. I am ready for this."

Luc nodded slowly and went back to the map. "As the soldier checks her papers, two soldiers always check the back of the truck. They will raise the canvas and check the cargo. I always leave a few bottles in a box at the end of the truck bed for the border soldiers. I have been doing this for many weeks and it is expected. I have prepared for this day. I always knew I would help any way I could, and with unique access to the border crossing, I figured I'd better build up some trust.

They stared up at him and Mason chimed in.

"Which barrels will we be in, ones at the back of the bed or closer to the cab?"

Luc stood up and looked at both men, "You will be in two barrels closest to the cab of the truck. The plugs on your barrels have been removed so you can breathe, and the barrels will be turned towards the cab so you cannot see the opening. We will remove the tops of the barrels and allow you the room to get in them, they will be in place on the truck. I hope you are ready for this because we cannot load the other barrels until you are positioned. You will be in there for some time, thirty minutes to load, twenty minutes to the border, and then another thirty until it is safe for you to get out. Can you do this?" Luc said in their direction.

Sully nodded, "Yes we can do this; we must do this."

"I can't have any noise while the soldiers are checking the barrels. The truck will be running causing some background noise but if you cough or sneeze or move, they will find you and then we are all dead. Do you understand? If you are found, we all die right there on the spot. There will be no questions, they will slaughter us and leave us in the field. Then they will come here and kill everyone on this property. We are taking a massive risk doing this and I believe we can do it, but I must know you will do as I say when I say it. I do this run every week and know how it works. I will get you across the border, but you must cooperate."

"We are in your hands. You have our word we will do as you say. Thank you for doing this for us," Sully said staring at Luc.

"We will get you in the barrels in twenty minutes. Get ready and only take what you need, the less there is to find, the safer we will be."

With that last message, Luc folded the map up and left the room.

"An hour and twenty minutes in a French wine barrel, how hard could that be?" Mason said shrugging his shoulders.

"Let's see if you still share that sentiment after you get out. Something tells me you won't be so dismissive as we unbend you in a field once we remove you," Collette said with a smirk on her face.

"I'll be fine," Mason said back to her.

"Let's get ready to go," Sully said as he stood up. "Only take your gun with you in the barrel. If it does go wrong, at least you have a fighting chance."

They collected their things and packed one bag to be stashed behind the seat under the hand jack in the floorboard of the truck. Collette returned after changing her clothes; she still looked beautiful to Mason, even though she was wearing some rags from the winery provided by Luc. Her hair was tied in a ponytail and she wore an old cap stained with grease from the truck. Her oversized pants were rolled at the ankles and a pair of brown boots made her an inch taller. She looked like a tomboy working at a garage.

"I didn't realize we had a mechanic with us," Mason said to Sully and chuckled.

"Very funny," she said, shaking her head.

Mason smiled and walked over and kissed her, "Those soldiers will be so struck by your beauty, they will have no need to check the truck thoroughly."

"Don't you worry about my beauty, just keep quiet in your barrel."

Mason smiled. "Not a peep."

They made their way to the truck bays where Luc stood with another man as a third man rolled a large barrel on to the back of the truck. Once on the truck the man stood the barrel up and began using a metal wedge and a wooden mallet to remove the top steel ring. He banged the wedge a few times and then moved it around the barrel top until the ring came loose. He removed the second ring and the wooden top. After doing the same on the other barrel, he loosened the third ring allowing the wooden sides to separate a bit at the top, giving the two Americans the room to climb inside.

Mason went first as Luc provided a small stool to stand on. He held Luc's hand as he climbed into the barrel, right leg first and then his left. He stood straight up, and the large barrel covered him up to his stomach. Sully followed into his own barrel.

Mason checked his Colt and looked up. "Ok, I am ready."

He shrugged his shoulders and twisted in a stretch to loosen his back a bit. He slowly lowered himself into the barrel until he was wedged against the wall on one side with his knees bent and his arms wrapped around his knees. There was no room to move. He figured that was a good thing because he would not be tempted to shift mid trip. He was fairly comfortable considering he was bent like a pretzel inside a wine barrel. The smell of fermented wine was intense, and Mason thought that might be worse than being cooped up for an hour and a half. The smell was overpowering and the top to the barrel was still off. Luc looked in on him, "How are you doing?"

"Wonderful," Mason said sarcastically

"You ready to be sealed up and become a barrel of our finest red?"

"I am; seal me up and let's go."

"Good luck, my friend, I will see you on the other side."

Mason took a deep breath as the top to the barrel was placed over the opening. The man banged on the lid for a few minutes and all sources of light disappeared except for the small two-inch plug hole which provided light and air. Mason shook his head at the smell and then remembered something an old friend had told him as he was driving across Paris with a decomposing body in his trunk, *"Breathe through your mouth."* With that thought, Mason started to focus on breathing in and out in a measured manner. He could hear his pal Sully being sealed in his barrel. Sully was in the Sancerre barrel and Mason wondered if it was as pungent as his. He should have checked both barrels and done a smell test before agreeing to be the red. Mason preferred red wine but maybe a Sancerre would have been the better choice.

"How are you, my friend?" Luc yelled as he tapped the top of the barrel.

"Never better," Mason yelled back, which got a laugh out of Luc.

Collette was not as cheery as everyone else. She looked at the barrel's size and could picture the position Mason was in. She felt terrible for him but this was the plan, the only way to easily navigate the border. She just hoped they would all make it through, Mason loved wine but she was sure he did not want to die in a wine barrel.

Luc and his men loaded six more barrels onto the truck. He placed the box of wine for the soldiers on the end of the truck bed and then closed the metal gate. Mason felt the bang of the gate and he knew they were done loading. A few moments later the truck engine started, and they began to move. Mason's barrel shifted a bit as the truck bounced around. Luc pulled onto the main road for his weekly delivery run, a woman he barely knew by his side and two men stuffed in barrels in the back.

19
Amboise, France

IN THE FRONT OF THE TRUCK, Collette watched as they drove down the Avenue De La Loire toward the town of Amboise. The rural grassy fields of the Loire passed by as the valley was just awakening. Passing several farms, Collette noticed the lack of humanity around; everything seemed deserted. A few horses grazed on the dewy morning grass, and one looked up as they drove by. The truck hit a ditch in the road and shook violently back and forth as Luc struggled briefly to control it and Collette wondered how Mason was doing in his closed quarters in the back. Luc did not say much as they drove, the conversation slowly dwindled, and she could sense his nervousness even though he put forth a brave face. He lit a cigarette as he drove.

"I have been taking the same route for many months and it relaxes me as I drive through the farm fields. In the summertime, you can smell the flowers in the breeze, and by September the sunflowers have arrived. It reminds me why they call the Loire 'the Garden of France.' It truly is a beautiful place. Unfortunately, some of that beauty has been stripped away by Hitler's ego. We knew he was mad, but I never thought he would control all of Europe."

Luc shook his head as they approached a roundabout. A German soldier on his motorcycle passed in front of them. Luc entered the circle and took the second exit toward Amboise; they were five minutes from the line. Signs had been erected notifying drivers of the approaching line of demarcation, some in French and some in German. The German signs almost yelled in their direction as they passed with large black letters, "*ACHTUNG*" at the top of each one.

The Loire River ran through the heart of Amboise dividing the city into two territories, Occupied France one,

Vichy France the other. Luc drove down the road until they reached the river, where he turned left onto the Rue de Bloise. The gears of the delivery truck grinded as he shifted from first to second, shaking the shifter and jamming it into gear.

The Chateau de Amboise rose above the landscape across the river as the city of Amboise came into view. The 1200-year-old Chateau was taken over by the monarchy in the 15th century and served as the royal residence of King Charles VIII. The towering Chateau sat on the hill overlooking the river and was always the first thing one saw as they approached.

The streets were empty except for German troops along the river. They passed a few more *"ACHTUNG"* signs as they got closer. Collette soaked in the scene as she took as many mental notes as possible. She noticed two patrol boats on the river, one anchored to the other side and the other leaving a wake as it disappeared under the stone arches of the bridge.

Soldiers looked up from their positions as the wine truck approached the checkpoint. Two soldiers, leaning on their motorcycles, watched them pass in between puffs on their cigarettes.

As Luc pulled to the mouth of the bridge, a German sentry emerged from his guardhouse and approached the truck. Guard houses sat on both sides of the entrance to the bridge. Painted in the colors of the Third Reich, red, white, and black, they housed the communications for the bridge. Collette watched as the scene unfolded in front of her. The sentry approached Luc's window as he lowered it. Luc recognized him as someone he had dealt with on previous trips and nodded as he approached.

"Papers," the sentry said as he looked past Luc toward Collette. She briefly captured his stare until she was startled by a tap on her window; she cranked it down.

"Your papers, *Fraulein*."

Collette retrieved her identification papers and handed them through the window. Her hand shook slightly as she let them go. She looked straight ahead as the man studied them.

"You are French?" the soldier said coldly.

"Yes," she replied nodding her head slightly.

The soldier studied her papers as Collette tried to calm her churning nerves. A few moments felt like hours until the man spoke again, "You appear uncomfortable?"

"She is new on my route; it is her first time crossing the border." Luc said as he leaned over.

The soldier dipped his head and looked in at Luc.

"I was not speaking to you," he said narrowing his eyes.

Luc raised his hands as a gesture of understanding and leaned back in his seat.

"Are you nervous, *Fraulein?* Is that true, your first time?"

"A little bit," she said sheepishly.

"What do you have to be nervous about?" the man said slowly as his gaze penetrated her soul. "You are French, correct? This is your homeland? You should not be nervous in your homeland."

"I am sorry. I used to visit Amboise when I was young; it is difficult to see it this way. I remember coming here and playing on the rocks down by the river's edge. I guess it hit me harder than I thought it would."

"You used to play over there on those rocks?" He stared directly at Collette as she nodded. He looked again at her papers and she studied his uniform as his head was down, the drab gray overcoat with the Nazi Eagle on the right chest, and his red Nazi armband on his left bicep.

"You should not be so nervous if you have nothing to be nervous about." He handed her papers back to her and gave her one last look before walking away. Collette exhaled and gave a glance to Luc who returned a reassuring nod.

The sentry on Luc's side was talking with a pair of soldiers in German and then turned back to him, "We need to check the back."

Luc stepped out of the driver's side and walked around to the rear gate of the truck. He unlatched the gate and it slammed down crashing against the bumper. The sentry and two soldiers stood looking at the cargo. Luc grabbed the wooden case filled with wine bottles and handed it to one of the soldiers. Another soldier at the back hopped into the truck.

Inside his barrel, Mason could hear the commotion and surmised they were at the checkpoint. He had lost feeling in his legs long ago and the smell of Cabernet Franc had become the norm, so it no longer bothered him. He could not fully make out the conversations taking place, but he could hear someone nearby tapping the barrels. He did not need to worry about moving since he could not, but he held his breath as the tapping grew louder. The soldier was tapping the top of the barrels with the butt of his rifle, listening for any discrepancies in sound. Luc had replaced Mason and Sully's barrel tops with a much thicker wood, so the dull thud of the rifle butt sounded like a full barrel of wine. Mason heard the tap just above his head and then a tap on the barrel next to him. Satisfied that the barrels were filled with wine, the soldier made his way out of the truck. As Mason listened, the voices grew more faint. Luc closed the gate with a bang and Mason exhaled. The sound signaled the end of the search, and one step closer to getting out of his barrel.

Luc popped back into the driver's seat and Collette felt the weight slowly lifting off her shoulders. The metal gate at the entrance to the bridge was manually opened by a sentry and Luc pulled up onto the stone bridge. The barrels in the bed shook side to side as they turned onto the crossing. Collette's sentry stared at her the entire time they drove by. She pretended not to notice him, but she felt his eyes following her. As they crossed the bridge toward occupied France, Collette leaned forward to look in the side mirror. The soldiers at the checkpoint were resuming their duties except for one man who was still staring at the truck driving away. She leaned back and focused in on the Chateau de Amboise directly in front of her, its traditional medieval flags replaced with the red Nazi flags of the Third Reich. Two large banners hung on the castle turrets and dropped down about forty feet in length. There was no mistake, Amboise now resembled Berlin.

They reached the other side and a small garrison of

soldiers waited as they slowed down. They were waved through and Luc turned left onto Rue Charles Guinot. The road would take them to their first delivery and into the countryside where they would be safer. Collette noticed the patrol boats as they drove next to the river. The sight of so many German soldiers in the small town of Amboise was unsettling and she knew this was only the beginning.

After fifteen minutes of relative calm they were in the fields of the Loire once again. Their first stop was in the small town of Montrichard, where they would unload some wine and two men who had probably lost feeling in their bodies long ago. Thanks to Luc, they were now in occupied France. Collette felt as if she had been traveling for days but she was happy to be back in the place of her birth. She wanted to find Anna's parents and the first step was getting here. She just hoped that the soldier at the bridge would forget all about her.

They entered the town of Montrichard and passed through the main square. A few German soldiers sat at an outdoor café as the truck drove by, otherwise the town was quiet. Luc turned onto Rue de Vierzon and reached the entrance to the winery. The wine caves of Sylvain Winery stretched into the mountain for several kilometers and the bottling room was also located underground. The delivery truck filled with wine and two men in barrels pulled up the small sloping driveway and into the courtyard of the winery. Luc pulled past the main entrance and down the side of the mountain toward an opening. The turn was tight as he drove into the cave opening. Two large wooden gates were opened fully to allow the truck through. A man waved them on, and they entered the troglodyte cave. Lightbulbs hung from the ceiling wired together to provide light deep into the cave. A tractor was parked on the right side of the cave next to a table covered with wine bottles. Several crates were stacked against the wall and the faint markings of Sylvain Wine Company could be seen stamped on the side. The gravel and dirt floor extended as far as the eyes could see. Luc pulled to the side and shut the engine off. The man closed the wooden gates as Luc emerged from the truck. They exchanged pleasantries in French, and he introduced the man to Collette.

"Collette, this is Alain Sylvain, his family owns the vineyard."

She shook his hand and thanked him for his help.

"It is my pleasure to help, I am only glad that there is someone to help. These past few months have been exceedingly difficult, we have managed to maintain a business, but the Germans are pressing harder every day and I fear it may not last. We have had to enter a terrible business deal with them to continue operations. If I must be in business with these pigs, I will do everything I can behind the scenes to hurt them. Speaking of which, we better retrieve your friends."

Alain retrieved some tools and jumped in the back of the truck. He slipped between the barrels to the two closest to the cab. Mason could hear the sounds and he hoped it meant it was time to be released. Alain wedged a bar under the metal strap and removed it with a few taps of a mallet. He pried the wooden top off and looked in. Mason shielded his eyes from the light.

"Welcome to the war," a man with a French accent said staring at him." Let us get you out of there." He reached in and grabbed Mason by the shoulders slowly helping him to stand up. Mason braced himself on the sides of the top of the barrel as he struggled to regain feeling in his legs. Alain released Sully next and helped him to his feet. Both men waited a few minutes for the needles and pins to dissipate, before attempting to fully remove themselves from their barrels. Collette smiled at Mason, "You made it." she said in a surprised, sarcastic tone.

"My head has made it here; I am not quite sure about the rest of me." He put his hand on his chest. "Everything below this hurts." He looked at Sully, "Yeah, that was pretty brutal." Sully agreed with Mason's assessment.

A few minutes passed and they pulled themselves out of the barrels and were helped down onto the dirt floor of the cave. Mason bent down and stretched every inch of his body.

He looked at Collette, "I may need a massage later."

"I'll get Sully right on that for you," she said smirking at him.

Mason looked around at the cave, "This place is huge."

"We have seven kilometers of wine caves; they provide the optimal temperature to bottle and store wine all in a natural environment. My family has been making wine here since 1886."

Luc interjected, "We better move, we have to get back on the road."

"Yes, of course," Alain replied. "I will unload the barrels. You can start bringing the cases over."

He pointed to the crates along the wall. They would replace most of the barrels with cases of wine for delivery to their destinations.

Alain very quickly used the barrel winch to remove all the barrels except for the two empty ones. One by one, they loaded fifty cases of wine into the back of the truck. Twenty cases of red and thirty of white. The vintages for French delivery were in the newer wooden cases with Sylvain clearly stamped on the side. The older cases were destined for the German occupying troops and then eventually shipped to Berlin. The vintages bound for Germany were some of the worst years they had. Alain decided that since the Germans knew extraordinarily little about wine and liked everything shipped to them, he would ship them the worst ones they had and keep the better vintages for the French people. He packaged them in the older crates to make them look better.

The Germans considered the older looking crates to be vintage and therefore, better wine. Alain had discovered their lack of wine knowledge by accident. He mistakenly sent three cases of the worst vintage he had, which ended up in Berlin. Word was returned to him that those three cases were highly received by Herman Goring and his minions. A Frenchman would have spit it out but apparently the German high command was very much enjoying its spoils of war.

Alain initially put up a fight explaining that his best

vintages were in high demand and he would be sent into bankruptcy if the Germans continued to take his best. All the while being more than happy to send his worst wine to Germany. He loved to tell the story of the German wine liaison demanding that all the same vintage go to Germany. He would have to stop himself from laughing sometimes as the liaison laid out the demands. Alain and his workers had walled up several areas of their caves to protect the legitimate best vintages he had—another way he could conduct business with his occupiers while rendering them fools.

Mason and Sully hopped into the back of the truck, the ride to their final destination would not require them to be back in their barrels, only stay hidden amongst the cases of wine. A cache of weapons from Alain was deposited in one of the barrels to help arm the resistance. That barrel was sealed to keep it out of sight.

Luc pulled back out onto the street with his passengers headed for the small town of Lien. There, they would make a delivery of wine and weapons to Marie Riberau at Café Saint Joanna. From there, they would begin their fight.

20
Lien

AS THEY CAUTIOUSLY TRAVELED THE road toward Lien, a car appeared behind them following at a safe distance. There were so few cars on the road it was hard to ignore. Mason and Sully noticed it right away and watched the car through the flap on the back of the truck. The winding streets would make the car disappear and reappear. Mason had no idea if Luc and Collette were on to this car or not. Luc had maintained the same speed as they drove through the valley. Mason and Sully checked their weapons and kept a close eye on the vehicle behind them. They reached a roundabout and Luc slowed down to allow a woman on her bicycle to cross in front of them. The black Renault appeared around the bend and slowed to a stop several car lengths behind. Mason pulled the flap slightly and looked through the opening, he could make out at least two people in the front, the driver was in a military uniform.

"We've got company," Mason said as he looked at Sully.

Luc started around the roundabout and picked up speed; he was clearly feeling the same way as his two passengers in the back.

"What do we do?" Collette asked as she watched the car through her side mirror.

"Do you think they have noticed back there?" Luc asked with his eyes on the road as he picked up more speed.

"Mason doesn't trust anyone, so yes I am sure between he and Sully they're quite aware of the situation."

"I am going to try to pull over because if we try to outrun them, we'll have half the German army on our tail. If we stop, hopefully they will just look at our papers and let us go. I will explain my situation and let them know they are interfering with deliveries for their superiors. It is the best we can do right now."

Collette agreed; she had a feeling her friend from the bridge had sent these men to follow them. She felt responsible and knew she had to do better.

Mason and Sully felt the truck start to slow down, they had known it was only a matter of time, a fully loaded delivery truck would never outrun anyone. Luc drove down a deserted road, fields on both sides including a sunflower field on the right side with six-foot tall flowers everywhere. Mason smiled, admiring Luc's tactic. The sunflower stalks provided them some cover on one side. The truck slowed to a stop on the side of the road. Mason and Sully ducked behind the cases of wine; weapons drawn. The sound of another set of tires on the gravel side of the road and then the opening and closing of two doors was clearly audible through the flap.

The two soldiers approached opposite sides of the truck and appeared at the windows at the same time. Luc had his window down as they arrived. When Collette noticed the man on her side, she followed suit.

"I need to see your identification papers." The soldier's booming voice caught Luc off guard.

"I work for the Sylvain Winery and I am just making my weekly deliveries."

"We will see about that," the man said as he took Luc's papers.

The man at Collette's window said nothing as he stared at her. She calmly sat still, smiling slightly, as they waited for his partner to say something. He was clearly the man in charge.

"We will need to check the back," he finally said, handing the papers back through the window to Luc.

"Of course," Luc said. "Can we do it quickly, I am due for my delivery to Lieutenant Volmer in Lien. He does get rather upset when I am late. You know how he is? Is he your commandant?"

"Open the back," The man said with a death stare.

"Ok, but let's try to make it quick."

"We will take as much time as we need."

Luc slowly got out and slammed the door louder than usual, sending a clear signal that they were headed for the rear of the truck. He walked slowly past the soldier who had placed his hand on the holster on his right hip.

"You—out of the truck." The other soldier said firmly to Collette. She obliged and he followed her back to the rear of the truck. They stood there, the two Germans, Luc, and Collette, a field of sunflowers to their right, and a fully loaded wine truck in front of them. Luc stepped forward and unlatched the truck gate. He opened it and let it smash down on the bumper making a clanging noise as it banged a few times before coming to a stop. He took a breath and flipped the canvas flap up onto the roof. It stayed for a moment and then slid back down so he stepped on the rear of the truck and flung it farther on to the roof exposing several wooden cases of Sylvain wine stacked neatly in the back.

"Step back," one soldier said as he approached the truck. He looked around and checked the cases visible to him. His partner grabbed a case from the top and placed it on the ground. He grabbed a bottle and handed it to his superior. The man looked at Luc for a moment as he turned the bottle in his hand. Written on the bottle were three words and a date," Sylvain Cabernet Franc 1935" He studied the bottle and then walked over to the truck. Holding the bottle from the bottom, he smashed the top of it on the metal rear of the truck. The top broke apart shattering leaving two thirds of the bottle in the soldier's hand. He once again looked at Luc and began to pour it on the ground. He removed his right glove and poured some on his fingers. He tasted the wine dripping from his fingers and licked his lips. He wiped a drip from below his mouth and then poured the rest out.

"Wine is not my drink of choice." He looked at his partner. "Check the rest of the truck."

With that, his partner climbed into the back of the truck. Mason crouched lower as he sensed the man only five feet away, barely out of sight behind the wine. He shot a glance at Sully and pointed toward his eyes, then in the direction of the German soldier, telling Sully he could see him in the truck.

The soldier pulled bottles from the cases closest to the rear gate and then worked his way farther into the truck. Clearly, the bottles were filled with wine. He climbed over a few cases and almost lost his balance bracing himself on the side of the truck. When he straightened, he looked down and right into the barrel of an American-made Colt revolver. Before he could speak, the bullet pierced the skin between his nose and his left eye shattering his cheekbone. He was jolted backwards, and on his way down, took a few cases with him. The sound of glass rattling and breaking filled the truck. Sully jumped up and fired a shot at the soldier standing outside, hitting him in the arm. The shot threw him backwards as it entered his arm below his right shoulder. He tried raising his pistol as Luc pushed him from the side sending him staggering on the uneven terrain toward the sunflower field. He fell awkwardly into the pit on the side of the road. After a split second, he got to his feet and disappeared into the field.

Mason climbed over the fallen cases of wine, jumped out of the truck, and followed him, pushing sunflower stalks aside as he ran. He could see the soldier faintly ahead through the flowers. A shot rang out and whizzed by Mason's shoulder as a stalk exploded next to him. He stopped and crouched down where he had a clearer view. Smudges of blood stained several stalks as he walked by. He proceeded cautiously through the field, stopping at one point to listen for any sign of the soldier ahead. The large leaves from the sunflowers made it hard to see clearly. He looked up at the flower heads with their bright yellow leaves surrounding the dark brown cylindrical center swaying in the breeze. As he stopped to listen one more time, he heard a moaning noise faintly to his left. Mason squatted down and saw the black boots of the soldier through the stalks about ten feet away.

The boots started to move toward him, and Mason fired, hearing a wince and then a thud as the man crumpled through the stalks and fell before him. Mason rolled him over; his bloody face and chest were covered in dirt and sunflower petals. The man gasped for breath as he tried to raise his pistol. Mason kicked it out of his hand and watched the man take his final breaths. He left him lying in the field, surrounded by thousands of sunflowers—perfect cover for a body. He raced back out of the field as Sully dragged the other soldier from the truck toward him. He grabbed the legs and the two of them dumped the other man far into the field.

"We have to leave now. They will come looking for these two. There is a trail just past this field where we can dump the car. Sully, get back in the truck. Mason, you drive the car to the trail; we will pick you up. Go down the trail until you reach the tree cover, leave the car, and we will wait back at the entrance on the road."

Luc was proving to be a good man under pressure. Mason jumped in the car. He raced past them and turned onto the dirt trail, which was the width of two tractor tires with tall grass in between. Mason pulled in between two large trees and parked the car. He threw the keys deep into the field and ran back to the street. The truck was idling as he hopped in the back and they were off.

"That was close," Sully said as Mason settled back in.

"A little too close," Mason replied as he grabbed a bottle of red. He pulled the cork out and took a swig. Handing it to Sully, Mason exhaled and wondered again if their mission was over before it had even begun. There would be questions about these two men and eventually the car would be found. Hopefully, they would all have disappeared before anyone came looking for them.

They reached the outskirts of Lien and Luc pulled the truck into the square, he backed into an area next to one of the buildings.

"Wait here," Luc told Collette as he jumped out of the truck. He went around to the back door and unlocked it.

Everything was clear so he returned to the truck, opening the flap.

"Let's go," he said to Mason and Sully. He collected Collette from the front and led the three of them through the door and into the basement of Café Saint Joanna. He left back through the door and returned with their things.

"You will stay here until contacted. Do not leave under any circumstances. I will try to find out any information on our little confrontation. After my delivery I will head back across the line through another checkpoint. If we are suspected at all I will be collected there. You must stay safe; it is more important for you than for me."

"Thank you," Sully said extending his hand. "We could never have done this without you."

"You are correct," Luc said, smiling as he shook all their hands. "I should see you in one week for my next delivery, if not, I am…" He took his finger and ran it across his throat in a cutting motion.

He left through the door and locked it from the outside. The three of them stood there in the basement. Food supplies and some old kitchen equipment surrounded them. A small table and chairs were in the middle of the room, an old couch in the corner. Mason sat down and looked around. "I wonder if there is any food down here. I'm starving."

"Really? That is your first thought…food?" Collette replied shaking her head.

"It's not like we can do anything else. Besides, I was stuck in a wine barrel all day."

"Oh, here we go…" she looked at Sully "I will never hear the end of this, his wine barrel odyssey."

Sully smiled. "It was pretty tight."

A noise quieted everyone; someone was coming. The three went behind some old kitchen equipment and Mason and Sully drew their weapons. Sully leaned out and stood up lowering his gun. Mason stood as well, and they saw a woman staring at them. She was beautiful and was holding a tray full of food. Sully approached her, took the tray of food, and placed it on the table. He placed his gun next to it and then grabbed the woman. He brought her in close and looked in her eyes. She said nothing as Mason and Collette looked on. After a few moments, Sully leaned in and kissed her. The feeling was clearly mutual as the couple kissed for what seemed like an eternity. Mason and Collette looked at each other and then emerged from behind the equipment.

"I guess you two know each other," Mason said, breaking the silence.

Sully turned around and smiled. "This is Marie Riberau; she owns the café. She will be our hostess in France…and yes, we do know each other."

"Thank you both for coming; it means so much to me and my people." She stepped forward and shook their hands. "I have brought you some food, you must be hungry. Please eat."

Mason looked at Collette, "How nice. I hadn't thought about it, but now that you have offered." He smiled and she slapped him on the shoulder.

As Mason engulfed the food, a man came down the stairs through the back door. Mason's jaw dropped as he recognized him right away. He walked over to Mason "How are you my friend?"

Mason reached out his hand and they shook, "I'm good. It is so good to see you alive and well." Collette came over and embraced the surprised gentleman. Mason was still in shock. He was told that they would most likely run into each other, but he was not sure when. He owed this man his life and Collette did as well. Mason knew instantly that they would now be in better shape with Paul Ganoux involved. Ganoux put his hand on Mason's shoulder, "Thank you for coming."

21

MARIE EXCUSED HERSELF AND LEFT the others. She had a café to open upstairs. They all agreed to meet back upstairs after hours and Ganoux would lay out the plan going forward. Mason, Collette, and Sully would rest downstairs; Ganoux had some errands to run, he would return later to brief everyone. He thanked the three for coming once again and disappeared out the back door.

Mason turned to Sully. "You knew about him?" he asked, referring to Ganoux.

"I did. He has been providing information to London on a weekly basis about troop movements and buildup, checkpoints, and the overall gravity of the occupation. When we discovered the information about Kliest ordering the assassinations of our operatives, Ganoux immediately gathered information. When I found you, I knew little about Kliest but since, we have acquired significant information about him, and most of that information has come from Ganoux. I am sorry to keep both of you in the dark, but it was too risky. Had we been caught, you would not have revealed what you do not know; it was just safer that way."

"How do you know Marie?" Collette asked as she sat down at the table.

"Marie and I have known each other for some time. I used to do some intelligence gathering in Paris and I would meet some contacts in this town at her café. We struck up a conversation one day and we have remained close."

"I can see that," Mason chimed in smiling.

Collette shook her head as she looked at Mason.

"She's an amazing woman with what she has been through to still be willing to fight back. I put Ganoux in touch with her when he was gathering names for possible resistance fighters. She was on board immediately; though not a native French woman she considers this as much a homeland as any."

"Ganoux worked for my father for many years. He is a good man to have on your side. I feel better knowing he is with us."

"We can use all the good men we can find," Sully said as he looked around for a spot to lie down. "We should get some rest. It will be a long night ahead. Our job has only just begun. Finding answers about the Totenkopf, information on Anna's family, and Kliest will not be easy but it is what we have come to do."

Silence overcame the room as the three began to contemplate the mission they had volunteered for. No, it would not be easy, but Mason liked his odds with Collette, Sully, and Ganoux by his side. He and Collette sat down on the couch and slowly dozed off, Sully found a blanket and curled up on the floor with his head on a burlap sack.

Ganoux returned around 6:30 p.m. and found the three of them sitting at the table. They had rested for several hours and spent the last two listening to the noise upstairs and taking note of their surroundings. The café seemed busy for occupied territory. Ganoux explained that it was a favorite of the German soldiers, which made it ideal for information gathering and trust building. The downfall was the enemy was always around, so caution was of the utmost importance.

Marie locked the door to the café at 7:00p.m. and came to the basement to retrieve the others. They entered the upstairs and gathered around two tables in the middle of the room. Marie was still busying herself behind the bar when Ganoux began to speak.

"First off, thank you all for being here. Though some of us are meeting for the first time, I guarantee each and every one of you can trust the other with your lives, and there is a very good chance you will have to. I have been collecting intelligence for months now. Sully and I have been in contact on a weekly basis. Here is what we have established. The German Reich is in full control of Europe. After invading Poland on September 1st of last year, it only took them nine months until the surrender of Paris. They seem like an army of immeasurable force and that is why we need to begin to fight back—not face to face but in the shadows with clandestine missions. The German army has settled into the area and they have placed a Lieutenant Volmer in control of this town and the surrounding area. Recently Volmer suffered an assassination attempt while standing over there. He was shot by a member of our resistance, a very brave member who gave his life for the cause." Ganoux walked over to the spot where the lieutenant fell, "Fortunately for us, Marie was able to save Volmer's life and prevent him from bleeding out on her floor. Not only did she save his life but in the process gained his trust and his adoration. It was our plan to get Marie into the good graces of Volmer; he has a soft spot for the drink and beautiful women. The Fuhrer has directed his various commanders to celebrate the occupation of Paris and our friend Volmer is hosting a private celebration in two weeks. He has invited his direct commander for a secret meeting."

Ganoux turned to Mason and Collette, "Kliest will be here on that night. We do not know why they are meeting; it has been kept noticeably quiet. We know he is coming in for the celebration but this meeting is separate. We believe it has something to do with cargo which arrives by train at the station outside of town. I have been watching the trains arrive from Paris and while they usually carry troops and material back and forth, there is always one car that is diverted into a warehouse away from the others. I have not been able to get a look at the cargo but I suspect something especially important and very secret is in those train cars. I had a plan to destabilize the bridge leading into Lien, but we cannot do anything with that until we know what is so valuable that it is hidden in our little train depot. We must find out what they are hiding in those cars and why it is so important that Kliest himself is coming here. Kliest is smart." Ganoux looked around at everyone. "He is very smart. We must be incredibly careful and pay attention to our surroundings at all times."

He turned to Sully. "I know you found a list of your operatives. We must always consider the fact that you were meant to find it and that we are walking into a trap. I would not put it past Kliest to sacrifice his own people to get us all here. Mason, you and I beat him at his game, and he is not the kind of man to let that go. With military operations seemingly in control for the moment, he may be plotting his revenge against you, me, and Collette."

Marie put some wine on the table with several glasses along with some bread. Mason poured the wine for everyone as Ganoux continued. "Collette, we have gathered some information about Anna's parents. We do not know its exact nature but there is a holding camp in Drancy, a town outside of Paris, which we believe is a camp for prisoners of war. We think people are being processed there before being shipped out of Europe. I am trying to gather some more information and we have people there trying to get documents with names. Sully has people in London who will get us word if anything comes up.

As far as weapons go, we have stashed what we can in the mausoleum of an old family here in Lien. Carolina has befriended the priest of the local church, so she has established access in and out of the cemetery with little issue. We can rely on her to transport any weapons back and forth. Carolina is also our baker; her family owns a small bakery on the outside of town. She provides most of the bread for the Germans and Marie's café, which will prove quite helpful."

Ganoux turned to Phillipe, "Phillipe here, helps out Marie at the café every day. His family owns a farm in the hills on the edge of town and has been farming for generations. Phillipe is also an expert in mixing chemicals together. He has developed several lethal combinations which they have used to rid his animals of disease and prevent further spreading. His methods also work remarkably well on humans. If we need to dispose of a body or two, he is your man."

Phillipe nodded his head at the group. Mason had thought he was just a dishwasher and helped clear tables. He did not look like a man who could hurt anyone, let alone dispose of bodies.

First, we will try to find out more information about the train yards, Drancy and Kliest's visit, then we will perfect our plan.

"Our plan?" Mason asked looking around at everyone.

Ganoux continued, "Our plan is to kill Kliest and Volmer the night of their celebration. Our best way to disrupt the precision of the German army is to take out their command. Volmer, as a means of winning Marie's affection, has asked her to cook for the celebration, which gets us in. Collette, you will pose as Marie's assistant and you will need to gain access with Marie before the celebration. Marie will bring you with her to meet Volmer so she can introduce you. Charm him if you can, it will make your job easier.

Collette and Carolina will help Marie with the catering at the party. Our goal is to poison everyone there, including Kliest, with a cocktail mixed by Phillipe and baked into the food and mixed in the drink at the celebration. Collette will mix the poison with the wine and champagne. The attendees will become ill in the days following and one by one succumb to their mystery illness."

All the information was a lot to decipher, Mason looked around at his new family, the seven of them together would try to pull off a monumental task that, if successful could encourage resistance fighters all over Europe to quietly rise up against their captors.

Seven people…, male, female, old, young, all with one goal, the murder of two high-ranking German Officers. Marie: the Temptress, Phillipe: the Chemist, Carolina: the Baker, Ganoux: the Mastermind, Collette: the Executioner, Sully: the Detective and Mason Wright: the Ghost.

22

GANOUX LED MASON AND SULLY through a field outside of town as scores of beech trees swayed above them. Darkness had come, the temperature had dropped, and the gusty wind picked up. Mason rubbed his hands together as they crossed the grassy field.

"Through those trees, we can get to the top of the hill and get a view of the station and the railyards. The next train is due in one hour. We should be in position in twenty minutes."

"What are we looking for?" Sully asked quietly as Ganoux walked in front.

"I want you two to help me figure out why a rail car is always diverted to a warehouse while the rest of the train moves on. Three pairs of eyes will be better than one. We may have to go down for a closer look. We need to find out what makes the one rail car special."

"How many troops?"

"That's the thing." Ganoux stopped and looked at them. "The station is guarded by a full garrison, yet the railyard only has guards at the entrance with very little security inside. It is fenced in and patrolled out front. As far as I can tell, once we are in, it will be quiet. The warehouse where the railcar is located usually has three guards around, but they don't do much other than stand around and smoke."

They reached the tree line and disappeared, swallowed by the branches of several evergreen trees. It was noticeably colder in the forest and Ganoux slowed down once they were in.

"I'll take the lead, you two separate and follow," Ganoux directed. "Allow roughly fifteen feet between us, just enough to see each other. Should we run into trouble at least we will not all be standing next to each other. Mason, you go to the right, Sully, you to the left."

The two men did as they were told, and they continued through the forest toward the rail station. The terrain began to rise as they reached the bottom of the hill. Mason climbed over a downed tree and cut his right palm on a sharp broken branch. He pulled his hand away quickly. "Ouch," he said quietly. He shook his hand in the air and wiped some blood away with his left hand.

Continuing up the hill, the faint sounds of civilization could be heard ahead. Ganoux put his right hand up and stopped. He crouched down and Mason and Sully did the same. They were approaching the road which circled the hill above the station. The dirt road was more of an access path than a well-traveled road. It led to a water tower which graced the top of the hill. Ganoux slowly approached the clearing and looked in all directions. He saw and heard nothing. Mason and Sully joined him at the edge of the trees.

Satisfied, Ganoux gave the go-ahead. The three men jogged across the dirt road into the field on the other side. They had lost the benefit of tree cover as this side was more field than forest. A few trees still stood but most had been felled to help build the wooden railyard buildings below. The faint sound of an engine could be heard in the distance and they stopped for a moment. The engine sound grew louder, and they realized it was heading their way. They ran over to one of the few trees and crouched behind it. It grew from the ground and split into two trunks about three feet off the ground. Mason and Sully crouched near the ground as Ganoux looked out from between the trunks. The engine was close now and Ganoux could see the light from headlights bouncing off the trees across the road. He got lower as the KFZ 11 Standard Personnel Vehicle approached. The German equivalent of the American Jeep, the KFZ 11 appeared over the hill slowly moving down the path. Three soldiers occupied the vehicle as it drove by, two in the front, one in the back. The passenger side soldier scanned the right, while the soldier in the back looked left.

The soldier riding in the passenger seat motioned to the driver with his hands and the vehicle slowed to a stop. The soldier got out of the vehicle and said something to the other two. He turned and walked toward the brush laughing. He puffed on his cigarette and secured his rifle on his shoulder. Mason, Sully, and Ganoux simultaneously readied their pistols preparing if he got any closer.

The soldier stopped about ten feet from them and took one last puff of his cigarette. He flicked it away, then unzipped his pants, closed his eyes, and took a deep breath as he urinated in the field ten feet from them. Mason glanced at Sully with a look of disbelief as they could hear the urine hitting the dirt. The other two soldiers were laughing in the vehicle, and one yelled to the soldier relieving himself. The man, still with eyes shut, yelled something back as he finished up. All three shared a laugh as he zipped up his pants. He turned and headed back to the vehicle, lighting another cigarette on his way. Once situated, the soldiers drove away towards the water tower, the wheels of their vehicle spinning on the dirt road. Ganoux just shook his head as they all looked at each other.

"He'll never know how close he came to that piss being his last," Mason said smiling.

Ganoux started walking again keeping low to the ground. They had reached the edge of the hill and the terrain started downhill towards a fence on the edge of the cliff. Mason slipped on a loose rock and briefly lost his footing. His right foot slid down the slope on the dry dirt. He balanced himself on a tree and paused a second before continuing. They reached the fence line and laid down on their stomachs. Below to the left was the Lien Train Station, a small station, with four tracks. Tracks One and Two headed north toward Paris, tracks Three and Four headed south towards Bordeaux. Had this not been war time, Mason would have brought Collette along and hopped on the train to Bordeaux to visit his favorite vineyards.

On track Four sat one rail car from a freight train originally used to carry coal or raw materials. The metal railcar had sides three feet tall and was uncovered. This car had been transformed into an armored train car. Four soldiers sat in the back behind a Flak 30 anti-aircraft gun. A large spotlight was beside the rail car pointed skyward. Some guards patrolled the platforms on both sides with their rifles shouldered, lit cigarettes hanging from their mouths. They walked back and forth slowly surveying the area. Other than German troops, no civilians were waiting. The station was a stone building, paint faded and nondescript. A weathered, rusted sign was mounted on the side of the building. It read "LIEN" in capital letters with some small writing below it. The white sign with blue letters had seen better days, as had Lien itself.

On the southbound line just past the station, was a third track which veered off to the left through a large wrought iron gate and into the train yard. Mounds of wooden railroad ties were piled against the fence along with crates of spikes. The track split into two tracks inside the yard, one came to a dead end after fifty feet, the other disappeared inside a wooden warehouse. It was this warehouse which interested Ganoux. He had watched them disengage a car from the train at the station and divert it into the warehouse. He had witnessed this several times. The large sliding wooden door was then closed so the train car was sealed inside, with a small group of soldiers standing watch. Whatever it was, it was something important. In the morning, the car would be reattached and sent back up north. The Germans were unloading something, and they did not want to be seen.

A few moments after 9 p.m., the train rolled into Lien. Since the Germans took over the railways, one thing was for sure, they were more precise, and everything operated with German efficiency. A handful of townspeople had gathered on the platform to meet people from the train.

Several soldiers emerged from the train after spending some time in Paris; they quickly disappeared into the station. An old man with a large brown bag exited and was met by a much younger man and woman. The old man could barely walk as they left the station, but when offered help with his bag, he refused.

The resilience of the elderly, Mason thought to himself. Resilience or stubbornness, there was a fine line. He thought briefly of his own dad and hoped he was doing well in upstate New York.

Mason's dad had become ill a few years ago and had to give up his life of archaeology. Mason saw the old man from the train and pictured his dad refusing help from anyone. Not because his father wanted to prove he could do it alone, the bags he carried were usually filled with rare and priceless antiquities, so he never let them out of his sight. His father told him once, "Mason, always assume the guy next to you wants what you have." That turned out to be the case when Mason helped Collette's father move some priceless art works out of France. He came face to face with the ugly side of fine art and without Ganoux's help, he would be lying dead somewhere in or around Paris.

The train whistle broke the silence as the steam train pulled away and continued its southbound route to Bordeaux.

"We can scale down the hill over there and approach the rail yard from that side over by those trees. We'll cut the wire fence and slip in and out," Ganoux said, pointing off in the distance. They agreed and started their descent with Sully taking the lead.

Sully held onto the tree branches and bushes wherever he could to prevent himself from slipping. Mason followed and tried the same approach. Ganoux had done this a few times so he went last and chuckled at his two American friends who looked like they were holding on for dear life. At one point, Sully lost his footing and held onto a branch as debris scattered down the side. Mason pulled him back up and agreed to take lead. Sully was more than happy to give it up. As they reached the bottom, Mason jumped down from the edge onto the stone side of the tracks, his feet sinking into the small stones. Mason checked for any German troops on the tracks. He could see the railcar with the anti-aircraft gun mounted on top down the tracks, by the station. The soldiers were concentrating on the sky and each other and no one was looking their way. They quickly scampered across the tracks and into the trees.

After a few minutes they reached the edge of the rail yard. Ganoux produced some wire cutters and started to cut the fence. He cut an opening large enough for one person and Mason volunteered for the reconnaissance mission. He slipped through the fence and hid behind a large construction machine. He was about thirty feet from the back of the warehouse with the train car. As he looked out from under the tractor, he could see three figures out front standing around in the darkness. There was little light in the rail yard; all he could see was the orange circular light of the cigarettes burning as they inhaled. He counted three cigarettes—three small orange lights blinking on and off as they puffed. He slid around the back of the tractor and, crouching low, jogged over to the corner of the warehouse. Once there, he looked in the dirty windows. He could not see much so he rubbed the glass with his sleeve, smudging the windows more. He noticed one light on inside and the large black shape of a railcar. He found a door in the rear, an old wooden door with six glass panes. He tried the handle and it would not turn. The lower pane on the left was cracked so Mason wrapped a rock in his sleeve and gently nudged at it until it separated. He moved it back and forth until it released. He pulled out one half of the cracked pane and then the other.

Reaching his hand in, he unlocked the door, opened it, and slipped in. He was now inside the barely illuminated warehouse. With the only windows on the sides, he needed some light to navigate the warehouse or he would be knocking into things left and right. Ganoux had given him a flashlight but it would be too bright to turn on fully, so he removed his coat and wrapped the flashlight in the sleeve. He turned it on, and a dull ray of light shown through his sleeve. Mason slowly walked around the warehouse. It was empty for the most part; a workbench on the left with assorted tools hanging on the wall, some train parts on the right. As he approached the rail car, he noticed two piles next to it. He could not make out what they were, but one had boxes of some shape and the other looked like a pile of rags. As he approached the pile of containers, he heard the soldiers laughing outside the main door. He froze as he made sure they were not opening the door. Confident they were not, he continued toward the pile. As he reached it, he bent down to pick up the box shape and realized they were suitcases and trunks piled together. As he picked one up, it opened and swung down. It was empty. He picked up another one and the same thing happened. He gently placed them down wondering if the Germans were disposing of people's luggage left on the trains. Seemed strange to him, hiding a rail car full of empty luggage. He walked over to the pile next to it and reached down. He picked up some rags, and after a closer look realized it was clothing, a pile of clothing. He looked back at the suitcases and then at the pile in front of him. They must be stealing people's belongings, bringing them here, unloading them and then sending the car back to Paris. Anything valuable would be kept, the rest destroyed. He looked around and noticed a large machine against the wall to his left. After a closer look, he realized it was an incinerator. He noticed a few suitcases at the base. He rubbed his fingers across the front and black soot covered his hand. Mason shook his head in disgust.

He looked back at the railcar and stepped towards the ramp leading to the platform in front of it. The ten-foot wide ramp served as a loading and unloading dock. He walked gingerly up the ramp and the floorboards squeaked under him. He reached the top and tried to quietly open the sliding doors to the railcar; they were padlocked shut. Stepping back to look at the car, he noticed a small opening in the side of the car with wrought iron bars protecting it so nothing could get in or out. The small window was roughly eight inches by sixteen inches. Mason listened for a second for the soldiers out front. He didn't hear much so he walked over to the window. He unwrapped the flashlight and held his hand over the beam as he raised it up. He shined the light in the opening and looked in. In a split second of shock, Mason immediately stepped back and dropped the flashlight. It crashed onto the wood making a loud thud which filled the room as he stumbled backwards tripping over some wooden planks on the dock. He fell off the dock and onto the stones, banging into some metal barrels. The clanking of the metal barrels made a loud noise. Startled, he quickly jumped up and made his way back to the door. The sound was heard by the sentries outside, as the large wooden doors at the front of the warehouse started to open. Mason closed the back door as the front doors slid open wide enough for the soldiers to come running in with flashlights and rifles drawn. The soldiers ran around the warehouse searching for the root of the banging noise they had heard. One walked up the dock with his rifle and noticed the flashlight on the ground.

"Alarm, alarm," he yelled at the other two. One of the others ran to the wall and pressed a large metal knob. Immediately, the alarm sounded loudly over the railyard and station as Mason ran from the warehouse past the tractor and to the fence line. Ganoux and Sully saw the fear on Mason's face as he approached and knew right away, he was responsible for the blaring alarm. They helped him through the fence and all three ran back across the tracks. Some German soldiers were running down the tracks toward them as shots rang out over their heads. Mason jumped up into the bushes and helped Sully up. Ganoux pulled himself up and started back up the hill. As Mason gained his footing, he followed Ganoux and Sully. Another shot rang out over his head, the leaves in the trees above him exploding like fireworks.

The German soldiers were yelling in their direction as they approached from the tracks. Mason secured his Colt as he ran up the dirt path. Ganoux and Sully were in front and Mason dodged the branches as they snapped back at him. They ran up the hill back toward the water tower and the clearing by the dirt road. Mason could not tell if the soldiers had followed them into the woods or remained on the tracks. He was not about to stop and find out. He kept climbing the hill, his insides burning from exhaustion. He caught up to Sully who was visibly struggling to get to the top. Ganoux, looking like he was on a nice evening stroll, calmly climbed, reaching the clearing at the top first. He paused when he reached it to look for anyone or anything waiting for them. Mason and Sully arrived in tandem, both men with hands on their knees huffed and puffed as they stopped.

"We must go," Ganoux said looking at them. "We can't rest here."

Mason nodded and stood up. Sully, coughing, also stood up and staggered forward. Ganoux led them across the dirt road and back into the woods. He would take them to Carolina's farmhouse where they would lay low. It was closer to their position, just over the ridge to the right and down into the valley. The shots had ceased, and it appeared no one followed them up the hill. It was hard enough for the three of them to make the climb—it would have been nearly impossible to do that with full soldier's uniform and gear. Ganoux methodically maneuvered them down the hill and into the valley. They reached the rear of the farmhouse and made their way to the back door. Sully stumbled along, his lungs burning from the trek. Mason held his own, but he too was burning inside. Ganoux opened the door and they settled in the kitchen. Ganoux went around checking the house for anything. He pulled the curtains back a bit to see the surrounding area and have a look. Everything seemed calm but he was sure the Germans would come looking at some point.

He returned to the kitchen where Sully and Mason were drinking some water, still noticeably out of breath, Sully especially.

"You need to get in better shape," Mason said, looking at Sully with a grin.

"I am used to being driven around London, not running and climbing through the woods. Not used to this outdoors stuff. I'll be fine. What the hell did you see in there?"

Ganoux looked at Mason, "Were you able to see inside the railcar?"

Mason nodded as he tried to calm his breathing.

"What was inside? Weapons? Supplies?"

"No" Mason said in between breaths. "It was nothing like that."

"Then what was so important that they hid it separately?" Sully asked as he filled his glass with water from the sink.

"They're not transporting weapons or supplies, they're transporting people, the car was filled with terrified people. I was so shaken by the sight; I dropped the flashlight and fell backwards into some metal barrels. I guess that is what alerted the guards, and then when they found the flashlight, they sounded the alarm."

"People? Were they prisoners of war?" Ganoux asked still trying to wrap his head around it.

"No." Mason nodded as he looked at both men. "These were not prisoners of war, these were civilians, terrified civilians. All their belongings were piled up next to the railcar in front of an incinerator. Men, women, children's stuff. I looked in the car and all I saw was eyes—sets of wide eyes as far as I could see. They must be crammed in the car. In the brief seconds I saw them, I heard a frail voice from an elderly man. He said three words to me as I looked through the opening in disbelief—'Please help us.' I am not sure what I expected but that sure as hell was not it." Mason said, trailing off as he sat down rubbing his face with his hands.

Ganoux took a deep breath and no one said anything. There was nothing to say. He had watched for several nights as one train car was diverted to the warehouse. He assumed weapons, supplies, even spoils of war. He never thought for a second that the diverted railcar was a prison car. The three men looked at each other as silence engulfed the kitchen. Words seemed so inconsequential at this moment. Each man's thoughts turned to the poor people jammed in the railcar and the fate that lay ahead for them. Mason stared at the table, Sully straight ahead, and Ganoux at the floor. No man said a word, they did not need to, they all shared the same thoughts, but at the moment, there was nothing they could do about it.

23
Paris

COLLETTE AND MARIE BOARDED THE train bound for Paris and found their seats. The three-hour train ride would drop them at the Gard d' Nord train station where they would board the Metro to the Latin Quarter. They were on their way to meet a contact who may have some information for Collette about Anna's parents.

The pair settled into their seats for the ride and Marie immediately noticed two men walk by and sit across the aisle from them. She recognized one of the men dressed in a long black leather coat as he passed and sat in the row behind them. She had seen this man at headquarters when she was summoned by Volmer following the attack on his life. He was one of the men at the entrance checking identifications as she entered; it was no coincidence that he was on this train. She did not recognize the other man.

Collette noticed Marie's concern as the train moved forward. The noise from the rails drowned out most of the talking in the cabin.

Marie leaned over and whispered in her ear, "We have company, two men behind us on the other side. I recognize one from Volmer's headquarters. I am sure the Lieutenant keeps tabs on me, so we will have to get creative when we get close to Paris. We can't afford to have any company tonight."

Collette nodded slightly as she sat back. She constantly had to remind herself how different things were from just a few months ago. This was her country, but she was a foreigner as far as these men were concerned. The feeling made her justify the reason she was here. The hardest part was having to accept that this was the way it was for now. How long would it last? No one knew. Germany controlled all of Europe and word was, they would go for England next. So many leaders were either dead or in exile, it was hard to even know who could counter Hitler. Churchill and Stalin were the last hope, and both wanted the United States to enter the war. Roosevelt was still hesitant, citing the American people as the deciding factor, and they did not want to enter a war across the world that, up to this point, did not include them. So, for now, this was the world. Japan was slowly conquering Vietnam and Cambodia while fighting a war with China, The Philippines would be next, along with the islands of the Pacific. Italy had begun their campaign in Egypt and Libya, and war was all around the world except for The West, but no one expected that to remain the case. People quietly hoped it was not *If* war would include the United States, it was *when.*

As the train reached the suburbs of Paris, Marie leaned into Collette, "When we are approaching the station, I will go to the restroom. Once stopped, you exit the train and meet me on the platform for the Metro. This will split up the two of them, Volmer's man will follow me, he will be hard to lose, so you must do everything you can to shake your man. If we can get to the Metro and have only one man to lose when we split up, he cannot follow both of us."

Collette had an idea on how to lose her tail. She had done it once already in Spain, so she felt confident she could do it again. The train conductor announced the arrival in Paris approaching and Marie gathered her things. She stood up and walked toward the front of the car. People had begun to stand and crowd the aisle. Marie slipped through an elderly couple who were moving at a snail's pace. The husband was putting on his coat as Marie snuck by. The rather overweight gentleman clogged most of the aisle as he raised his arms into the sleeves of his wool coat.

Collette remained seated and watched for Marie's shadow to pass by. Within moments the man in the long leather coat walked by and reached the older gentleman with the coat. He waited impatiently for a second and then forced his way through, knocking the man back into his row. The older gentleman said something in French that despite the beauty of the language, was clearly an insult directed at the pushy man in the leather coat.

Collette removed a small mirror from her purse and pretended to apply some lipstick, while she glanced behind her at the second man. She moved the mirror side to side as she touched her hair. She noticed him sitting sternly looking forward. He had an angry face, the kind of face that is not approachable. As Collette stared at him, he moved his eyes and caught her stare in the mirror. She quickly glanced back into the mirror and pursed her lips, pretending to spread the lipstick around.

The train stopped and a burst of steam could be heard outside as the conductor announced the arrival in Paris. Collette rose from her seat and pulled her coat tight. She secured her red hat and tied her matching scarf around her neck. Evening was setting in and the temperature was dropping. She made her way into the aisle and moved forward. She stopped and let the older couple out of their row and the man thanked her with a nod. She followed them slowly off the train and onto the crowded platform. A woman walked by her and knocked into her with a large suitcase. Collette stumbled sideways and said something under her breath. She stood for a moment and looked around; she saw some German soldiers slowly approaching glancing from side to side as they watched the platform. Their machine guns rested against their chests as they methodically walked. She moved forward toward the exit sign and into the station. The crush of people got worse as she approached the stairs, six people across funneled down to two. She grabbed the handle and started up the stairs next to a young woman holding some yellow roses. The color of the flowers stood out against the misery of the train station. She hoped the flowers were for someone special and admired the young woman's confidence in carrying them out in the open. Collette wondered if she was making a statement to their occupiers. She hoped the young girl was, and for a split second, it brightened Collette's day. She greatly admired this sign of youthful spirit; it was surely needed.

At the top of the stairs, Collette turned left and looked for the *Toilette* sign. She found the bathrooms down the hallway and entered the Mademoiselle side, slipping into the first stall. She stood there for a few minutes and waited until the bathroom was less crowded. Two women were chatting at the sink about their useless husbands, Collette waited impatiently for the conversation to end. She felt bad for the husbands and understood their plight as these two women were rather brash and quite annoying. After they left, Collette emerged from her stall and looked under the others; they were empty. She pulled out matches and went to the trash can, opened it and proceeded to set fire to the newspapers which lay on top. They simmered and began to smoke. She threw a roll of toilet paper from the counter in the trash and it ignited right away. Satisfied with her arson, she left the bathroom as two women were entering. Collette became panic stricken and yelled, "Fire, Fire."

The two women screamed, and Collette walked out in a panic. They followed her out yelling in French as chaos ensued. Collette quickly left the scene and walked briskly toward the Metro sign. Two security guards passed her on the way toward her fire. She hopped down the steps and darted through the waiting passengers slipping behind an advertising column situated at the end of the platform. The circular column was pasted with posters of events happening in the city. One caught her eye as she hid behind it, an American style show at the American Café d' Paris. She smiled and shook her head thinking of Franz "Lucky" Leiter, a French gangster who owned the American Club and had a love-hate relationship with Mason. She was quite sure he was profiting nicely from this occupation, catering to the German elite with his food, music, booze, and girls.

Collette peeked out from the column looking for the man from the train and was startled by a woman standing in front of her. The disheveled woman approached her and asked her for some change. Collette stared at the woman for a moment, the old lines on her face, the sad eyes, the rags she wore for clothing.

She had an idea, an idea that would help both of them. She reached in her pocket and pulled out some money, handed it to the woman. Collette then removed her hat and scarf and placed them on the woman, tying the scarf tightly around her neck and securing the hat. She smiled at the woman and cupped her cheek. The woman thanked Collette profusely and wanted to hug her, but Collette interrupted her, "Quick, you must hurry, the train is leaving." Collette turned her around and ushered her toward the open door of the Metro. Once on the train the woman found an area to stand on the crowded train.

Collette ducked back behind the column and caught a glimpse of the man who was following her. She glanced quickly and noticed him walking briskly back and forth, looking at the crowd entering and exiting the train cars. He walked to the edge of the platform and looked inside the train at the crowd. The bell rang, signaling the doors to be closed and the man found what he was looking for—the red hat. He saw the red hat at the front of the train car and immediately jumped through the doors as they closed. He stood shoulder to shoulder with the crowd as the train pulled away. Collette emerged from her hiding spot as the sound of the Metro pulling away filled the station. A few people ran down the steps and stopped as they realized they had missed the train. She stared at the man on the train as it pulled away; he was focused on the red hat at the front of his car. She smiled at the thought of this man eventually realizing he was following a red hat and scarf on a sixty-year old woman.

She waited on the platform for the next Metro train. Five minutes later it pulled in, the doors opened, she stepped inside and held the rail next to the door. The Metro pulled out on its way through the underground of Paris. Collette looked up at the map above the door and counted the stops until Denfert-Rocherau. Four stops until her exit. She wondered about Marie and if she had lost her tail or was still weaving her way through Paris. They were to meet at the Medici Fountain near the entrance to the Luxembourg Gardens.

Collette walked casually up the steps of the Metro stop at Denfert-Rocherau and onto the streets of Paris. Dusk had begun and the streets were sparsely populated. She glanced around for any people taking an interest in her, but everyone she saw was keeping to themselves as they passed by.

As she reached the top step, she noticed the entrance to The Catacombs across the street, sealed for many years the wrought iron door was the entrance to several flights of stairs down into a world of six million bones. Mason had spent some time down in that world retrieving some stolen paintings for her father a few months ago. She did not think at that time that she would be back in Paris anytime soon. She walked down the street a bit further approaching the intersection of Denfert-Rocherau and Montparnasse. A couple strolled by her arm in arm, clinging close together to stay warm. Collette stopped at the light and waited for a few cars to pass, two people on bikes rode by as she stepped into the street. She jogged across the street and turned onto Boulevard Saint Michel. The opening to the gardens was up ahead on the right. A few German soldiers hung around the entrance checking papers as people went by. They seemed to be randomly selecting people to harass. Collette was sure she was next, a woman out at night by herself.

A soldier approached and asked for her papers. She retrieved them from her inside pocket and handed them over.

The man stared at her for a moment as she handed them to him, "You are not nervous out alone?" he said with an air of arrogance.

"Should I be?" Collette replied.

"Well, you never know, a beautiful woman like yourself alone in the big city, things happen."

Collette threw up in her mouth as she listened to this man, "I can take care of myself."

He nodded as she looked at him and after a few moments he returned her papers.

"Be careful *Fraulein*."

"You're a pig." She replied with a smile in perfect French. The man looked at her with a crooked smile clearly unsure of what she said.

She grabbed her papers and started into the gardens. As she walked down the dirt and gravel path, she was surrounded on both sides by perfectly manicured trees, three rows on each side of the walk. Boasting over one hundred statues, fountains, and monuments on its grounds, the Luxembourg Gardens were a sight to behold. During the spring and summer months, fresh flowers were abundant on the grounds, but things had changed, of course, and all the beauty of the gardens had been replaced with German soldiers and wartime defenses. The Luftwaffe had taken over the palace on the grounds and for now, the gardens remained open, but any day that could change.

Collette reached the steps leading down to the center of the gardens. The large lake in the middle rippled softly in the wind. The path split into two as it went around the grass and the lake. She stayed to the right as she headed toward the Medici fountain on the other side of the lake.

The Medici Fountain commissioned by Maria d' Medici, then Queen of France, is one of the jewels of the garden. The fountain features Polyphemus discovering the two lovers, Acis and Galatea, below him on the rocks. Commissioned in the 1600s and then refurbished several times, the last reconstruction took place in 1866. A long pool of water leads away from the fountain, decorated on the sides with ceramic urns. The fountain was designed in the classic Italian renaissance model, after Medici brought with her the visions of gardens from the family villas in Florence and Rome.

The palace stood directly in front of her as she walked. Several soldiers stood out front and there was a spotlight visible on the roof. A large red Nazi banner hung down from each side of the front door leaving no question who the residence now belonged to. Collette reached the edge of the lake and walked toward the fountain. She stopped on a bench and sat for a moment pretending to adjust her shoe. She glanced back in the direction she came from but everything seemed ok. A man stumbled along looking in the trash bins for a bite to eat, eventually tripping on the side of the path and falling onto the grass. Two German soldiers walked to him and picked him up. They dragged him away into the shadows toward the entrance.

There was no sign of Marie yet, Collette would give her until 6:30 p.m., if there was still no sign, she would proceed on her own. This was no time to hesitate or second guess, if there was a chance of finding out some information for Anna, she had to do it with or without Marie.

She waited patiently until she saw a woman approaching. Collette headed to the fountain and the woman got closer. Marie smiled as she reached the fountain.

"You made it, thank God." Collette said as Marie stopped in front of her.

"You alone?" Marie asked.

"Yes, my man is following an older woman wearing my hat, I suspect he is somewhere in the Metro system. You?"

"Yes, I was able to lose him at the train station. He got caught up in some chaos, apparently someone started a fire in the ladies' bathroom."

"I heard something about that," Collette smiled.

"Let's go, we need to walk up the hill to the Sorbonne, we will meet my contact at a café off the main square."

Collette followed as Marie led them through the gate and across the intersection onto Rue Soufflot. They walked three blocks and arrived at the Place de Pantheon, the large mausoleum where France entombed the remains of famous people in their history. Inside, Emile Zola, Victor Hugo and Alexandre Dumas were among the almost 50 people laid to rest inside this magnificent stone structure. The Pantheon was surrounded by a ten-foot tall wrought iron fence and the cobblestone square was usually lit with spotlights on the French flag towering over the roof. The German army had removed all flags in the city and replaced them with the red and black Nazi flags.

Marie stopped at the corner of Soufflot and the Place de L'estrapade. She got her bearings and they proceeded down the dark street looking for the small French café on the corner. As they approached the door it swung open and a man and woman loudly stumbled down the step onto the street. Marie stepped back as they walked away. Upon entering the café, Collette unbuttoned her jacket and took a deep breath, they had made it to their rendezvous point. Marie secured a small table in the corner, large enough for four people. They sat and ordered some coffee. The waitress brought over some bread and two glasses of water along with a carafe.

The door opened and an older man entered wearing a long wool coat, he removed his hat and glanced around the room. He saw Marie at the table and slowly walked over and sat down.

"Hello Marie," he said softly.

"Jonathan. how are you?" she replied with a smile.

"I am old and in failing health, I only hope to see my country back in the hands of my people before I die." He coughed into his hands.

Marie introduced Collette and they exchanged greetings.

"So, did you find any information on the family of Anna Dressler?" Marie said quietly to Jonathan.

He coughed again, a raspy cough of someone who smoked cigarettes for too long. "I found out some things from my daughter who works in the office of personnel for the French government. Her office has been taken over by the German Army and she has been retained as a secretary for the office staff. As she was filing some papers, she noticed some documents on the desk of her superior. She glanced at them for a moment and noticed the name was followed by the age, hometown, and then a relocation destination.

She found this strange because all she ever dealt with was confirming people's addresses, a way for the Nazis to keep tabs on undesirable citizens. The addresses next to the names on the list she saw all originate in Germany, and they end up in France. They are all Jewish names. She was working late one evening and she went back into his office to retrieve the pile for a closer look. The names were all women on one set of documents, men on the other. At no point were they together. I think these people were taken from their homes and shipped here. I don't know why but they seem to originate in Germany and end up somewhere around Paris." He coughed again and took a drink from his glass of water.

"I fear the worst; rumors have been coming out of terrible things committed against the Jews in Germany. I don't know why they are moving people to France from Germany, but I don't think it is for their freedom, I believe they are being systematically eliminated somewhere in this country."

Marie sat back against her chair, the look on her face said it all. Collette had heard the rumors and in her conversations with Anna had envisioned the atrocities. The thought of a country shipping people in railcars to their death was unimaginable. Maybe they were sent to factories or work camps; she refused to believe the worst, partly for her own sanity and partly for Anna's family.

"I managed to find some information on the name you gave me." He reached inside his coat and handed Marie a note. She opened it and it had some writing on it: 27, September 1940 Dressler, Female 17, City: Saarbrucken, DE - Lien, FR.

Marie handed the paper to Collette, she looked at it for a moment., "That's Anna's sister. She must still be here in France somewhere. Can you find out where she is being shipped and when?" Collette pleaded with the old man.

"My daughter already has done a lot for this information. I will see if she can find out more, but it will be difficult." He coughed into his hand again, "She doesn't have access to everything, and I cannot ask her to risk her life for two strangers. I am sorry."

"Please, if she can find out anything, it would be very much appreciated."

The man put on his hat and stood up. He nodded to both and turned to leave. Marie and Collette sat quietly at their table. How would they find her, she could be anywhere?

"We should go back," Marie said faintly reaching across the table and covering Collette's hand. Collette slowly nodded but said nothing.

The two exited the café and headed back in the direction of their Metro. They turned the corner into the square and noticed a man up ahead leaning down and fumbling with something on the ground. Marie directed them behind the tree for a closer look. The man stood up and looked through a wallet of some kind. Unsatisfied, he tossed it aside. Collette caught a glimpse of what was on the ground; it was Jonathan, and he was motionless. The man looked around and walked past them towards the front door to the café. He opened it and went inside. Marie and Collette ran to Jonathan's side, he had blood all over the front of his coat, he was coughing, and blood was bubbling at the side of his mouth. He looked up at Marie, "Get out of here, he is looking for you."

They stood up and ran to the corner as the man emerged from the café. He caught a glimpse of the two women running toward the Pantheon. He quickly ran past Jonathan, and onto the cobblestone street. Marie and Collette ran full speed across the Pantheon square, passing a man walking with his bicycle who stopped to watch as the two women ran by. As their pursuer ran past him, the bystander quickly jumped on his bicycle and disappeared into the night peddling as fast as he could. Marie reached the end of the square and she and Collette split up, Marie heading up the Rue des Carmes, while Collette continued up the square past the Bibliotheque St. Genevieve of the Sorbonne. The man stopped for a moment as he watched both women run in opposite directions. After a few breaths, he started after Marie up the Rue des Carmes.

Marie ran up the sidewalk and past the few cars on the street. She was headed toward Rue de Ecoles. Collette realized the man was no longer behind her and had gone after Marie; she slowed to a jog and turned onto Rue Clotilde, heading in Marie's direction. She ran up the sidewalk and reached the next intersection. Looking around the corner she noticed the man in the middle of the street looking every direction before choosing one. He continued running straight up the road. Collette continued in that direction.

Marie reached the end of the street and hid behind some parked cars. She heard the footsteps of the man running toward her. He slowed down to a walk and looked around. Marie crouched down low and could see the man's feet as she looked under the car. He was approaching her car slowly. She inched forward as the man passed. She walked around the back of the car as he reached the front. He looked around and saw nothing. She peeked out and noticed a knife in his hand. He was carrying it by his side, the streetlight reflected off the blade. She leaned back against the car and pondered her next move. Marie could not outrun him, and she could not fight him off; she needed something to use as a weapon. She looked around—there was nothing. She was trapped. The man continued around the car toward her. As he reached the back of the car, she lunged at him hitting him in the face with all her might. She was a tough woman and stronger than she looked. The man stumbled backward, and Marie kicked him between the legs; he crumpled down in agony as she took off. Yelling something at her in German he gathered his strength and set off after her. Marie's lungs were burning, and her feet were sore from running on the cobblestone street, back in the direction of the Pantheon. She reached the corner of Rue de Lanneau and turned the corner. Collette was at the top of the street. Marie saw her and ran in her direction. Collette saw her coming and close behind her was the man chasing her. Marie ran up the sidewalk as Collette looked around for something, anything she could use to help. She found a garbage pile and a large piece of lumber. She grabbed it, cutting herself on the sharp edge. Marie was close, so Collette crouched behind the steps to the building on the left. As Marie ran by, Collette readied herself. She stepped out and with all her strength swung the piece of wood, hitting the man in the face as the wood snapped in half. The man fell onto his back with a thud. Collette ran over to him as he lay there moaning. She reared back and kicked him in the head, leaving him bloody and motionless.

Marie walked back to her and they stood over him. She stared at him for a moment but did not recognize him. He began to regain consciousness, so Marie took over this time. "You killed my friend," she said angrily. She kicked him in the ribs with her boot twice with all her strength and then in the side of the head. Blood flew from his mouth as his cheek hit the ground.

"Let's go." Collette said in between breaths. She put her hand on Marie's shoulder to calm her down. Marie looked at her and sighed.

"We can't leave him here on the sidewalk."

Collette agreed, so they dragged the body into the shadows behind some garbage cans, and then walked away toward the Metro.

24
Lien

Still shaken from their encounter in Paris, Marie and Collette joined the rest of the group as they reconvened in the basement of the café. The room was somber. Mason was uncharacteristically silent as he sat on the couch with Sully. Ganoux, too, said nothing as he busied himself setting out papers at the table. Phillipe and Carolina had not yet joined them; they were upstairs cleaning up after the day. Mason stood and embraced Collette as soon as she entered the room. The look on his face told her something had happened. She could always read his emotions clearly. He told her many things without saying a word. If they ever played poker, she would wipe him up.

"What happened?" she asked as she looked into his eyes. "Something happened, I can tell."

Mason nodded but said nothing.

"Are you okay?" she asked again as she ran her hand down the side of his face slowly.

Marie and Sully were having a similar exchange nearby. Ganoux sat silent at the table, a book in front of him and a knife next to it. He was thumbing through the pages slowly and kept picking the book up and looking at it from all different angles.

Mason finally spoke up as he backed away from Collette. "We need you and Marie to sit down. There is something we need to tell you."

With this ominous warning Collette and Marie locked glances. The two sat down and looked at Mason.

He started with a deep breath and then recounted their day. He arrived at the part inside the warehouse. "As I looked in through the bars of the train car, I saw people, terrified people, their eyes looking back at me. I don't think I will be able to forget that scene ever," Mason said, his voice trembling. "They are transporting humans in that extra car. Where they are taking them, we do not know but the car was filled with people. All their belongings were piled up outside the car. They are being brought here, stripped of their things, and then shipped out from here, one car at a time. I imagine this is happening all over Europe, people being shipped in cattle cars, crammed together."

Mason looked at their stunned faces, both Collette and Marie stared blankly as the gravity of the information sunk in.

They gave each other a knowing glance. The final piece of the puzzle had been solved. They had the information listing Lien as a destination but not knowing what that meant, it was just a stop on the rail line. Now it was more than that. The people on the list of names were being shipped through Lien, stripped of their belongings, and then shipped out like livestock.

Marie spoke up, "My contact in Paris gave us a sheet of names with personal data and a destination on it. We found Anna's sister's name on it; she is due to come through Lien in two days. Now we know where she will be and what will happen to her. We need to get to that train car in two days and get her out."

"Can you get some more specific information from him?" Sully asked as he grabbed a chair and sat down next to Ganoux.

"No, he was killed tonight outside the café after we met."

"By whom?" Sully asked noticeably concerned.

"A man I didn't recognize. He came after us, but we managed to get away. We left him lying in a doorway. I am fairly sure he will have a tough time breathing for a while—if at all. I kicked him in the ribs several times and then in the head. Not sure he was breathing when we left him."

Sully looked at Mason and they were thinking the same thing, "How did anyone know you were meeting in Paris?"

"I don't know but Volmer's man was following us from the minute I left. We lost him, though," Marie continued.

"Johnathan was a good man…trustworthy. He took a huge risk meeting me. I would guess he was followed and maybe someone in the office of personnel saw him removing the information or copying it and said something. If the Germans are transporting people to camps—or worse—that is a secret that they would kill to protect. Even some of the French people are cooperating with the Germans, so honestly, you cannot trust anyone. A reward is being offered to Parisians who turn in anyone who is conspiring against The Reich."

"If we have a chance to rescue Anna's sister, we have to get her off that train. We must find a way. Anna deserves to have someone in her family back. With her being this close, I couldn't live with myself if we did nothing." Collette's exasperation showed in her voice.

Mason walked over to Ganoux who was still fiddling with the book. He had not said a word the whole time, but Mason was sure he was absorbing all the information like the machine Mason always believed he was.

"What do you think?" he asked as he reached the table.

Ganoux looked up at him and put the book down. "This is what I think. You want Kliest who will be here in a week, so you will have your long-awaited reunion with him."

He turned to Sully, "You want to avenge your agent's death so yours and Mason's objective is the same…Kliest."

Marie, Carolina, Phillipe and I want to disrupt the German occupation as much as we can and that will happen when we take out Volmer and his staff at their gathering."

He turned to Collette. "Collette, I have known your family for a long time, and I owe your father my life. I know you are here to find Anna's family, and I believe she deserves an answer as to their whereabouts, so I think we should do everything we can to get her sister off that train and back to her. The rest of us have come here for revenge and death, it would be nice to actually come out of this having saved a life or lives. This horrible war will take so many lives, if we can give one back, at least maybe we can feel a sense of purpose other than death in this whole godforsaken situation."

Mason spoke up. "I agree but that warehouse is guarded twenty-four hours a day and now after our little run in, I am sure there is more protection than ever. That is going to be nearly impossible to pull off."

"I know, so we will have to hit the train before it arrives at the station. Create a diversion which stops the train and get her out somehow. We will work out the details. The train arrives at daybreak so we will have some measure of darkness, but not for long. The cattle car is the last car so we can approach it from behind without being seen. I don't think they will be guarding the car as it is in motion because no one knows what's in it."

Mason looked around the room and everyone seemed to nod in agreement. Ganoux was right; it could be the one good thing that came out of this mess.

He looked back at Ganoux. "What are you doing over here?"

He showed Mason the book. "Ever read this?"

Mason grabbed it, "*The Count of Monte Cristo?* Yes, of course."

Ganoux pulled out a small Colt pistol from his pocket and he opened the book. He rifled through the first few pages until he reached page fifty. Mason's eyes peered in as he looked at the open book. Inside starting on page fifty was a cut out which extended deep into the book in a strange shape. Ganoux had cut out the pages in the shape of the Colt. He placed the gun inside the cutout and closed the book.

He handed it to Mason, "You may need some protection when you meet Kliest. You will never get a gun in there so I will have Marie and Collette place the book on a shelf when they go see Volmer tomorrow. Marie has requested to see the space they will be entertaining in. This way you have a little firepower if you need it."

Mason looked at the book and moved it around in his hand.

"That is brilliant. I love that it is an American made gun tucked away in a famous French novel about revenge. That is well thought out." He smiled and handed the book back to Ganoux.

"I thought you would appreciate that." Ganoux smiled, taking back the book.

Sully came over to the table. "Marie and I are going to turn in. It's been a long day for everyone and honestly we don't get much time together."

"You don't need to explain, we all could use some rest. We'll see you tomorrow."

Mason watched as Marie and Sully left and headed upstairs. He could see the love they had for each other despite an awful situation. Having the distance between them and now a war on top of it, he wondered how it worked but it did. Sully constantly looked at her adoringly and she returned his affection.

Marie led Sully into the back of the café and pried up the floorboard. He watched as she retrieved the journal she kept. He thumbed through it and smiled when he reached the middle. Attached to the top page was the pen he had given her.

"You still have this." He pulled it out and looked at her.

"Of course; I write all the important information with that pen. I told you I would hold it for you to make sure you came back for it." She smiled as Sully chuckled to himself.

"You know I came back for more than the pen."

"I sure as hell hope so," she said lovingly pushing him in the shoulder.

She took the journal and they disappeared into the back room of the café.

25

MARIE AND COLLETTE ARRIVED AT the front gate to the German Headquarters, the former Hotel Lien. The entrance to the courtyard extended down a gravel driveway to the front of the hotel. As they approached, the sentinel came out of the guard house.

"Halt, what is your business here?"

"We have a meeting with Lieutenant Volmer."

"Papers," the man said sharply.

He inspected both sets of papers and then went back in the guard house. He telephoned the hotel and had a brief conversation in German. When he returned, he asked both ladies to open their purses for inspection. He started with Collette. She opened her bag and he rifled through her belongings: a brush, a wallet, some lipstick, and a scarf. After making a mess of her stuff he handed it back to her. He turned to Marie as she opened her bag. He peered in and more of the same, a brush, wallet, and a hardcover copy of *The Count of Monte Cristo*. He stopped and looked at her, "You like to read?"

"Yes, you should try it sometime," she replied with sarcasm.

"The Count of Monte Cristo," he said as he looked at the cover. "I prefer German writers," he stated as he returned her bag. "Proceed to the entrance and they will show you in."

He stepped aside as the two women closed their bags. Collette took out her scarf and wrapped it around her neck. The guards raised the gate and Collette and Marie proceeded down the driveway toward the entrance to the Hotel Lien.

The hotel, now sporting Nazi red banners on either side of the grand entrance was a Lien staple for many years but looked a shell of itself, now transformed into Nazi headquarters. They passed the anti-aircraft gun in the parking lot. Surrounded by sandbags, it was an imposing figure in the center of the lot. German soldiers stood around smoking and talking. One man was laughing as he told a story to the other two.

Collette and Marie walked past a few German troop carriers. The Opel Blitz trucks carried a dozen soldiers plus cargo. They were painted the now familiar colors of the German Army camouflage of olive and tan. Next to them were two black Rolls Royce command vehicles. Both had little red Nazi flags mounted to the front corners of the vehicle. The convertibles were sitting with tops up and shined as if brand new.

As they reached the front entrance men were coming and going out of the headquarters, up and down the steps. An older man, who Marie recognized from her last Volmer meeting, approached and stopped in front of them, *"Fraulein Riberau...this way."*

He led them up the stairs and inside to the lobby of the hotel. The check-in table was manned by two German soldiers. A large, framed picture of The Fuhrer hung on the wall behind them. As the three approached, the two German soldiers behind the desk snapped their heels together and raised their right arms in salute, *"Heil* Hitler," they said as the officer approached. He nodded as they walked by. They followed him to the winding staircase and proceeded up. Collette grabbed the large wooden bannister as they climbed to the second floor. A man saluted as he passed them on the way down.

The officer led them down the hallway to a waiting area. They sat down on the couch and he left, closing the double doors behind him. After a few moments, the doors opened, and he reentered. He turned and extended his right arm. "Please, this way."

They followed him down the hallway to another larger room. Upon entering, Lieutenant Volmer stood up to greet them. He said something to the man he was with, who then saluted him and quickly exited the room. The doors were closed leaving Marie, Collette, and Volmer alone.

Volmer approached with a slight smile on his face. "My beautiful guardian angel, thank you for coming. As you can see my arm is healing nicely thanks to you." He raised his arm up and down showing his dexterity.

He grabbed Marie's hand and leaned down to kiss the top of it. He stood and turned his attention to Collette, "My, my, who do we have here?"

"Lieutenant, this is my friend from Paris, Collette. She has come to help at the café for a while.

Volmer seductively glanced her up and down and grabbed her hand. He raised it to his mouth and placed a soft kiss on it. "Mademoiselle, the pleasure is most assuredly mine."

Collette smiled and wished him a good morning. "It is nice to meet you. You are a disgusting pig," she said in perfect, beautiful French. Marie had assured her that Volmer knew no French at all, but he always asked her to say things to him in French because he adored the language. She initially stuck to random sentences but as he drank more, she would wish death on him and tell him constantly he was a fat pig. He would laugh and say how beautiful the language was.

"Please come sit down so we can discuss our little soiree, as you might say in French. Volmer seemed to think he was charming both ladies. As they sat, three glasses of wine arrived with some cheese and bread. Volmer raised his glass and made a small toast, "To my two beautiful visitors, thank you for coming, you have made me the envy of the entire town." They tapped glasses and Marie replied in perfect French with her beautiful smile, "Drop dead."

Collette kept her composure even though inside she was laughing.

"So, let us get down to business." Volmer said as he put his glass down. "I am having my superior down for the weekend and I want to have a nice private gathering for him and a few guests. Marie, I would like you to provide the food, an authentic French meal. Everything, wine, cheese, escargot, meat, and dessert. Spare no expense; make sure the meal has the best of everything. I would like to impress with the presentation. Please do not have that old man who works for you appear in the dining area, I only want the two of you to be serving."

Marie chimed in as she put her wine down, "I will be cooking and Collette will be helping me in the kitchen, you can't possibly expect me to do both. My friend Carolina will be baking the bread, I will have her serve and the two of us will join you later if that is ok. If you want everything perfect, I need the time in the kitchen to make it that way."

Volmer paused for a moment and relented. "Very well but keep that smelly old man out of sight."

"Phillipe is my friend, don't say that."

"Of course, I am sorry." Volmer said filling his wine glass again.

Collette was amazed at the power Marie exhibited over Volmer. He acted as if she was the one in charge which was perfect for their plan. Collette could not be in the dining room with Kliest, he would recognize her right away.

Volmer continued, "This is an important night for me and you. If it goes as well as I envision, we will all be rewarded in the end. I stand to become very wealthy and you stand to become my personal chef. We can do great things together."

Marie's insides churned at the thought of cooking for this vile man every day.

Collette spoke up, sensing Marie's turbulent insides, "We will do everything in our power to have a memorable evening. It will be so good you will think you have died and gone to heaven."

"I like your ambition, *Fraulein* Collette. I don't need to die to go to heaven; I believe I am sitting in heaven right now with the two of you." He smiled and sipped his wine, still proudly believing his charm was seducing the two beauties in his midst.

"Let me show you the space we will be entertaining in." Volmer stood and stepped back. He motioned toward the doors. He opened them and led them down the hallway to some stone spiral stairs leading up. The hotel was built on a hill so there were several levels and stairs. They followed Volmer up the stairs and into a hallway lined with large glass windows. He stopped to point out the pool outside and the view of the countryside. The three stopped for a moment and Collette and Marie feigned their interest in Volmer's tour of the hotel. He continued through the hallway and out the wooden French door onto a stone patio. They walked across the patio and onto a dirt path which led away from the main hotel toward a separate building. German soldiers were stationed on the grounds patrolling the edge of the trees quietly back and forth.

They reached the doors to the separate building; Volmer opened them into a large space decorated with wood and stone with a large rustic table in the middle. Ten large wooden chairs surrounded it, and three separate tables adorned the walls around the room. A unit of shelves on the right side of the room held some small statues and some books., the fireplace at the far end of the room was trimmed in stone with a large wooden mantle. Above the mantle hung a picture of the *Fuhrer.*

Collette wondered if all these Hitler pictures had been sent to these places to hang. Was there one man in charge of making sure Hitler was everywhere in their occupied territory? *I guess that is what happens with a dictator, he wants his picture everywhere.* She found it creepy that everywhere they went Adolf was looking down on them. Volmer walked around the table explaining to Marie where the food and drink would be presented. He assured her she would have everything she needed to complete her cooking. The separate kitchen area was larger than her café kitchen and was quite nice. She had attended private events in this area before and was familiar with the setup.

Volmer leaned against the table under the Nazi flag on the right side of the room, "I trust you find this space acceptable?"

"It will be fine," Marie replied.

As Volmer looked around, Marie gave Collette a glance telling her it was time to stash the book. Collette walked toward Volmer and pointed out the window to the countryside slightly obscured by the tree line, "What a beautiful view," she said as she poured some more wine for both of them. Volmer's back was to Marie as she slowly walked over to the bookshelf and began admiring the selection.

"Oh my gosh, I am such a mess," Collette said as she spilled wine on her sweater. She acted flustered, looking for a napkin. Volmer handed her a handkerchief. As she grabbed it, she made sure to rub his hand a bit accidentally on purpose. He was putty in her hands as he studied her cleaning her sweater.

"Is there a restroom where I can clean this up a bit?"

"Of course," Volmer said smiling. "I will show you." He turned to Marie, "Excuse us."

"Collette, would you like for me to go with you?"

"No, I'll just be a minute."

She followed Volmer out into the hallway and down to the restroom doors.

They both returned a minute later, Volmer certain his charm was working on Collette. Little did he know she had nearly vomited in the bathroom just from rubbing his hand.

Volmer poured the rest of the wine and they exchanged drab conversation just to appease him. He boasted about his leadership skills and how Berlin was keeping a close eye on him for promotion. He explained how the chain of command worked and why he was so admired by his peers. If he did not have another meeting, they would have been there all day and Collette might have killed him right then just to get him to shut up. A man came to get the Lieutenant for his next meeting.

"My apologies that I need to end our quite lovely time."

"Thank God," Marie said in French with a sad, frown on her face.

He led them out past the bookcase which now housed a 1933 copy of *The Count of Monte Cristo* with an American Colt inside. The gun was now stashed; if all went well, they would not need it, but it gave them some measure of hope just in case.

The doors closed behind them and they were led away from the building back toward the main hotel. The next time they would be there, they would be serving a lavish dinner which would prove to be the last supper for Volmer and all his guests.

26

THE CREW GATHERED AT CAROLINA'S farmhouse to finalize the details of their train heist, except they weren't stealing jewels or gold, they were hoping to rescue a train full of frightened people and get them to safety without the German soldiers, train conductors or engineers knowing.

Ganoux started the conversation. "I have spoken to Sidonie Martineau at Chateau Chenonceau and she has agreed to help us. Her Chateau lies on the Cher river which also happens to be the demarcation line between occupied and free territories. She will offer us safe passage for the refugees, but we must be incredibly careful. The German army patrols the Cher river looking for people crossing illegally, and they will not hesitate to shoot."

Collette took over, "We are looking for Anna's sister Sarah; she is seventeen years old with shoulder length blond hair, we think." She distributed an old family photo Anna had given her. The photo was years old, so it was not much to go on. "We have heard rumors of prisoners having their heads shaved regardless of man or woman. Since we cannot justify saving one person and leaving a train filled with others, we will try to rescue as many as possible. We don't know what kind of resistance we will face, as the Germans are keeping this all hush hush. We are hoping for a couple soldiers and the rest, train engineers."

Marie stood up. "I have arranged transport with Luc from the train to Chenonceau. He makes a monthly delivery to their cellar, so it is not uncommon for him to be in that area. He will meet us on the road beyond the trees so we need to be as quick as possible, he cannot wait forever because the Germans randomly patrol the roads in the area. He will be at the end of his deliveries so the truck will be empty. Hopefully, we can fit everyone in and get them to the Chateau quickly and quietly."

"The train will be here in one hour so we must go and get

in position," Ganoux said as he stood.

They left the farmhouse in two groups; Marie and Collette drove away while Ganoux, Sully and Mason disappeared up the hill into the trees on their way to the fields beyond the hills where the train tracks snaked their way across the valley. They had picked a spot for the heist in a clearing around a bend where the train would approach a crossing. The crossing was near a wooded area, Ganoux had picked the spot hoping the front of the train would be at the crossing in the woods, while the rear car of the train would still be in the clearing.

Ganoux led the way through the woods and into the clearing, the tall grass swaying in the night breeze.

Mason slapped Sully on the back. "You ready?"

"Well you are all excited. Need I remind you last time we were near train tracks we almost got pissed on and shot?" Sully said to Mason as he looked over at him.

"I know but we didn't have either of those things happen, did we?"

"Nope, but we came close to both."

"When this is all over, are you heading back to London or you going to stick around with Marie?"

"My plan is to go back but don't either one of you say anything. London is where I can do the most good but I have not discussed this with her."

Ganoux looked back at Sully. "I am not sure Marie would go with you."

"I wouldn't ask her to. She is happy here with the café and the little thing you have going on. She believes in you and the whole idea of resistance. I couldn't ask her to give that up unless she wants to. I don't like the idea of being apart again but I will let her decide."

"What about you?" Sully asked Ganoux

"I am here for however long it takes. I will continue to try to grow the resistance. People from other countries are showing up in France eager to fight back but they can be reckless when discretion is needed. I do not need the Germans retaliating every time some young Belgian decides he wants to firebomb a German vehicle. This is not his country, the people who bear the brunt of the retaliation are not his people, so there is a disconnect sometimes between doing more harm than good. It is a fine line we walk but walk it we must."

Mason thought of Collette and Marie driving to the crossing and hoped they would be okay. He hated to be away from her in the war zone, but it was the only way this would work. Besides, as she told him many times, she could take care of herself.

They reached the clearing, and the tracks could be seen ahead. The tree line they stood at offered some measure of cover but the clearing leading to the tracks was a good fifty feet long so they would be severely exposed if things went wrong. The three of them crouched down and surveyed the area. Behind them the forest extended for a bit until the edge of the road where Luc would be waiting.

Mason took a deep breath, "You know, we have no idea what kind of shape these people are in, or how many there are. If they have been sealed in the train car for a long time they may not be able to move quickly across rough terrain."

Sully nodded as he looked straight ahead. "Unfortunately, we won't know that until we see them. I just hope her sister is on the train. We are trying to rescue someone we have never met before, who doesn't know us, and just hope she trusts us enough to go with us. These people are terrified, and they may not willingly run through the woods with three strange men to a waiting truck to be shipped to safety."

"Hey Sully...how about some optimism, okay." Mason said as he looked over at him with a smirk.

"You're right. Sorry."

"Just stick to the plan," Ganoux said staring straight ahead at the tracks.

MARIE PULLED THE 1937 CITROEN 7B around the bend and the train crossing was in sight. She gently pulled up the incline and the car shook as they pulled onto the tracks. She turned it off and the two of them exited the car. She walked to the front and raised the hood. Looking inside, she reached in and pulled at the coil wire cable, it came off and she tucked it away in her bag. Collette looked on from over her shoulder.

Marie stood up and wiped her hands on a handkerchief, "That should do it, we are officially broken down. Now we wait for a train."

AFTER SEVERAL MINUTES, Ganoux could hear the train approaching and as it chugged around the bend in front of them, they noticed the cars: one engine, two passenger cars, two supply cars, and one cattle car in the back. The steam from the engine filled the air as it approached, and then the sound of screeching brakes as the train started to slow down. The sound was music to the three men at the tree line; it meant the diversion had started. Now they needed the engine and passenger cars to disappear in the trees far enough to leave the last car exposed.

MARIE WAS ON THE SIDE OF THE CAR waving her scarf in the air as the approaching engine came into view. She waved her arms back and forth as Collette stood behind the car. They both heard the brakes screeching as the massive engine rolled closer. Marie and Collette moved farther away from the car and after a few minutes the train came to a stop about ten feet from their car.

The train brakes by the metal wheels were smoking as the train sat there in a menacing form looking straight at the tiny car. They began to hear the screaming voices of the conductor as he exited the engine and stood on the rail with his hands motioning every which way. He looked as though he was throwing a tantrum. In the first passenger car, two German soldiers emerged and went quickly down the steps jumping onto the stone trackside. One soldier stumbled and quickly regained his balance. Both men started running toward Marie and Collette with machine guns drawn. The two women immediately backed up a few paces with their arms raised as the soldiers approached. The conductor was still yelling at them in French, but his voice was failing him, so it was virtually impossible to understand what he was yelling. They heard a few curse words and "stupid women" thrown in between breaths.

The soldiers reached the car and began yelling at them in German, as the conductor screamed in French.

THE TRAIN STOPPED AND MASON, Sully, and Ganoux waited a few moments before moving. In the distance the sound of a yelling man was audible. The last car was stopped about fifty feet in front of them. If it was filled with people, you would never know it.

Mason looked at Sully, they both nodded and stood up. The two inched their way into the clearing, bent down slowly, and began to advance toward the train. As they reached the edge of the field where they could see down the tracks toward the crossing, they slowed and glanced down. More voices were audible now, a mixture of yelling and screaming. No one was in their sight, so they jogged over to the back of the train car. Mason grabbed the metal rail and pulled himself up onto the first step at the rear of the car. He stepped over the chain hanging between the railings to prevent anyone from climbing on. He reached the platform attached to the back of the car and waited as Sully remained on the ground as a lookout. Mason climbed alongside the car and reached the metal rungs which covered the opening of the car. He prepared himself for the sight once again of prisoner's eyes looking at him. He took a breath and looked inside and the eyes of the terrified looked back at him. He could hear whimpering coming from inside the car.

"Does anyone speak English?" he quietly whispered into the car. The eyes just stared at him, some looked away, but no one spoke up. "God damnit, does anyone speak English? I am trying to help you."

"A faint voice in the back finally spoke up. "A little."

"Tell everyone in the car that when I open these doors you have to move quickly out of the car and into the woods. Can you do that for me?"

"Where are you taking us?"

"That is not important right now, what is important is you move quickly and quietly, we need to get away from here as fast as possible. Now please just do it."

The woman spoke in German to the car in a clear quiet, voice.

A few voices talked back to her and a conversation ensued in German.

"We don't have time to discuss. Tell them to move when the door opens, if they do not want to, they will be left behind in a situation which I can assure you will be very unpleasant. I am offering you a chance at freedom."

She conveyed Mason's words and finally looked back at him. "They understand."

Mason stared at the eyes in the train car, he saw some figures but mostly eyes as if they were floating in air. He did not like this feeling; it was like talking to ghosts. He climbed down off the car and told Sully they were ready. The two split up and went to opposite sides of the car to look down the tracks toward the crossing to see if anyone was coming.

"YOU MUST MOVE THIS CAR NOW," the German soldier said to Marie in broken English.

"I don't know what is wrong, it just stopped." Marie said playing a hopeless pretty woman.

The soldier stared at her and Collette, his unhappiness evident. The other soldier had his weapon still pointing at them. His partner put down his weapon and walked over to the hood to have a look; he stepped up on the bumper and leaned into the engine. The light on the train was a blinding spotlight but gave the soldier something to see by. Marie and Collette stood together under guard from the other man whose gaze never left them. The soldier under the hood reached in and played with some wires but with no luck. He jumped down and barked orders to the other in German. He yelled down the tracks in German and two more soldiers jumped down onto the gravel track side. While the one kept the two women at bay, the other soldiers convened next to the engine to discuss their problem. They decided to push the car off the tracks and leave the two women stranded. They did not care that they were beautiful, they needed to keep moving, and none of them were particularly interested in helping an enemy with a broken-down car. As Marie and Collette stood watching, three soldiers put down their weapons and convened at the rear bumper. One ordered Marie into the driver's seat and instructed her to put the shift in neutral. Marie pretended that it was stuck for a few moments and then eventually got the car into neutral. As the German soldiers began rocking the car back and forth, they were having little success moving it forward. Marie made sure of that by intermittingly pressing the brake.

MASON AND SULLY CONVENED at the side door to the railcar. Mason produced a pair of bolt cutters and snapped the lock. Grabbing the metal handle, he slowly pulled on the door to the car. It barely moved so he put a little more effort and the door began to open. He stopped once he had it open a few feet. He looked inside at twenty or so completely terrified women. He looked at Sully who looked to the tree line and Ganoux, who gave a thumbs up. Mason nodded and spoke quietly to the woman inside who spoke English, "You need to tell them to follow my friend here. He will lead you to the tree line and eventually to a waiting truck to take you to the free French border." She repeated Mason's orders and the women looked from the woman to Mason as he stood in the doorway. The women stood, some holding small suitcases, and some carrying canvas bags or blankets.

"You need to tell them they cannot bring anything other than themselves. We have limited room; we can only take people, not their belongings."

The woman spoke in German to the car and immediately most of the women began talking back to her. One woman approached Mason and hit him on the shoulder with her bag.

He backed up and looked at the woman, "I am trying to help you," he said firmly and slowly to the woman who was ready to swing again. "Look lady, it is either you or your bag, not both." His liaison instructed everyone to drop their things or they would not be able to go. Begrudgingly, most of the women relented and almost all of them looked at Mason with scorn.

The women started to emerge from the car as Mason waved them on, they formed a single file line and followed Sully to the tree line. Approximately fifteen women in dresses and coats emerged from the car. Mason's liaison was the last woman who exited. She grabbed Mason's arm as she reached him, "You have to understand what these women have been through, they have been separated from their families and thrown in a rail car. They are tired and scared. You must understand."

"I do, but we need to go quickly, or we are all dead." Mason ushered her off the car and onto the grass.

"Thank you," she said before turning and following the others.

Mason nodded and turned back to the car. He pulled the side door closed and crept around the back again for another look. The car had been removed from the tracks and two soldiers were walking toward the rear of the train. He turned and began to run in the direction of the others. Most of the women had made it to the trees. Ganoux looked up and saw Mason running toward him with both arms in the air pushing toward him.

"We have to move," Ganoux said to Sully and they ushered everyone into the woods and away from the tracks. Mason reached the edge of the field and turned as he crouched down in the grass. He looked under the train car and could see the feet of the two soldiers walking toward the back of the train.

Sully joined him, "What are you thinking?"

Mason looked at him, "I am thinking if they look in the car, our little escape will be short-lived."

They watched as the two soldiers reached the back of the train. They stood for a moment on the tracks and lit cigarettes. They glanced around and then crossed the tracks to Mason's side. He pulled out his Colt and readied for the possibility of an ambush.

WITH THE CAR OFF THE TRACKS, Marie raised the hood again and reattached the wire. The German soldiers had left them and were walking back to the train. The conductor had climbed back up into the engine room and was waiting orders to proceed. Two soldiers were instructed to check the train for anything suspicious and they had wandered to the back where they were currently smoking cigarettes under Mason's watchful eye.

The soldier in charge yelled to the back of the train and his two soldiers finished their cigarettes, tossed them aside, and began their final inspection. Seeing nothing out of the ordinary, they started to head back to the front of the train as the engineer was starting the train forward. They hopped onto one of the cars for the short ride to the Lien station.

Marie and Collette needed to get going. Marie turned the car on; it sputtered at first but started. She jammed the shifter into drive and pressed the gas pedal to the floor. The rear tires spun, kicking up dirt and gravel as the car took off. They fish tailed off the roadside and onto the pavement gaining speed as the tires hit the road.

The conductor watched with surprise as the two ladies who had stopped his train dead in its tracks drove off in their broken-down car.

MASON AND SULLY RACED INTO the woods and caught up with the others. They had reached the road and were loading into Luc's truck. Ganoux was helping the ladies in as his two partners arrived. He could tell by their expressions that things were okay.

They helped the last two ladies in the truck, hopped in, and closed the flap. Luc jumped in the driver side and Ganoux in the passenger side. Luc hit the gas and the rumbling wine truck started up the road away from the scene. Mason pulled the flap back to make sure they were not followed. The truck raced away, and he sat back down a little bit shaken.

"That was close," he yelled to Sully startling the women seated around him.

"We made it this far but it's not over yet." Sully said, cautiously optimistic.

"I just hope Collette and Marie got out of there." Mason replied to him as he shook his head at the situation.

He sat back and the woman across from him spoke up, "Where are you taking us?"

"Hopefully to the border and then into the unoccupied zone."

She looked at him, "Thank you for caring enough to do this. I have been separated from my family for some time now. My brother fled to America last year, and my younger sister was shipped to France a few months ago, I have no idea if either one is still alive. My parents were taken, and I have not heard anything about them. I was sure I would be killed once I was loaded into that train." She started to well up with tears as Mason looked up and got a good look at her. He noticed the resemblance even in her emotional face as she wiped tears away. They had found Anna's sister.

He smiled at her. "Is your sister's name Anna?"

The woman looked up at him in disbelief as her face went blank.

Mason leaned in and touched her hand as he began to tell her who he was and why this all was happening.

She began crying hysterically and hugged Mason with one of the tightest hugs he had ever received. She cried on his shoulder as the truck rumbled down the road on its way to see a woman who would help them with their next phase of the escape.

27

AS THE SUN ROSE IN THE SKY, Luc drove the truck through the rolling fields of the Loire Valley at a rate of speed it was not designed for. He had to be reminded by Ganoux several times that they were not carrying wine but rather, people in the back. Luc would nod and apologize as he chain-smoked cigarettes.

"I'm sorry," he said as he mumbled in French under his breath.

"Don't apologize to me, just take it easy. We have a group of terrified women in the back with Mason and Sully, we don't need to tip over or we are all in trouble."

Luc pulled off the gas a bit as they entered a roundabout. The streets were mostly empty at this time as he followed the turn-off marked with a white metal arrow and black lettering reading 'Chenonceau 6' signaling the distance in kilometers they were from their destination.

In the back of the truck, Mason took a deep breath as he felt the eyes of many women upon him as they bounced back and forth. Several women closed their eyes and prayed silently with every turn as Mason thought of Collette. One young woman looked about 17 or 18; she had a hat pulled tight. She was clearly terrified, and Mason had not heard a word out of her. One of the older women was trying to protect her from the reality of the situation, so Mason could not imagine what was going through her mind.

He jolted as the truck turned wildly through a roundabout and he put his hand down to prevent himself from falling over onto the terrified sixty-year-old lady next to him. She looked at him with a blank stare as he smiled and nodded. She did nothing in response, so he gave Sully a glance and focused back in front.

Luc lit another cigarette as they drove down the Allee de la Charmaie toward the D40 for the last few kilometers. As he exhaled, he noticed the vehicle approaching. Ganoux sat up and noticed as well. He banged on the wall of the back of the truck hoping Mason would pick up on the signal. Approaching was a German troop car, and Luc shot a gaze over to Ganoux who motioned with his hands to calm down. Luc slowed to a manageable speed as the car approached. He and Ganoux stared straight ahead as the car slowed and passed them on the left. The second they were clear, Luc focused on his rearview mirror watching the troop car slowly disappear around the bend. He exhaled the deepest breath he could, as if he was holding his breath the whole time. Ganoux felt a twinge in between his shoulder blades as he relaxed for a second. They reached the intersection of the D40 and turned left. In the back, Mason rolled a bit to his right as they turned. He had heard the banging from Ganoux in the front and peered through the flap to see the German troop car pass them. He sat back and waited for another signal, but none came so he figured they were in the clear.

Luc downshifted, grinding the gears as they approached the entrance to Chenonceau. He pulled through the wrought iron gates and onto the gravel path. The driveway up to the Chateau was lined with thirty-foot tall trees whose leaves had turned the shades of fall. Luc gently pulled the truck down the driveway past the empty flower urns, which usually held magnificent growing rose trees and lemon trees.

Mason knew they had entered Chenonceau and that they were one step closer to freedom, though far from it. The truck stopped and Luc shut down the engine. Mason and Sully jumped up and told everyone to stay put. Mason lifted the flap and they hopped out the back onto the gravel driveway. Mason looked back down toward the gates and it was clear for now. Ganoux and Luc joined him at the rear of the truck.

Luc threw his latest cigarette down. "The wine cellar is over there in the Domes building next to the Apothecary."

Mason and Sully looked over at the sprawling building easily longer than a football field. The Domes building was designed and built by Catherine Medici when she took over the Chateau in the sixteenth century. The long white building with a brown cedar roof had housed a military hospital during World War I and now was home to an Apothecary and underneath the building, a wine cellar.

Ganoux spoke up as he looked around, "Let's get everyone into the cellar. I will head up to the Chateau to let *Madam* Martineau know we have arrived.

Everyone agreed as Luc lit another cigarette. He offered one to Mason and Sully who declined. Luc puffed away, sporadically coughing in between breaths. He fidgeted with the lock and chain from the back gate of the truck as he smoked and coughed away.

"You sure you should be smoking?" Mason said as he approached him, "You don't sound too good and we need you to be focused.

"It relaxes me," he said to Mason as he continued to jiggle the chain. He swore in French as he played with the lock.

"I can see that," Mason said sarcastically as he stepped in and simply removed the chain and unlocked the gate. He lowered the gate to the bumper and threw the flap up on top of the truck exposing their cargo of frightened ladies.

Sarah stood up, "Are we safe?" she asked, standing at the back gate.

"Not until we are across the river. We are moving into the wine cellar until we can get you into the Chateau. Can you tell them to, in a quiet and orderly fashion, come to the gate one by one and we will help them down? Then follow the one in front of them over to that building and down into the cellar. Ok?"

Sarah nodded and turned to the others. After a few moments of back and forth she turned back to Mason, "Ok, they understand."

Mason reached out to Sarah and she grabbed his hand as he helped her to the ground off the back of the truck. The three of them began helping the other women off the truck and then they followed Sully over to the Domes building. Sarah and Mason were the last two at the back and he turned to Luc. "Thank you. Get back safely and for your own sake, stop smoking." Mason chuckled as he shook Luc's hand.

"Be safe. See you on the other side," Luc said as he closed the back gate and walked around to the cab. He started the truck and the sound of the wheels on the gravel filled the air as the tires spun a bit before lurching the truck forward. He turned back in the direction of the entrance and pulled away.

"Let's go," Mason said to Sarah and the two jogged across the grass and met the others at the building. Sully had gone in and down the stone steps to the winery. Each woman gingerly followed, grasping the iron railing with conviction. They reached the cellar underneath and one by one found some room to sit on wine barrels or old wooden cases. The cellar extended the length of the building and was filled on both sides with wine barrels. Their supply had dwindled since the start of the war and many of the barrels lay on their sides empty. The stone walls provided the ideal temperature for wine storage, and at its peak it could house several thousand bottles.

Mason stood outside with Sarah until the last woman entered. Sarah started in and Mason was about to follow when he noticed a vehicle turning into the grounds from the front entrance. He walked out on the grass to get a closer look and noticed right away the troop car resembled the one they had passed on the road. He ran back to the cellar door and hopped down the steps to the bottom. As he entered the cellar, he caught his breath. "We have company."

At the same time, Ganoux exited the front of the Chateau and stopped in his tracks as he saw the German car approaching. He backtracked, turned, and quickly disappeared back in the front door.

The car slowly pulled into the area of the Chateau front and came to a stop near the Guardhouse turret situated to the right of the entrance. Mason crept back up the steps for a look and saw the car parked. A German officer got out of the passenger seat and wiped off his uniform as he looked around. The driver came around, took the officer's coat, and handed him something. Two other soldiers climbed out of the back seat and stood around the car. The officer began to look at the item he was handed, and Mason could see the man was holding a camera. He began taking pictures of the Chateau and the surrounding grounds.

Sully closed the door to the cellar and locked it, leaving the women inside as he and Mason stayed out of sight on the steps. The two soldiers began to walk away from the car with their rifles shouldered. They were soaking in the sights of the beautiful grounds. They started to come in their direction as the officer wandered closer to the entrance with his driver.

Mason looked at Sully. "We can't have them come in here."

Sully agreed and they decided if the men got close enough, Mason would confront them as a worker on the grounds to divert their attention. Sully headed back down the stairs to the bottom and looked in the room opposite the cellar. He returned with a shovel and some gloves and then headed back down and out the back entrance. The two men got closer and Mason decided they had come far enough. He grabbed the gloves, slipped them on and grabbed the shovel. He popped out of the doorway and propped the shovel over his shoulder. He walked across the lawn pretending to be oblivious to the German soldiers at the end of the building. He stopped at a flower bed and began digging when he heard the German speak up, "Halt...you there."

Mason turned around as the two soldiers walked quickly toward him with their rifles no longer shouldered.

He turned and acting surprised and backed up a few steps.

The soldiers reached him, "What are you doing here?"

"I am the gardener." Mason replied in his best attempt at a French accent.

"And what are you doing?" the soldier asked firmly.

Mason looked at his shovel and back at the soldier, "I'm gardening."

The soldier looked around at the barren flowerbeds and the empty urns. "There is nothing to garden."

"It may look that way, but you must keep the soil fresh so that the flowers come back in the spring," Mason said, making it up as he went. The two soldiers seemed confused by him.

"I need to plant the bulbs for the spring; come here I will show you." Mason turned and walked toward the garages at the end of the Domes building. The two soldiers hesitated and then followed Mason over to the garage. As he reached the garage door, he opened the side door and walked inside. The two men followed him into the garage and as they stood in the open area, Mason turned around. The soldiers looked around. "There is nothing here."

"That's right." As Mason got the words out, the shovel head came swinging through the air and struck the soldier in the back of the head. He dropped to the ground out cold, leaving Sully standing behind him. As the shovel hit the first soldier Mason lunged at the second and grabbed the rifle from his hand pinning it against the man's chest. Sully grabbed the second soldier around the neck and with a quick motion, snapped his neck. After letting go, the German fell in a heap to the ground next to his partner.

"Thanks. I was running out of things to say. They seemed to be confused by me." He smiled as he looked at the two men on the ground.

"What do we do now? Eventually the officer is going to wonder where his guards went."

Mason thought for a moment and then looked at Sully, "Ever wanted to be a German soldier?"

"Not really," Sully said. "But I think I know what you mean."

The two stripped the uniforms off the soldiers. As Sully was removing the jacket from the live one he began to come to. He looked at Mason and snapped the neck of the second soldier. It did not faze either one of them, they were simply doing what needed to be done to get everyone to safety.

They put on the German uniforms and looked at each other, they did not look half bad, clearly not the ideal size but it would do. Grabbing the rifles, Mason and Sully emerged from the garage and looked around a bit. The officer was returning to the vehicle and he yelled something in German to his guards. He got in the back of the car and his driver in the front. Mason and Sully walked briskly toward the car and as they approached the officer again barked something in German. Sully walked along the driver's side as the officer turned to Mason. His eyes went wide as he looked at the American in an ill-fitting German uniform.

"What is this, who are you?"

"The gardener." Mason replied with a slight smile as he fired one bullet into the officer's forehead. Sully did the same to the driver and then silence again set in over the grounds of the beautiful Chateau.

28

MASON AND SULLY GAVE THE women a scare as they returned to the wine cellar wearing German uniforms. They had put all four bodies back in the German military vehicle and drove it to the water's edge. From there, they pushed it down the embankment and watched it disappear under the waterline. Noticing the uneasiness in the room, they quickly removed their military caps, and everyone relaxed a bit except for the woman who had hit Mason with her suitcase, she peered at him with a scowl.

He turned to Sarah, "Why does that woman hate me so much, she does realize I am trying to help her, right?"

Sarah smiled, "She told me you remind her of a neighbor in Hamburg who turned her in. That is the reason she doesn't trust you."

"Ummm…she does know that I am not him?" he said trying to make light of a tough situation.

Sarah shrugged her shoulders. "I'm not sure," she managed a slight smile.

Mason sat down on a wine barrel and they began the waiting period. Ganoux had not returned yet with confirmation that they would indeed be allowed to cross through the Chateau into free territory. He looked down at his German uniform and shook his head slightly. Less than a year ago he was working at the Metropolitan Museum of Art in New York under a highly prestigious staff, dealing with antiquities. He had been quite happy. Since then, he had barely escaped with his life out of France once, and was now sitting in a 16th century wine cellar surrounded by fifteen women, one of which thought he was the enemy, wearing a German army uniform, awaiting word for safe passage to free France. He wondered where Collette was, and if she and Marie would arrive soon. If she saw him like this, he was quite sure she would have an interesting greeting for him. He laughed to himself at the thought of her reaction. He also thought of this whole ordeal and how he was no closer to Kliest at this moment. His payback would have to wait but they had a good plan for the gathering back in Lien and he was not leaving France without Kliest's head on a platter—figuratively of course.

Sully poked his head in, "They're here."

Mason jumped up and left the cellar. He climbed the stairs two at a time and arrived outside as the car pulled up. He and Sully stood staring at the car as it screeched to a stop and the dust cloud dissipated. Collette and Marie exited the vehicle, stopping short as they saw the two German soldiers standing there waving at them. They looked at each other as they walked closer.

"You two have joined the other side?" Collette said as they approached.

"You don't want to know. How was your ride over? Any trouble?"

"Once we left the train, we snaked our way through the valley trying our best to avoid main roads. We did well, only passing some locals. Thank God for Collette, she navigated us through." Marie said as she wiped some dirt off Sully's uniform.

"These uniforms may come in handy, especially if we can alter them a bit. They don't exactly fit you two," Collette said as she tugged at Mason's uniform top. "You need to lose a few pounds for it to fit nicely."

"What are you talking about? I think I look good," Mason said looking down at his uniform.

"Of course, you do. Where is everybody? Were you able to get everyone here?" she said, smiling.

Mason took Collette's hand and led her across the grass to the doorway leading to the cellar. They walked down the stairs and turned into the room. The women sat quietly as Mason and Collette entered the room. Mason led Collette over to Sarah who stood up. She put her hand over her mouth as she began to cry. Collette looked at her and knew immediately it was Anna's sister. She reached out and embraced her as they both cried in each other's arms. Collette stepped back wiping tears from her face.

"She looks like you. I cannot wait for you to see her. I have been promising her since day one that I would do everything to find her family. I can't believe you are standing here."

Sarah wiped her tears and she nodded, "Honestly, I never thought I would see anyone from my family ever again. I was sure we were being sent to be killed. When Mason opened the door to the rail car I was confused because he didn't look like a German and when he told me the story of Anna at the train station and how you were so compassionate with her, I knew there was a ray of hope that I might actually see her again. Tell me about her. How is she?"

Collette sat next to her and began at the beginning, Sarah hanging on every word.

Mason met back up with Sully and Marie at the doorway. As they were talking, footsteps could be heard on the stone steps. Sully turned and glanced up to see Ganoux walking down the steps. He looked at Sully, "Nice outfit."

"What's the deal?" Mason asked as Ganoux entered the room.

He looked around. "Oh, good, you both made it," he said to Marie after seeing Collette across the room. "We have to wait until dark and then in groups of five we will head to the Chateau. The Germans up the patrols at night so we need to be quiet and quick. The sun goes down at roughly 6:30 so the first group will go at 7. I will take the first group over and once we are in, I will show a light through the upstairs window in this direction and then the next group can start over. Germans patrol the river in twenty-foot motorized boats, usually manned by four soldiers. A machine gun on the bow can cut you down from a hundred yards away. Once we get through the Chateau, we must still be vigilant because they will not hesitate to fire into free territory. They have been instructed to not pursue anyone into the free side, but they will shoot. Germany has yet to realize that people are trying to escape through the Chateau because no one has been caught. We do not want to be the first ones. This route can be a continuous route for refugees if we protect it, like your Underground Railroad during slavery."

Ganoux looked at both Mason and Sully and then around the room. He was distracted by a voice at the top of the stairs, where the daughter of Sidonie Martineau stood. Ganoux spoke to her in French and motioned her down. She carried a burlap sack on her shoulder as she walked through the shelter to the far end where a makeshift table had been set up with two boards across two wooden barrels. Ganoux followed her and she put the sack on the boards. She opened it and pulled out four loaves of bread and a large triangle of cheese. She produced a large bread knife and began slicing the loaves. Ganoux asked her something and she pointed to the corner as she responded. He walked over, leaned down, and grabbed two ceramic jugs. He walked to the side entrance and dislodged the iron bolt lock, pushed open the old wooden door and disappeared outside. He returned a few minutes later holding the two jugs, water splashing out of both while he walked. He put both up on the table and asked the women to come up one by one to get some food and drink. Sarah relayed the message and walked over to the oldest woman. She said something to her, and the woman stood up and walked slowly to the table, followed by the younger shy girl. As they approached, the older woman stopped and turned around and shook her head while saying something to Sarah. She approached the woman and with a caring hand helped usher her to the table while talking quietly to her. When they reached the table, she spoke to Ganoux, "She is afraid…she thinks it may be poison. You must understand what we have been through. No one has offered to help us so you can see her feelings."

Ganoux nodded silently and then looked at the woman as he grabbed a slice of bread with cheese. She looked at him cautiously as he took a large bite out of the slice. He swallowed it and then took a large sip of water. The woman looked at him and then Sarah. She slowly lifted her hands and Ganoux placed some food in her palms. The woman nodded and said in a barely audible voice, "Danke."

"My pleasure," Ganoux answered with a reassuring smile.

A line began to form once Ganoux waved everyone up. The women took their food and then once they ate, lined up for water. Mason, Collette, and the others watched as one by one these incredibly brave and trusting women got some food and drink. Mason noticed the interaction and sense of calm that came over the room as they ate. Ganoux opened a few bottles of wine which were passed around the room. Mason sliced off some of the Comte cheese and took a bottle for himself and Collette. He sat with her and they shared the cheese and wine as if alone on a picnic. He marveled at her beauty and her calm. She smiled at him as he ran his hand through the side of her hair. He took another drink of the Vouvray and relaxed for a bit. The next step in the process would have to wait for a few hours until darkness set upon the Loire Valley.

29

GANOUX OUTLINED THE PLAN for everyone. He, Collette, Sully, Marie, and Mason would take the groups up to the Chateau main entrance. Each group would consist of five women. Three trips would be required to get everyone safely to the entrance and into the Chateau. Once inside, they would gather in the upstairs Gallery until everyone was there. The Gallery window shutters were locked so no one could see in or out. The river ran under the Chateau and the Gallery was on the second floor. If the German river patrols came, they would be directly under the Chateau as they passed and at any noise or sign of life, they would open fire. The Germans had orders to shoot on sight anyone trying to escape the occupied territory. It was negotiated that no person on free soil should be harmed but Germany did not obey the rules of war.

Once inside, Madame Martineau would lead the way to the back entrance. Again, groups of five would advance one at a time until they were all safely in the unoccupied zone. Ganoux explained the route from the wine cellar to the main entrance. Mason and Sully held up a map of the grounds as Ganoux spoke.

"At the top of the stairs, everyone will go to the right and follow the path to the end of the building. Once you have reached the end, you can see the river across the gardens. Your guide will check for any patrol boats and only when it is clear will you continue." He spoke slowly so Sarah could relay the instructions to the ladies gathered around.

"From the end of the building, once it is clear, you will walk briskly across the stone path toward the guard tower. You must be quick and silent as you will be exposed until you reach the tower. Following the path up to the first bridge, you will cross the moat onto the forecourt of the castle." He ran his finger across the map towards the turreted stone tower which stood across the moat from the main entrance. The circular white stone Marques Tower was restored in the 16th century. It was all that remained from the earlier castle which stood on these grounds. The original tower served as the Castle Keep until restoration and had housed the guards of the Chateau until war broke out.

"Once at the tower you will again rest at the entrance to the second bridge which leads to the main entrance. Does everyone follow so far?"

Sarah asked the room and there were several head nods mixed with verbal acknowledgements.

He continued. "When your guide tells you it is clear, the group will proceed to the front entrance to the Chateau. Madame Martineau will be waiting to open the door and let you in. You will gather in the main entrance until everyone has arrived and then we will proceed upstairs to the Gallery. We have a lamp in the Chateau that I will turn on and off twice. You will be able to see it through the window when we are clear and ready for the next group. The guide for the following group must wait at the top of the stairs to see the Chateau window. With luck on our side, in a few hours we will be on the other side and on your way to freedom."

Mason and Sully put the map down and Mason laid it out for everyone to look at. Sarah conferred with the group as they decided on the first five women who would go. Two of the ladies were very tired and older than the rest so they were picked to go first so they could rest in the confines of the Chateau rather than the damp, cool wine cellar. Sarah suggested that the other in the group be younger in case the older women needed some help getting to the entrance and made sure the younger woman stayed with her friend. Ganoux would lead the first group of five.

They gathered at the top of the wine cellar steps. Ganoux glanced out toward the Chateau and listened carefully for any sound of a boat motor. Satisfied everything was calm, he motioned for the ladies to proceed. One by one they shuffled their way toward the end of the building, passing large barn-style doors and several empty stone urns. They kept close to the building as they were instructed. Ganoux followed behind the last woman, making sure everyone was okay. The first woman stopped at the corner of the building. She was in her fifties and winded from a lifetime of smoking. She held onto the stone sill at the bottom of the double, six-foot arched windows, as the others arrived. Ganoux reached the end and passed to the front of the group. He raised his finger to his lips signaling the ladies to be quiet. They all stared at him with their wide, frightened and tired eyes.

He checked the direction of the river and downstream; everything looked good. The branches from the trees on the riverside blowing in the wind was the only sound he heard. Ganoux turned to the woman behind him and motioned to her that it was okay to move to the next stop. She crouched down as she walked quickly across the gravel path toward the entrance to the first bridge, the other four in tow. She had regained her breath long enough to make it there without incident.

Ganoux arrived last again and quickly looked upstream and downstream. He paused for a moment and then he led them to the base of the Marques Tower. The women caught up to him after a few moments and they all crouched down with their backs against the white stone of the tower. Retrieving a pair of binoculars from his jacket pocket, Ganoux slid to the edge of the tower where he looked downstream. He could see the ripples of the river hitting the shore on each side but nothing else. The wind had picked up causing the minor disturbance in the trees and the water. He turned and looked the other way. About one half mile upstream was a set of stone steps leading down to the water's edge. Two iron posts with a chain hanging prevented access to the water. The chain slowly rocked back and forth in the breeze. All was quiet except for the sounds of the night. He came back to the women and nodded slightly. The first woman pushed away from the tower and began her walk up the small hill onto the entrance bridge. Water slapped the stone base of the Chateau as she crossed the bridge to the massive twelve-foot wooden doors. Designed for

Thomas Bohnier and his wife, Katherine, the doors were adorned on the top section with the family crests of both families, The Bohnier crest on the left and the Briconnet on the right. The doors were exquisitely painted in an aged copper green with the bright colors of the crest made for an impressive welcome. Two smaller doors were cut in the bottom of each door.

Ganoux arrived and slightly tapped the door on the right. Three knocks, a pause, and then three more. The door creaked as the handle turned and it began to open. Standing in the doorway was an older woman wrapped in a white gown with a black scarf around her neck which hung down to her waist. She greeted Ganoux and he stepped aside allowing the five women to enter. He entered last and closed the door behind him. The seven of them stood in the Grand entrance with its high arched Renaissance-style ceiling. Two statues stood opposite each other on marble pedestals. One of M. Bohnier, the other his wife Katherine. The Chateau was a touch warmer than the wine cellar but not by much. Madame Martineau led them into a room on the left which was much warmer as a fire burned in the large stone fireplace at the far end. Several chairs were set up near the fire so Ganoux motioned to the women to please come and sit. They anxiously sat and rubbed their hands together in front of the fire. The smoker coughed a bit as she struggled to regain her breath, having held it for most of the way out of fear.

Ganoux walked over to the lamp positioned on the table by the window. He reached under the shade and turned the knob. The light flickered and lit up. He turned the knob again and it went out. Repeating the process one more time, he then left the light off.

He returned to Madame Martineau, "I will wait for the others by the door. Can you make sure these ladies are okay?"

"Of course, you go, I will make sure they are warm enough for the final journey through the woods."

Sully and Marie saw the signal and started out to the end of the building. They reached the end and Sully listened for anything. He turned to Marie and put his finger to his mouth. They both listened and a small whir from an engine could be faintly heard in the distance. He peered around the corner crouching down to get a look beneath the blowing tree branches. He saw nothing but the noise was getting louder. They waited for a minute and the noise dissipated. Feeling comfortable he began walking toward the bridge with his group. A few steps before the bridge the area around them was flooded with light. Sully dove to the ground along with everyone else as a light searched the area back and forth. Sully crawled over to the stone wall to have a look. He slowly peered over the edge and noticed a German patrol boat no more than fifty meters away. The sound of the engine stopped; it had been turned off and the boat and its crew floated nearby. They must have heard something and were scanning the landscape. He could faintly make out voices of the German soldiers in the distance.

Sully sat upright with his back against the stone wall and motioned to Marie to keep quiet and stay low. They could not remain here; they were sitting ducks. Sully thought for a moment.

Mason saw the scene unfolding in front of him from the top of the steps. He could see the seven figures lying on the ground by the entrance to the bridge as a light scanned the area illuminating the tower base and the bridge as well as the grassy knoll. Ganoux could see the searchlight through the shutters in the room opposite where the women had gathered. Mason had an idea. He told the women with him to stay where they were; he would be right back. He asked Sarah to tell them in German because he was sure they did not understand, but they all nodded at him. He went down into the cellar and out the back door searching for some rocks. He found some baseball size rocks on the ground and grabbed two. He made his way along the back of the building until he was at the corner and could see the boat to his right. Crawling on the ground he arrived at a large oak tree, the trunk three times his size. Mason considered himself a pretty good athlete and he hoped he was good enough for his plan. He loosened up his shoulder a bit and then reached back. He took a couple steps and launched the rock as far up in the air and as far as he could. It hit a branch in the tree and ricocheted to the ground to his right. The thud it made along with the branch noise caught the attention of the spotlight operator. The light moved from the grounds to the tree and the area to Mason's right.

Sully recognized the movement of the spotlight and immediately the seven of them ran up the first bridge and arrived at the tower. They all breathed heavily as they sat with their backs against the tower base. Mason watched from behind the tree as the spotlight searched the area one more time. Finally, the engine roared to life and the patrol boat pulled away and disappeared under the Chateau and continued upstream. Everyone waited until the noise was out of range before they moved up to the front door. Ganoux opened the door and everyone entered. One woman was crying and sniffling, shaking with fear as she was led into the room with the others.

Mason came back through the wine cellar and gathered his group. Sarah was one of the five as was the woman who had hit him with her bag. She had softened to him but still had a stare that would make anyone uncomfortable. They gathered at the top of the steps. Collette and Sarah began the trek to the end of the building, Mason following. He closed the door to the wine cellar and caught up to the others. They reached the tower with no problems and as they waited to go the final distance to the front door, Mason heard the faint sound of the patrol boat, it was on its way back. He decided they could not stay here, they needed to make a run for it. Sarah led them across the bridge as the patrol boat moved closer to the Chateau. Mason was the last to go, as he reached the bridge the woman in front of him tripped on the small incline and fell onto the bridge. Mason almost fell over her, he was so close behind her. He stumbled and then caught his balance. She had been watching out for her scared, younger friend and lost her footing. Mason reached down with both hands and dragged the woman to her feet as she held onto him with vice-like hands staring at him in fear. He ushered the younger woman ahead as he helped the older one. The younger woman was paralyzed with fear. Sarah reached the door and knocked as fast as she could. Ganoux opened it, saw Mason struggling to get the woman to her feet, and ran past everyone to help the younger woman to move. He and Mason pulled them to the door and inside. Collette closed the door and pushed the large metal bar through the lock.

Mason stopped in the front hall and let go of the woman he had just carried inside. She held onto him still with fear in her eyes. The younger woman stood there trembling with fear as Ganoux tried to calm her down.

"You're okay, you're okay." Mason said slightly out of breath. A tear rolled down her cheek as she slowly let go. Mason walked her into the room with the others. He sat her in front of the fireplace and tapped her shoulders as he nodded at her. She grabbed his hands and squeezed them tightly. Mason had no idea what this woman did for a living; she said very little but had hands of steel. He slowly loosened her grip and walked over to Ganoux at the window.

"Follow me," Ganoux said as he raced out of the room. They went up the stairs to the second floor and into a darkened room. They reached a window overlooking the river and saw the patrol boat approaching. It was slowing down toward the stone steps waterside with the hanging chain. The boat stopped and two soldiers hopped out and stepped over the chain. The spotlight shined on the riverside showing them the way.

Ganoux looked at Mason. "They are coming here." He didn't need to say anything else as both men ran out of the room and back downstairs.

They arrived in the room where everyone was waiting. Collette noticed immediately the concern on Mason's face as he entered. Ganoux found Madame Martineau and explained the situation. She nodded and left the room immediately.

He told Sarah that they all needed to go downstairs to the kitchen right away. She relayed his message and the women looked on with a mix of fear and surprise as he led them out of the room and down the stone steps to the bottom floor. They turned right and arrived in the large kitchen. Copper pots and iron pans hung on the wall. A large cast iron stove, easily measuring ten feet, sat in the middle of the room. As they squeezed into the room, Ganoux led them into the pantry area. Shelves with food and supplies hung on both sides. Sarah explained that everyone needed to squeeze in and be as quiet as possible.

Mason stayed upstairs until the last of the women left the room. He quickly helped Madame Martineau put things back to normal, moving most of the chairs up against the wall. He exited the room and headed for the steps downstairs when someone began pounding on the door. He secured his Colt and disappeared down the stairs to join the others. Madame Martineau waited until he was out of sight before approaching the door. Mason reached the kitchen where the pantry was filled with people, so he and Collette along with Sully ducked into the fireplace. The five-foot tall behemoth could have held ten people. Mason pushed aside a large metal cauldron as he crouched inside, weapon drawn.

At the door, Madame Martineau grabbed the handle and slowly swung the door open, even as the pounding continued along with a loud voice yelling to open the door. She calmly turned the handle and opened the door. Two German soldiers stood there staring at her, weapons drawn.

"What can I do for you?" she asked in a welcoming voice as she stared into the eyes of the enemy.

30

"GOOD EVENING FRAULEIN, my name is Major Von Raupt. I am wondering if there is anyone in this Chateau with you?" The Major was dressed in his military uniform, his *Waffenrock* coat was a pressed, form-fitting grey coat with eight buttons. On each collar were the *Litzen*, an insignia in shiny silver that looked like the Roman Numeral two. A few metals hung from the Major's chest over his heart. Madame Martineau took in all the information she could as she stood staring at the German major who spoke firmly but calmly.

"May we come in?" the Major said as he pushed the door open and walked by her. She gazed at the Major for a second and then stepped aside. "By all means."

The soldier with Von Raupt also entered and they stood in the large entrance hallway. The soldier kept his eyes on her as the Major looked around the foyer.

"I'm sorry, I didn't get your name?"

"My name is Sidonie Martineau and I am the Matron of Chenonceau. I am here alone."

"That is a beautiful name. Are you sure there is no one else on these grounds with you? We have reason to believe you may be hiding some refugees on your property."

"Major, you asked me if there was anyone in the Chateau with me and I said no. As far as the grounds, I have a gardener who helps me during the day, but I believe he has gone for the evening. I can assure you I am alone, and I do not appreciate the insinuation that I am not."

The Major pivoted in his shiny black boots and smiled slightly at the woman. He stared deep into her eyes, "Perhaps I was mistaken but I would like to take a look around—with your permission, of course." He walked over to the table against the wall and admired the blue hand-painted ceramic bowl, "This is very beautiful," he said, changing the subject.

Mason stood at the top of the stairs out of sight listening

in on the conversation. He was still in his ill-fitting German uniform and he held his Colt against his chest. He had come this far with the rescue, and if he had to kill a German major to make it through the evening, he would. They needed to move soon because all the women were tired and hungry and to ask them to survive a firefight in a sixteenth century Chateau was too much. Sully stood next to him with his gun drawn; Ganoux stood at the bottom waiting for any signal from the top.

The Major turned around and gazed again at Madame Martineau. He walked slowly over to her, the heels of his black boots echoing as they hit the Italian marble floor. He stopped directly in front her and his deep blue eyes bored into her soul, "May I call you Sidonie?"

"No, you may not, Major. We are not friends or acquaintances. You are in my Chateau accusing me of something which I have told you is not true. I do not believe that we need to exchange pleasantries. I would rather you look around or leave. I am tired from a long day. I have also been fighting a cold, so I need some rest. Do you understand?"

"Well *Frau* Sidonie, I only ask to be polite, but I will do whatever I feel necessary, because I can."

The Major smiled a wicked grin giving his soldier an order in German. As he spoke, he stared directly into Sidonie's eyes. She returned his gaze and said dismissively, "Then get it over with."

The soldier immediately headed up the stairs and checked the top floor. After a few minutes of his boots shuffling from room to room, he reappeared and shook his head. He checked the rooms on the main floor and returned with the same response. Mason and Sully moved back down into the kitchen and moved everyone out of sight. Mason closed the pantry door and he, Ganoux, and Sully hid at the end of the hallway with a clear view of the stairs. If the soldier came down, they were prepared to act if they needed to. They heard the boots on the stone steps as the soldier descended. Mason peeked around the corner as the soldier arrived in the lower level. He quickly looked in the kitchen and then turned and headed toward Mason. He walked slowly searching for a switch to turn a light on. Ganoux had removed the bulbs from the overhead light. The soldier pressed the switch, and nothing happened. He pressed it again. With no light he approached the room at the end of the hall slowly inching forward. Mason readied a knife. If the soldier came into view, he would use it. The soldier glanced in the darkened room and listened intently. Mason's heart was beating like a small marching band and the lump in his dry throat was growing by the second. He stretched his fingers around the knife. The soldier took a deep breath and then turned and left. He shuffled up the stairs back into the entrance where he assured the Major the woman was alone.

The soldier stood in the doorway as the Major silently looked at Madame Martineau.

"I do hope you feel better," he said as he started to leave. "Oh Sidonie, one more thing. If I find out you are helping people escape to the free zone, I will personally come back here and..." he paused for a moment and took a step back toward her, "let's just say, it will be most unpleasant for you."

He stared at her for a moment and Sidoinie could feel the coldness in his stare. She was shaking inside but remained calm on the outside. The Major turned and left followed by the soldier. Sidonie closed the door and locked it. She turned and leaned against the door exhaling as she closed her eyes. Mason peeked around the corner and saw her standing there visibly shaken. He waited a few moments until she stood back up straight.

"She caught his eye and nodded. "It is okay, they have left."

Mason looked back down to Ganoux, "He's gone."

"We should wait until we see the boat leave." He said as he passed Mason. "I will go upstairs and watch. Do not let anyone out until I say it is okay."

Mason nodded slightly and Ganoux disappeared up the stairs.

Mason looked at Sully. "If they do leave, they will return. It's only a matter of time before they discover that their little patrol that was driving around these parts never returned. Once the boat guy hears that, he will come right back here with half the army and tear this place apart. We've got to move quickly, and we've got to move now."

Sully agreed. "We have come this far; we are going to figure out a way to get these women to safety. We only have a few days until the dinner at the German Headquarters, Marie must get back and start doing preparation. Volmer, I am sure, is wondering where she is. We are far from done, my friend."

"I didn't come all this way not to get Kliest. I will have plenty of energy left to kill that asshole."

"You and me both. He ordered the death of my friends and he will pay for that."

Ganoux returned. "The boat has gone back upstream but it will be back. I imagine sooner rather than later so we must move. I am sure Luc is getting impatient waiting for us. He has probably run out of cigarettes."

Mason chuckled at the thought of him nervously sitting at the edge of the woods in an empty wine truck waiting for twenty people to suddenly appear out of the woods.

They followed Ganoux down to the pantry where they informed the others of what had transpired.

Collette shot Mason a worried glance and he mouthed silently to her, "We'll be fine." He winked at her and she managed a faint smile. Ganoux led the group back upstairs and they assembled in the Medici Gallery. It extended one hundred eighty feet from the Chateau across the river to the other side and was directly over the famous arches which formed the foundation of the chateau. Its black and white marbled floor and magnificent hanging lights gave the aura of a famous museum. Several statues were mounted on both sides of the gallery and its eighteen large windows provided plenty of sunlight on a nice day. The Gallery was used as a ballroom by the Medici family for gatherings.

Unfortunately, the eighteen windows also provided little

cover for everyone standing there at the moment. Even though they were shuttered, light still seeped through and if someone were watching from afar, they would see the many shapes inside moving around. This made Ganoux and Mason nervous, so they wanted to move quickly. Sidonie joined them and approached Ganoux with a set of keys. The door at the end of the Gallery to the south opened to the other side of the river: their doorway to freedom.

Sidonie shuffled her way to the end followed by her twenty guests. She fumbled with the lock and then inserted the key. The bolt made a loud bang as it disengaged. She pulled on the large handle and the door opened slowly.

Mason and Ganoux went out first, each looking down his side of the river for any activity. They slowly walked down the large stone steps onto the dirt path which ran parallel to the river. They quietly looked around and then back to each other. Convinced no one was around, they motioned to Sully to begin the parade.

One by one they helped the women down the stone steps and onto the path. Sully led them away from the Chateau and into the woods toward the graves of several prominent former owners of the Chateau. The moonlight peeked through the trees and gave them a little light to walk by. Collette and Marie followed the end of the group as Mason and Ganoux made sure they were clear.

Ganoux went back up the stairs and thanked Sidonie for all her help. She deflected the praise back to him.

"You are the one doing the good. I merely have a building here that can help. Be careful." She closed the door and Ganoux heard the deadbolt lock. He walked back down the steps and met Mason. As they started to walk into the woods, the shots rang out from across the river. They both dove to the ground as the trees exploded above them. They heard two German voices yelling as the shots continued. Collette and Marie quickly got everyone down to the ground. As Mason crawled to the edge to get a look, bullets raced over his head from the MG-42 machine guns. He could see the blast of fire coming out of the woods on the other side, as the Germans sprayed the trees around him with 1200 rounds per minute. He crouched on the ground as the fire concentrated on the stone wall in front of him. The bullets exploded against the stone and above him in the trees, leaves and branches raining down.

As Mason lay there, he felt someone on his side, he opened his eyes to see Ganoux lying next to him. *How the hell did he get over here in one piece. How does this man do it? In the face of complete chaos, he is always calm.*

"Wait here for my signal," he said to Mason as he slid his rifle to him, then rolled over and crawled back into the trees. Mason grabbed the rifle Ganoux had left and tried to position himself, but the bullets were still hitting everything but him. Sully returned some fire from the tree line but without a target, it was hard to know where to shoot.

Mason held his breath until the firing stopped. He looked up quickly, figuring they had to reload at some point when a flare shot up into the sky from behind him. It illuminated the other side of the river and Mason focused on the area where the shooting was coming from. He could see two figures crouched near the edge, he aimed and fired three rounds. One figure hunched over and fell forward over the edge and splashed into the water. Sully fired his entire clip at the other man as he struggled to reload his machine gun. Mason aimed again and fired, the man's head exploded, and his body fell limp as he too splashed into the river. Rolling over, Mason dropped the rifle and started to breathe again. A few moments later, Ganoux showed back up with his trusty backpack. Ganoux always had a bag with him and now Mason knew why. He was always prepared for a situation. He wondered why he did not just pull a plane out of it and fly them all the way home to London.

"You okay?" Ganoux said, offering his hand. "We have to move, that flare just alerted every boat on this river, they'll be coming."

Ganoux barely got the words out and the sound of the boat patrol engine could be heard approaching from the west.

They both looked quickly and then ran into the woods to meet the others. They were barely inside the trees when the bullets began flying again. These were louder, faster, and deadlier. Whole branches crashed down on them as they ran. Collette and Marie had gathered everyone, as they all ran for their lives. The German patrol boat was firing at will into the free zone violating every part of the treaty agreed upon with Marshall Petain.

Mason and Ganoux caught up to the others and they all ran as fast as they could. Mason helped some of the women down the debris-laden trail One woman fell onto the ground and Mason ran by, dragging her by the arm into the trees. He shielded her as a branch fell on them.

The woman glanced at Mason with her eyes wide with fear. It was the woman who distrusted him but now began to see him as her guardian angel. She was bleeding from her forehead from the fall.

A break in the firing gave him a chance to get her back up. She stumbled as Mason brought her over to Marie who helped her gain her footing and catch up to the others.

Mason met up with Sully and Ganoux and they agreed to go back. The entire German army would be coming if they did not dispose of this patrol boat. Ganoux had an idea, as usual, and Mason and Sully agreed. It would be dicey. If it did not work Mason and Sully would be either captured or dead. With Marie and Collette safely away from the chaos, they headed out, walking slowly toward the spotlight which illuminated the woods. As they reached the end, they began waving their hands wildly at the boat. Sully yelled, *"Nicht schiessen."* Don't shoot in German. The two members left on the boat seemed confused as two men in German uniform came out of the woods. The Major who had visited the Chateau earlier yelled something in German and Sully continued yelling "Don't shoot." As the two stood there waving their arms distracting the patrol boat, Ganoux snuck around the flank and approached the boat from behind. The Major was losing his patience trying to figure out what was going on when the fire from Ganoux's rifle cut him down. The other soldier was soon lying in a pool of his own blood as Ganoux finished them off.

Mason and Sully put their hands down and stood in silence staring at the boat. Ganoux jumped on to the bow and threw a tie rope onto the shore. Mason picked it up and wrapped it around a tree. Ganoux pulled some dynamite out of his bag of tricks and placed it on the in the bow of the boat. After setting the timer for 5 minutes, he engaged the engines and then hopped off the boat. They released the rope, and the boat began to drive downstream.

Mason, Sully, and Ganoux disappeared into the woods to catch up to the group. *Are we finally free of German pursuit?* Mason wondered as they jogged down the path. He hoped so but he knew the reason he had come back to France was for something else. It was now time to turn his attention to Kliest and exact the revenge he had long sought. It was within his reach and he smiled at the thought of the look on Kliest's face as Mason watched the life drain from it.

31

THE GROUP REACHED THE EDGE of the forest and waited for the three men to catch up. Mason saw them up ahead and slowed to a walk just as Collette saw him and ran over. She wrapped her arms around him and held him tight for a minute.

The group was startled by a loud noise a few miles away.

"What was that?" Collette said looking at Mason.

"There is one less patrol boat in the German army."

"Everyone, follow me," Ganoux spoke up as he took the lead in front. He led the group across the field and through a small valley until they reached a road. He stopped and looked around. "Dammit Luc," he said to himself, then louder, "Let us rest here for a moment."

After a few minutes Luc emerged from the trees to the left, cigarette in hand. He whistled and Ganoux turned to see him. "Thank God," he muttered.

The women stood and followed Ganoux to the trees where he and Luc shook hands.

"Hello again. Any problems?"

"Only that you are extremely late. I have been sitting here for hours. I moved the truck into the trees to hide it from anyone on the road. I have been nervous that you wouldn't make it."

Mason walked up, "Good to see you pal, I owe you a carton of cigarettes." He smiled and walked by him.

Luc turned in his direction, "Yes, you absolutely do."

They managed to get everyone into the truck; the woman who had fallen sat next to Mason." When they met, she would not go near him, now he was afraid she would be coming back to London with him; she would not leave his side. He checked her forehead and it seemed okay, but she would need some tending to when they reached the winery.

The ride back to Sylvain was more leisurely than the ride

through occupied territory had been. The sun was rising, and Mason kept the back flap open to get some air. He thought of his dad and hoped he was well. He would have one hell of an adventure to recount for him back home.

The truck shook as they entered the winery driveway. Luc pulled into the courtyard near the entrance to the cellar. A few farmhands were waiting with blankets and water.

Once everyone was out of the truck, Luc led them into the cellar through large, wooden barn doors. The cellar was noticeably cooler. The troglodyte caves were naturally cool, perfect for wine storage.

As they entered the cave, they could see the shine of the light bulbs on the wine bottles stacked floor to ceiling. Mason had never seen so much wine; he felt as though he had just entered heaven. Hanging over each stack of bottles was a sign listing the type of grape and the year of harvest. Mason read each one as they passed as if he were on a tour. He was already making a list of the bottles he would be taking back to London. They passed a long wooden table with chairs where the winery would taste their annual harvest. An old grape press was on the right side against the wall with a black and white photograph above it of the original Sylvain family standing next to their horse and carriage.

Luc led them for almost ten minutes into the caves with wine bottles stacked as far as the eye could see. Mason had to ask—he could not hold out anymore. "Luc, how many bottles of wine are down here?"

"How many do you think, Mason?"

Mason looked around and then answered, "50,000."

Luc stopped. "Not even close."

"75,000," Collette yelled out. Luc shook his head. "Two hundred thousand," he replied, "give or take a couple hundred."

"Wow, I'd like to take a couple hundred," Mason said to himself as he stood in awe.

They arrived at a turn in the cave where barrels were stacked three high from the floor to the ceiling. Six of the barrels had been moved to form an opening in the middle. A large wooden wall was behind the barrels with decorative wrought iron slats running the full horizontal length roughly two feet apart. Luc pushed the wall, and a door opened in between the slats. You could never tell the wall had a door cut into it.

"Please, everyone." Luc motioned toward the opening. Marie and Sully entered first to a large room with blankets, wine, makeshift beds, and a large table covered with bread, cheese, and some sliced ham.

A large French flag hung on the far wall. The flag had a red Cross of Lorraine painted in the middle; it had been adopted as a symbol of the free French forces under Charles de Gaulle. The symbol was showing up subtly throughout the region as an opposition to the Nazi Swastika.

Everyone gathered in the room, Mason poured some wine and many of the women gathered for some food. Luc and Marie took a group to the bathroom, and several women just sat on the blankets and cried. They had been separated from their families, put on a train in Germany to an unknown destination, stripped of their belongings, and then rescued by complete strangers. They were overcome with emotions, both happy and sad. Mason's new friend stood next to him as he poured wine. He handed her a glass and surprisingly she took it. In one large gulp she drank it and held her glass back out. She wiped her mouth with her left hand and Mason filled up her glass again with a smile. She managed a thank you in broken English, and then she said *"Prost."*

After about an hour it was time for the band to break up. Collette explained to Sarah that they needed to leave for an especially important task, but they would be back. Upon their return, Sarah would go with them to board a plane back to England and be reunited with her sister.

Sarah wished them well and thanked each of them for the group. Mason's new friend did not want him to leave but eventually she allowed him to go. She gave him a big hug, nearly squeezing all the air out of him. They had come a long way in their relationship. First, she had hit him with her suitcase, now she hugged him goodbye.

Mason, Collette, Ganoux, Sully, and Marie exited the caves and found themselves staring at the wine truck once again. Luc was making his scheduled deliveries so Mason and Sully would ride in barrels in the back.

Mason remembered the odor of the red barrel, so he claimed white for this trip. Collette would ride up front with Luc, as she had the first time they crossed into occupied territory.

Sully crammed himself into the red barrel and Mason into the white. Marie and Ganoux would take another truck and drive back to Lien. They had French citizenship so they could pass through a checkpoint. They left first and everyone agreed to meet back in Lien at Carolina's farmhouse.

The truck pulled out and Mason immediately remembered how miserable this mode of transportation was. He closed his eyes and hoped it would be a quick trip, though he did enjoy the smell of the white barrel more than the red. He imagined Sully was cursing him right now as the smell of red wine engulfed him.

The trip was uneventful, a small holdup at the checkpoint but nothing major. By now, the German soldiers were used to Luc coming through. His new assistant in the front seat was a nice addition for the men at the checkpoint. A beautiful woman was rare for them. Collette played up the part perfectly as she was now more comfortable in that role. They pulled onto the dirt road leading to Carolina's farmhouse. Marie and Ganoux had already arrived. Mason extricated himself from his barrel and slowly brought the blood flow back to his legs. Sully did the same and they compared notes on their various aromas, having both rode in red and white wine barrels. Both agreed the white was a better choice.

With everyone settled around the kitchen table, Carolina pulled the curtains tight and locked all the windows. They had finally arrived at the reason for which Mason had come back to France—the plan to kill his nemesis Johan Kliest. Forty-eight hours from now the gathering at the Hotel Lien was to take place. Lieutenant Volmer welcoming his good friend Johan Kliest for a celebratory dinner party. Mason planned for it to be the last dinner Kliest would ever eat.

On the table in front of everyone were some items which would be used to take down the German command. The resistance, though small had managed to come up with some ingenious ways to hide things in everyday items.

The plan was to use a work truck to transport Marie, Carolina, and Collette to the Hotel Lien for the German celebration. They would be given access to the hotel's private cabin which had its own kitchen. A road leading in from the back of the property would allow them to avoid the main entrance. Mason was sure everything would be checked carefully so everything needed to be concealed perfectly.

Ganoux began explaining the items on the table in front of everyone, starting with the small black leather suitcase. The case was no bigger than a briefcase and when Ganoux popped the locks, he opened it to reveal an eleven-inch Type A Mark III short-wave transceiver with a range of 600 miles.

"This case will be stored in the truck's spare tire compartment and if needed can be used with the battery housed in the inside of the spare tire. The wires from the battery will be visible under the tire. Just attach them here…" He pulled out the connecting wires on the transceiver, "and you can radio all the way to London if you need to. This is to be used only to pass information in a dire situation. The last person alive must make the call to London to report on any useful information we have uncovered. Hopefully, we will all make it out of the Hotel alive and well and will have no need to radio London."

Ganoux next grabbed a log from the table. He pulled out a pocket-knife and used the blade to separate the log. The log was hollowed out and cut in two. A secret compartment inside held six sticks of dynamite. He removed one of the sticks and held it up for everyone to see. "These are useless without the fuses, so you must remember that the dynamite will need to be attached to these timers which hold the fuses. He removed the top from a gas can and pulled out three timers. Each timer had two long pieces of heavy tape attached to it.

"You attach two sticks of dynamite with the tape and then set the timer. You have forty-five seconds to get away, or you along with the dynamite will explode."

Mason smiled at Ganoux's gallows humor.

"Once again, if our plan goes as we believe it will, these may not be necessary. The log will be in the back of the truck along with the gas cans. Each can contains a bit of fuel in it in case it is poured out to check the authenticity of the can. The timers are housed in the bottom which is sealed with a light epoxy to hold it together. You need a knife blade to wedge the top off the secret housing.

Mason was enjoying this little show and tell. As usual, Ganoux was thorough and in complete control. His idea, his tools, his people, which added up to a well thought out plan.

Moving on, Ganoux picked up a group of pens from the table. He showed everyone the reddish-brown pen, and then removed the top to reveal a small vial of poison, "Everyone will be given a pen. The poison vial was developed by our very own Phillipe for a quick and painless death. You need to swallow the contents of this should you be in danger of being caught. We cannot risk being exposed or the resistance will be dead before it has even had a chance."

Ganoux's seriousness was evident as he looked around at everyone sitting there. He then moved to the final two items, a wooden case of wine, and a mechanic's oilcan. The oilcan was black and had a long, metal, funnel-like tube extending from the oil compartment measuring no more than eight inches long. Ganoux opened the top revealing a small amount of plastic explosive molded inside the oil compartment. "These are small explosive devices which can be used to blow a door or cause a diversion. The fuse is at the tip of the funnel, just light it and you have twenty seconds before detonation. Two of these will be in the back of the truck, one will be in the front cab."

Next, he moved on to the wooden wine box. He pried open the top to the case of wine to reveal six bottles of Sylvain Sancerre, a Loire Valley staple made from the Sauvignon Blanc grape. He removed the bottles one by one and handed them out to everyone.

"These are for your enjoyment tonight at our last meal before this plan goes forward tomorrow night. The wine for the event will be transported in these cases and a couple of them will have false compartments built into them." He grabbed the sides of the middle board on the side of the case and pulled it off. Ganoux reached in and pulled out a pistol and some ammunition. "The false crates will have six bottles of poison wine on top and pistols hidden inside. These, along with the pistol hidden in *The Count of Monte Cristo* book will be the only weapons available inside the cabin, use them wisely. If everything goes right, we should not need any of these things but learn them just in case.

With that the show and tell was finished and everyone relaxed a bit. Mason and Collette sat together on a couch in the living room quietly, Collette's head on his shoulder. Dinner that evening was spent discussing the plan as well as the recent escape from occupied territory with a group of scared but strong women whose story was going to shock the world once it can be told. Kliest and Volmer were transporting women and children, like cattle, around Europe. Separating them from their families, stealing their possessions and their dignity, while simultaneously starving them. Mason would make sure that both would pay for this with their lives. He knew he could not save every person, but he could eliminate the two men in charge.

32

MASON WOKE UP THE NEXT morning after a restless night's sleep. Collette was already up and sitting in the kitchen drinking some coffee along with Carolina and Marie. As usual, Ganoux was nowhere to be found. He told Collette he had to do some things. Sully was still asleep, having been up late on a radio call to London with Carolina's attic radio, and Phillipe had started early at the café to prepare the menu for that evening. While the rest of the group was rescuing the women from the train car, Phillipe, the chemist, was working on his batch of tasteless poison which would be baked into the meal for that evening. The menu would consist of some frenched chicken with *haricot verts* and a savory lemon butter sauce, a nice, tossed salad with balsamic vinaigrette dressing, homemade sorbet as a palate cleanser, and a cheese board for dessert along with Carolina's chocolate cake.

Phillipe's poison would be spread out over the course of the meal. His mixture was meant to cause a gradual slowing of the internal organs and induce cardiac arrest after several days of sickness. Most of the attendees were coming from out of town so by the time they returned to their posts, the poison would have worked its magic.

According to Marie, Sully had checked in with London and his people; no one had picked up any chatter about the secret dinner in Lien. Since there had been no talk in town about the missing women from the train car, this told him that Volmer and Kliest were doing this on their own; it was not a sanctioned German plan. The two of them oversaw shipping people to a secret location in France with their belongings and a promise of freedom. But first they would be shipped to Lien, stripped of all their valuables and then, sent back to the secret location. Sully was sure they knew the women were gone but could do little about it other than raise the security level for the next shipment.

"Morning everyone," Sully said as he entered the kitchen, clearly groggy from a long few days and nights. He sat across from Mason as he poured some coffee, "How are you doing?"

"I'm good." Mason replied. "How was your call with London?"

"Good, they were happy we were all still alive. No one has heard anything about this secret dinner tonight which is good for us. My people have dug up more information on Kliest. Apparently, he has a large estate outside of Berlin and he is quite the art collector. I guess that is why he oversaw stealing art for the Fuhrer museum. I imagine most of the items of value that he is stealing from these people are somehow making their way back to Berlin and onto his walls, or into his vault."

Mason agreed as he sipped his coffee, "In my experience in the art world, art collectors have a team of people behind the scenes helping them assess the value of their collection. There must be people who know what he is doing. No one can move that number of valuables without help. I know Volmer is involved but according to Marie, he is too concerned with drinking and womanizing to be fully trusted to run a smuggling operation."

As the two talked, Ganoux walked in and nodded to everyone. He carried some papers in his hand and sat down at the table. Mason looked at him. "We were just discussing the logistics of the smuggling operation that Kliest and Volmer are involved in, and we came to the conclusion that they would need people behind the scenes to move the amount of stolen valuables back to Berlin."

Carolina left the room and returned a few moments later with some neatly pressed German uniforms. Sully and Mason would be reprising their roles as German soldiers for tonight's event. Marie and Collette returned to the kitchen after freshening up; they were set to head over to the café with Carolina, to continue preparation.

Mason stood and Collette kissed him, "I will see you later, be careful."

"I will; you stay away from Kliest. He can't see you or we are all in trouble," Mason said as he gave her a hug.

"I will keep her away from him. Volmer will want to introduce me to everyone so this way, Collette can stay in the back," Marie said as she kissed Sully goodbye.

"Be careful. I didn't come all this way to lose you now," Sully said as he kissed her forehead.

The women left and Mason, Sully, and Ganoux sat silently for a few moments at the table.

Ganoux spoke up. "We have some supplies at the cemetery which will be needed for tonight. We should go together so the two of you will know which mausoleum it is in case I am gone."

They all agreed to meet out front in ten minutes to walk to the cemetery.

Ganoux led them back into town and through the square past Café Saint Joanna and then up the hill toward the Church of Lien. Sully and Mason walked together through town with Ganoux several feet ahead. Groups of three males would raise suspicion so they kept their group as a pair.

The doors to the church were open and a few people sat in the pews praying, no doubt for this whole godforsaken war to end. Two German soldiers passed by without incident, talking and smoking.

The people of Lien could go about their daily activities during the day; the only real source of interaction was at the checkpoints. Ganoux had discovered countless ways to avoid the checkpoints: through woods, near streams, and across fields. He confidently led Mason and Sully to the gates of the cemetery.

They stood outside the cemetery as Ganoux looked around. Mason and Ganoux would go in while Sully agreed to venture into the church.

Sully walked away and up the stairs into the front doors of the church. He sat in the next to last pew on the left side. Immediately he took note of who was in the church. Two women knelt with their hands clasped in prayer across the aisle from him. Another woman got up to exit the church with her head bowed down, resisting eye contact. A priest at the front near the altar busied himself preparing everything for that night's service. A handyman carried a ladder from the back and stood it up near the sign depicting the psalms for that evening. He climbed the rickety wooden ladder and began to change the page numbers. Sully turned and glanced outside, he noticed a German soldier walk by the entrance to the church and continue in the direction of the cemetery.

Ganoux and Mason walked through the cemetery gates separately and Mason followed behind him as they navigated between the graves and approached the above ground mausoleums.

The German soldier on patrol caught a glimpse of the two men walking through the cemetery. He noticed the man who was following, looking around suspiciously as he walked. The soldier decided to go in for a closer look at the two gentlemen.

Ganoux turned to Mason and pointed, "It's right over here." He walked up to the stone building with the name "Touleau." Mason noticed the grandeur immediately, the ornate stone urns at the entrance with the large wrought iron gates. They had wrapped around a few trees on a gravel path and were secluded from view when Ganoux unlocked the gates. He opened them and they both stepped in. Ganoux went right for the prayer box, he had just knelt to unlock it when a voice startled both of them. Mason turned to see the soldier standing there with his gun drawn. He yelled at them in German as they both raised their hands. The soldier approached them and motioned for Mason to move out of the structure. Mason slowly moved out and to the side with his hands above his shoulders. Ganoux stood inside as the soldier reached the entrance. He looked at Ganoux and then around the inside of the tomb.

"It's my family's tomb," Ganoux said in French as the soldier looked at him. The prayer box was open at his feet and Ganoux blocked it with his body. The soldier backed away and motioned with his hand for Ganoux to come outside. Mason stood to the side quietly as the soldier reemerged, backing up. Ganoux came outside, hands raised. The soldier approached him and in a quick burst landed the butt of his rifle to the top of Ganoux's head. Mason heard the crack of the rifle and watched as Ganoux fell to the ground, blood forming on his forehead. The soldier turned to Mason and pointed his rifle at him, saying something in German. Mason shook his head signaling he did not understand, and the soldier approached him. Mason leaned back as the soldier approached, expecting the same treatment as Ganoux. The soldier raised the rifle butt and then he slumped down, his eyes wide. He fell face-first to the ground. Mason could see the knife stuck squarely in his back. Mason looked up at Sully standing ten feet away. He exhaled and ran to Ganoux who was still lying on the gravel. Sully walked over to the soldier and grabbed his legs. He dragged him to the entrance of the tomb as Mason checked on Ganoux. After a few minutes, Ganoux began to come around. He glanced up at Mason with a dazed look on his face as he tried to shake away the confusion.

"You all right?" Mason asked his friend.

"I think so," Ganoux said, wiping at the blood on his forehead.

"What are we going to do with him?" Sully asked, standing over the soldier.

"Put him in the tomb. I think the top right is empty."

Mason went inside and pried off the stone tablet covering the top right burial chamber; it was empty. Sully helped him remove the tablet and place it on the floor leaning on the other side. They grabbed the soldier and lifted him up and into the stone burial chamber. Ganoux sat up, still getting his bearings as the other two replaced the tablet. Mason opened the prayer box and grabbed the guns and the knife from inside. He closed it up and came out. "What a brilliant hiding place. You can hide weapons, bodies, valuables, and then lock it and go."

"I was only planning on weapons, not bodies," Ganoux replied as he got to his feet. I have known this family for a long time. The thought of putting someone in there that is not a member of the Touleau family disturbs me, but we have no choice right now."

He threw the key to Mason who locked the doors. Ganoux stood there still straining to see clearly, the soldier had really got him good. The butt of the rifle was as hard as stone. He felt better after a few minutes and Sully left them to go back to church. After fifteen minutes, Sully noticed Mason and Ganoux passing the entrance to the church. He sat in his pew for a couple of minutes before making the sign of the cross, asking forgiveness for the killing of the German soldier. As he exited the church, he wondered if God gave forgiveness for the horrendous acts people were perpetrating during this conflict. He slowly shook his head as he stepped out into the air of the late morning in Lien.

33

MARIE, COLLETTE AND CAROLINA squeezed into the front seat of the Sylvain wine truck for the drive over to the Hotel Lien. The night which they planned for so many weeks had finally arrived. Volmer, in all his arrogance, was hosting his friends for a private party as the Third Reich controlled all of Europe. He planned on a celebration of victory in Europe. Since France had fallen, the Third Reich had begun their plans of occupation, enacting new laws, and systematically beginning the elimination of Jewish culture throughout Europe. New laws in Paris were meant to shame the Jews into closing their businesses and leaving. A new law was rumored to be coming, requiring all Jewish businesses to hang yellow signs in their windows with the words *"Entreprise Juive"* signaling a Jewish-owned business.

And for all the horrors of war, The German command in Lien would celebrate tonight with the finest food and drink around. As Marie drove the truck through the outskirts of town, she thought of the first night of occupation and how terrified everyone had been. *Would we all be forced out of our homes and businesses, run out of town and out of Europe, or worse, shot and left for dead.*

Marie agreed that night she would never give up her way of life without a fight. She knew it would be an uphill battle fought in the shadows and underground. The information gathering stage would soon lead to small victories and hopefully to pushing the Germans out of France one day. The odds were not good but if everyone gave up, France would never be returned to the French.

When she was contacted by Ganoux, they shared a similar vision of a clandestine war fought with the enemy right under their noses. Tonight was the climax of that first conversation. Start to eliminate the heads, and the bodies will eventually die. Her job tonight was to cook the best meal she could and serve it with a smile, flirt with the guests, and eventually poison them. Carolina had baked the bread earlier in the day and Collette was going to help in the preparation and execution of the plan. Mason and Sully, in their freshly pressed German uniforms were on their way through the woods heading to the hotel grounds.

Marie pulled onto the service road and stopped at the checkpoint. Two German soldiers checked their identification and did a check of the contents of the truck. They rummaged through boxes of food and bottles of wine and beer, boxes filled with cooking utensils and recipe books. Everything in the truck was for a catered party. The soldiers knew of the event, but low-level men were not invited and would not get close to the gathering. Their job was to secure the hotel perimeter and keep any unauthorized people out. The truck received the go ahead and Marie followed the road through the woods until she reached the rear of the hotel. She pulled down the rocky drive and parked outside the rear gate. Two soldiers opened the gate and ushered the three of them into the cabin where the party would be held. They were shown the kitchen area and then left to unload their possessions themselves.

Collette wore a white chef's coat and had her hair tied up in a knot on her head. She tried to appear as kitchen worthy as possible. She carried the box with the utensils and recipe books through the arched French doors of the cabin. The cabin, located in the rear of the hotel grounds, was a short walk up the gravel path from the main building. It was reserved for private parties and banquets. Marie herself had attended several weddings in the venue. Collette put the box down on the large metal preparation table in the kitchen. As she turned to head back out to the truck, a German soldier startled her as he had silently entered the room. She politely said, "Pardon me."

The soldier just stood quietly staring at her. He then looked around and backed up to the wall where he stood watch over the kitchen.

Marie entered followed by Carolina, each carrying a

wooden case. Carolina held the beer, and Marie the wine. They dropped each in front of the large walk-in refrigerator. The beer and white wine would be chilled, the red would be left in the case at room temperature. The soldier watched their every move as the three women conversed amongst themselves. They switched back and forth between English and French.

Marie laid out the knives and set up the pans she would be using. Collette unpacked the utensils and books while Carolina went back to the truck.

She returned with a large basket of fresh bread and a jar of olive spread. She placed the bread on the counter and the spread in the walk-in refrigerator.

Once everything was unloaded and brought into the kitchen, Marie began preparation. The first guests were due in a little over an hour, so she had some time to prepare the first course. It would consist of wine, beer, cheese, hummus dip, bread, flatbread, nuts, and fruit. Collette chopped up fresh berries and washed the grapes for the cheese plate. The selection of locally made cheeses was provided by a local dairy farmer and included Comte, Beaufort, Bleu d' Auvergne, two kinds of Brie, a creamy mild and an earthy Normandie Brie. The first course of cheese would be served as the guests arrive and featured the best cheese and berries available. The second serving of cheese with the dessert would be slightly different than the first. The second would be served with an added ingredient provided by Phillipe. Those cheeses were marked "dessert" in bright red on the waxy cheese paper. Hopefully, by the end of the meal, the guests would have plenty of wine and beer in them that any slight change in the taste of the cheese would go unnoticed. As Marie retrieved the vat of butter from the walk-in, the door to the kitchen opened and Volmer came strolling in. He was dressed in his formal military outfit, grey pressed pants with his grey jacket top, silver buttons, shoulder straps, a silver Nazi eagle embroidered over the right pocket and medals hanging over the left.

"Good evening everyone, how is my beautiful kitchen

staff?" he said with a big, arrogant smile as he walked across the room.

"Good evening, Lieutenant," Marie said, glancing up from her preparation duties. Collette said nothing and tried to look busy. Carolina was preparing the cheese board with such precision; she barely noticed the robust Lieutenant in the room.

He walked over to Marie as she turned toward him. "Ravishing as ever," he said smiling.

"Oh, please stop," she replied, shaking her head flirtatiously.

"So, are we all ready for tonight. I expect the first guests to arrive soon."

"Yes, we are ready to go. Carolina is preparing the cheese board and the first course. We will have it ready before anyone arrives. The beer and wine will be well chilled and served as guests arrive. "

"Very good." Volmer said as he admired Marie melting butter and garlic in a saucepan. "Smells wonderful already. I have some champagne to be served early on. As host, I will be welcoming everyone and saying a few words. I would like you to be by my side as I speak."

"I will be terribly busy preparing your dinner. You take me away for some time and things may not be perfect for your guests."

"You have these two lovely ladies to mind the cooking as I introduce you to my guests. It will be fine. I want to show you off to my friends so they can see how beautiful their cook is."

Marie sighed and relented, "Very well, but only for a minute."

"Take a quick walk with me," Volmer said, motioning with his right hand.

Marie looked at him for a moment and turned the flame off, then wiped her hands with a towel, throwing it down on the counter.

Volmer led her out of the kitchen, down the hallway and

into the dining room. A massive wooden table was set up, complete with place settings and pressed napkins.

"This is an especially important night for me, and I should very much like you to be a part of it. The world has changed my dear and you have an opportunity to lead a vastly different lifestyle now than before. I am in command of this area and I would like you to be by my side. I have treated you and your town very well since we took over and I wish to continue to do that. A lot of that depends on you. If you value your town, you have an opportunity to help them."

Marie slowly walked behind him as she looked over the table setup. The white china plates with the Nazi Swastika in black emblazoned on the bottom, the crystal glasses with the symbol etched in each one, the napkins pressed and bright white. It was making her sick just seeing it but hearing the words coming from Volmer's mouth were almost too much to bear. She stopped at the bookshelf and glanced at some of the titles together on the shelf as Volmer kept talking. Most of the titles were German authors who published propaganda books for the Third Reich. On the second shelf from the top were some classics, *A Tale of Two Cities, The Rime of the Ancient Mariner* by Samuel Taylor Coleridge and slotted next to that, *The Count of Monte Cristo,* a French classic about death and revenge, the one that mattered the most.

Volmer turned to Marie, "Think about my offer?"

Marie looked back at him, "Can we just get through tonight before we start making life plans." She smirked at her sarcasm and Volmer remained stoic for a moment, until he too, smiled back at her, "Of course, my dear."

34

MASON AND SULLY REACHED THE EDGE of the hotel property, crouched down in their newly pressed German uniforms, and checked out the surroundings. The large pool area was to the left of them, and the gravel path leading away to the right would take them to the private cabin where the dinner was taking place. Mason could see a few German sentries slowly walking the grounds. He and Sully would try to not draw any attention as they emerged from the trees. If they were found to be suspicious in any way, this would be an extremely short evening stroll. They both stood and wiped off their uniforms. Glancing down the hill at the sentinel by the pool, Mason waited until he turned back and began walking away from them. As soon as he did, Mason and Sully slipped out of the trees and slowly began walking toward the cabin.

The path snaked its way back into the trees briefly until it led to a grassy area where the stone and wood cabin was located. Several large cobwebs were visible in the trees next to the path as it continued past the cabin ending at the hotel's tennis courts.

They strolled toward the cabin to check things out. Reaching the opening, they noticed two soldiers manning the front entrance. Just beyond the front entrance a limestone path would lead down to the parking area where the truck was situated. Mason gave a slight nod to the two soldiers hanging around the front door as they came into view. One of them returned the gesture as Mason and Sully paused for a moment, the two soldiers guarding the entrance to the cabin paid them no mind. Many soldiers were given leave for the weekend to enjoy the festivities in Paris. They were replaced by newly recruited men just out of training. This helped Mason and Sully blend in, just two more Wehrmacht soldiers protecting the hotel.

"Shall we check out the grounds?" Sully said as they

turned and walked away from the cabin.

"Yeah, let's see what else we can find out."

They walked back past the area where they had emerged from the trees and followed the path which wrapped around to the large pool area. The pool was closed for the season and all the deck chairs were stacked in the corner. Some private villas had closed for the war since the Germans showed up. The small two person cabins overlooking the pool were sadly locked and boarded up.

Mason looked around as one of the sentries approached them. He stopped as Mason and Sully approached, "Cigarette?" he asked as the three stood there.

Mason had noticed that every soldier seemed to smoke so he had requisitioned a few packs from Luc. This way, they could blend in better. He promised to repay Luc for the packs when he returned, since he begrudgingly parted with them for the greater good.

He pulled a pack out from his breast pocket and shuffled one out of the opening. He turned the opening of the pack toward the sentry, who gladly pulled the cigarette out of the pack. *"Dank,"* he replied with a nod. Mason removed his lighter and offered it up. The sentry lit his smoke, nodded again with a smile, and continued his patrol.

Sully took a cigarette from Mason and lit it up. He had not smoked in years but if it helped them with their cover, he could do one or two. So far, their cover was holding up. They were just two more soldiers guarding the hotel grounds, strolling, talking, and smoking.

The hotel was a rustic building of wood and stone. It was situated on a hill and had several levels and secret passages. Built mainly of orange limestone, the stone structure blended in nicely with the lush vegetation surrounding it, the green of the trees and the stonework made for a stunning landscape.

Mason and Sully reached the top of a stone staircase which led down to the lower pool area. They paused and looked out over the pool and through a break in the trees, they could see the French valley in the distance.

They heard some voices down below as two German soldiers appeared on the stone patio. The men lit cigarettes and laughed as they spoke in German. Mason and Sully quietly listened as the two men below carried on a conversation. A third man appeared and ordered both men back inside. The men quickly stomped out their cigarettes and immediately disappeared back into the hotel. A few minutes later voices could be heard rapidly approaching. The two men who were smoking minutes before down below were quickly climbing the stone steps to the landing where Mason and Sully were standing.

Mason looked around and he and Sully quickly found the steps leading up and out of sight. Mason kept an eye on the landing as the two Wehrmacht soldiers passed by, followed by two more. Mason watched as the soldiers moved to the upper pool area and disappeared on the path leading toward the cabin. He had a feeling that the guest of honor, Johan Kliest was arriving, and the added security was for him. Mason was one step closer to his revenge.

He was startled by a German officer who appeared at the bottom of the staircase and started up toward him. The man was one of Volmer's men, Captain Hauptman, who immediately began giving orders to Mason and Sully. By the tone of his voice, he was not happy with the two of them standing around. He motioned with his hands toward the cabin and, though Mason could not understand him, he figured out most of it. He and Sully headed down the steps and up the path toward the cabin followed by Hauptman. Mason felt the sweat gathering under the brim of his Wehrmacht hat. He did not like being followed by the enemy, he felt vulnerable but at this moment there was nothing he could do. They arrived at the cabin and Hauptman slipped by them and continued down the path followed by Mason and Sully. They reached the parking area as a German high command black Mercedes Benz 770 approached. Nazi flags attached to the front, and the large round headlights almost blinding them as it pulled in. The car stopped and the driver emerged quickly, walked around the back of the car and to the passenger rear door. He opened it and a man got out standing tall in his officer's uniform, his medals shining, his boots polished. He removed his black gloves as Hauptman rushed to greet him. He stopped, clicked his heels, and raised his right arm, "Heil Hitler," he yelled vigorously. Giving a half-hearted reply, the officer handed the man his gloves and coat. Mason and Sully stood stoically in line with the other soldiers.

Mason watched the guest of honor's every move as he talked with Hauptman. He was standing ten feet from Johan Kliest, the man he had come back to France to kill. Ganoux had cautioned Mason to make sure Kliest did not see him, and here he was standing at attention in the reception line. Hauptman motioned to Kliest to head toward the stairs. He talked to Kliest like a young boy excited that his father was home. Kliest showed little emotion as they walked. Mason stood at attention next to Sully at the edge of the parking lot, his hat pulled down low. Kliest paid the guards zero attention as he walked, trying to hold the conversation with Hauptman.

Mason watched his every move as they approached the path leading up from the parking area to the cabin's front door. After the two disappeared, the soldiers relaxed and resumed their patrols. Mason and Sully waited a few minutes together before leaving the area. Sully watched as Kliest's driver turned the car around and backed it up next to the tree line, readying it for a quick exit. The driver began wiping down the vehicle using a white cloth. He carefully wiped the entire vehicle clean, knowing his boss would not stand for less.

Hauptman led Kliest into the foyer of the cabin, where he was greeted there by one of Volmer's underlings. "*Heil Hitler's*" were exchanged as the men stood together. Carolina was in the main dining area making last minute preparations to the table settings. The white porcelain Nazi plates shined alongside the polished Nazi silverware. She rolled the white linen napkins and slid them through the polished silver Nazi-emblazoned rings.

They entered the main dining room as Carolina was

exiting. She stepped aside with her head bowed, as the men entered the room.

The first attendees gathered at the side table covered with stemware and crystal decanters. Kliest stood and waited for one of the men to pour him a glass of Gewurztraminer, a favorite white wine from the French Alsace region bordering Switzerland and Germany.

"Where is Volmer?" Kliest asked, impatient with his absent host.

"He will be along shortly," Hauptman responded.

A few moments later two men entered the room, both of whom served on Volmer's staff, but were recently transferred to Paris. They stood erect as statues, when seeing Kliest and extended their right arms, "*Heil* Hitler."

Kliest raised his glass slightly acknowledging the two overly eager soldiers.

They both came over to Kliest to give a formal hello. Kliest was not interested in small talk, "Where is your boss?"

"He is on his way," one man responded.

"I have repeatedly been told Herr Volmer is on his way, but he never appears. I suggest one of you go get him. I do not appreciate having to wait for his presence."

"Yes, sir," the officer responded with vigor and turned to leave the room. As he did, the host of tonight's festivities entered the room with an arrogant grin on his face. Volmer walked in and immediately spoke with his booming voice. "Gentlemen, welcome. Johan, how was your trip?" he walked over to Kliest and snapped his heals together with a right-armed salute.

Kliest turned to Volmer stoically, "I do not appreciate waiting in a room full of subordinates for my host. Please make sure it never happens again or you will find yourself permanently among them."

"Yes sir, I apologize. With my injured arm, it takes a little longer to get ready."

Kliest looked at Volmer's shoulder and then back at him, "Allow more time to get ready and stop wasting mine.

Understood?"

Volmer stood silently and nodded. He had just been dressed down in front of his entire staff. Kliest left no one in the room questioning who was in charge. This might be Volmer's headquarters but Kliest pulled all his strings.

Kliest broke the awkward silence, "I am starving, where is this feast you kept telling me about?"

Volmer ordered his men to inform the kitchen that the food service could begin.

Carolina, Collette, and Marie were in the kitchen putting the finishing touches on the cheese and meat plate. The large trays of Brie, Gouda, and Comte cheese, mixed with slices of prosciutto, salami and French baguette, garnished with greens and artichokes, making the presentation as impressive as the food. Carolina always believed that the presentation of the food was as important as the taste, even if you were serving men you loathed. She believed in tempting the three senses of a meal, the sight of your plate, the aroma once your plate is positioned in front of you, and most important, the taste of your prepared dish.

Carolina was pouring champagne into large crystal glasses. The champagne was requisitioned from one of the best houses in France, Pol Roger. With the help of Ganoux, Marie was able to acquire several bottles of Pol Roger's best vintage. Everything Ganoux did was well thought out. Pol Roger was a prestigious brand and coveted by the German high command. It was also a favorite of Winston Churchill, so Ganoux could not think of a better brand to poison the German elite than a bottle of Churchill's favorite. He was quite sure that Winston would approve of the choice.

Carolina removed a small vial of clear liquid and using a dropper placed three drops into each glass; it disappeared amongst the bubbles. Phillipe had crafted the poison using ingredients to blend into food and drink. The small doses would barely alter the taste but over the course of a full meal and evening would add up to a sizeable amount which he had tested on some sick livestock on his farm. The dose killed a six-hundred-pound calf in two days. He was confident that two hundred-pound Germans would offer little resistance. Marie carried one cheese tray, Collette the other. Carolina carried the six glasses of champagne and they entered the dining room. Collette placed her tray down on the table immediately inside the door. She quickly exited back to the kitchen to remain out of sight. Marie placed her tray in the middle of the room on the table. Carolina went from man to man offering the poisoned glasses of champagne, one by one they left her tray.

Volmer grabbed the last glass and raised it in front of his face, "Welcome gentlemen. It is my pleasure to host you all here tonight, especially my good friend, Johan Kliest. Our victories so far in this fight have been plentiful and far reaching. I wish good health and prosperity to everyone here, and especially our beloved Fuhrer, *Heil* Hitler."

"*Heil* Hitler" rang out through the room loudly enough to be heard in the hallway as Carolina and Marie returned to the kitchen. They shared a sly grin as they reentered the kitchen. They would wait a few moments in case the champagne tasted odd. If it did, Volmer would be in the kitchen any moment. If a few minutes elapsed, the women knew it was on to phase two, the main course. The three waited in silence staring back and forth between them. As the minutes passed, each woman became increasingly confident in their plan. The demise of Volmer and Kliest had begun.

35

MASON WATCHED AS THE DRIVER polished the front bumper of Kliest's car. Sully was off patrolling the grounds and most of the soldiers had dispersed from the parking area. Two remained at the base of the path leading to the private cabin. Mason patrolled the parking area, nearing Kliest's vehicle from behind. The back of the car was against the rows of trees lining the parking area. The driver worked his way around the side of the car, bent at the waist polishing the lower portion of the passenger's side door as Mason approached him quietly. He glanced over at the two soldiers standing guard; they were immersed in conversation paying little attention to the parking area.

As Mason raised his rifle with both hands, the driver heard a sound and turned. Mason brought the rifle down onto the back of the driver's head with a loud thud. The driver collapsed to the ground. Mason stood up and checked the soldiers through the glass of the car's windows. They were oblivious to his presence as they smoked and talked. Mason laid his rifle down and grabbed the driver by the shoulders. He dragged the limp body through the trees and used the driver's belt to tie up his hands. He stuffed a handkerchief into the man's mouth, and then quietly snapped his neck. Sully had showed Mason the quickest way to silently end someone's life. He was not proud of it but needed to do it out of necessity.

Their uniforms were similar except for the hat. Mason switched caps with the driver and straightened his clothes. He brushed some leaves off the front of his uniform and adjusted his new hat. He had officially been hired as Kliest's driver. He quietly emerged from the trees, crouched down, and picked up the polishing cloth. He continued polishing the car and reemerged in sight of the two soldiers who paid him no mind. After finishing with the cleaning, Mason slid into the driver's seat awaiting the return of the Major, his new boss. Mason relished the thought of the look on Kliest's face when he saw him.

In the kitchen, Marie worked feverishly with Collette as Carolina walked the dining area replenishing everyone's champagne glass. The initial poison dropped in the glasses had now been dropped into the bottles of Pol Roger. So far, so good. The champagne was a hit with everyone, especially Volmer, who was downing twice as many glasses as everyone else. Carolina was worried that he might drop dead right there in front of everyone. Kliest had consumed three-quarters of one glass. As a respected Nazi, he never wanted to be too compromised, so he consumed alcohol in small quantities. Adolf Hitler did not drink or smoke and expected his command to be responsible. Most of them abided by the rules when they were near their Fuhrer but indulged when away from Berlin.

He looked at Volmer and could see the lieutenant's face getting redder with each sip. He was enjoying the cheese and meats with the bread, but frankly, the conversation was boring. Volmer droned on and on about all the accomplishments of the Third Reich. Kliest was a true Nazi but he also knew that the ease of their occupation of Europe would be met with a counterattack from Britain and Russia at some point. If Churchill and Stalin convinced Roosevelt to enter the war, their reign over Europe could turn out to be short lived. Kliest did not believe in the Thousand Year Reich; he was setting himself up for post war living. The riches he was accumulating would buy his freedom or safe passage to somewhere else in the world.

His pawn, Volmer, would be his ticket out. Men like Volmer were too arrogant to see the bigger picture. Volmer was drunk with power and well on his way to being drunk on champagne. If Kliest wanted to talk business, he had better have that conversation now before Volmer became incoherent. He walked over to Volmer, got his attention, and nodded. Volmer quickly put his glass aside, nearly knocking it over in the process. He excused himself from the conversation with two others and led Kliest out of the room and into an adjacent office. He closed the door behind them and turned to Kliest.

"We have had a very good month," he began. "Several of our trainloads have been very prosperous. I have two crates for you to take back to Paris."

Kliest listened as Volmer read a list of the contents of the two wooden crates on the desk. They were branded with the symbol of the Nazi Eagle. They were both padlocked, and the keys lay next to them on the desk.

Volmer read the list aloud: "thirty-six gold watches, seventeen gold rings, two hundred seventeen necklaces, twenty-eight diamonds, and three hundred twenty-one gold and silver valuables."

He elaborated on the last item, explaining the valuables ranged from picture frames to family heirlooms. All the items were stolen from the people forced onto the trains that came through Lien.

Kliest nodded slowly with approval as he grabbed one of the keys from the table and tried the lock on the case on top. It clicked open and he removed the key and pulled the metal latch back. Opening the crate, the sparkle of gold and silver stared back at him. He felt like a modern-day king opening his treasure chest. He pulled out a necklace decorated with green emeralds and small diamonds. He held it in his hands and admired the craftsmanship. Turning back to Volmer, he smiled, "You have done well, Franz."

Volmer smiled and offered an emphatic, "Thank you sir."

"Though I am concerned with the incident at the train yard." Kliest said as he placed the necklace back in the crate. He turned to Volmer whose expression had changed from pleasure to concern. "Were you not going to tell me about the men who got into the train yard?"

Volmer swallowed a lump in his throat. "Major, I assure you it was an isolated incident, and it was taken care of. Just a couple of local kids looking for food. I did not share the details because it is nothing you should concern yourself with.

Nothing will interrupt our supply route."

Kliest stared at Volmer as the silence grew longer and longer. Kliest's blue eyes stared Volmer down for a length just short of eternity. Volmer's sweat engulfed his brows.

"I am concerned, Franz. First, you are shot while drunk in a bar, then rumors of a so-called resistance begin circulating the country, and now a group of men start poking around the railyards. If I did not know better, I would think you have a small problem brewing right under your nose, but I feel you are too drunk or stupid to realize it. You have become oblivious to the war around you and have become complacent. I have taken matters into my own hands and out of yours. I suggest you tighten up your grasp on this little town of yours before it swallows you up." Kliest locked the crate and turned back to Volmer, "Franz, I like you, but this is business. I do not need any more friends; I need people I can count on. Can I count on you, Franz?"

"Absolutely, sir. I shall rededicate my command to establishing a tighter control of this area. I shall double my efforts. I have moved more troops to the railyard."

"I hope so for your sake, or you will end up disgraced. I will bury you in all the ways you can imagine. The name Volmer will never be heard from again...understand?"

Volmer stood tall. "Yes sir."

"Have your men load these crates in my car, I would like to enjoy a quick bite and then I am heading back to Paris."

Volmer nodded and the two returned to the dining area where laughter was filling the room as one of Volmer's men was describing his sexual conquests in every country. The laughter died down as Volmer and Kliest returned. Volmer pulled aside Hauptman and told him to have the crates loaded into the Major's car.

Hauptman grabbed two soldiers outside the cabin. Each man grabbed a crate and followed him down the path to the Major's waiting car. Sully carried the second crate, as he followed the two men in front of him.

Mason saw the soldiers approaching. He noticed Sully

trailing behind. Leading them was Hauptman, whom he recognized right away. Pulling his driver's hat down tight, he exited the driver's side.

"These are for the Major," Hauptman said as they approached. Mason nodded and proceeded to the back of the car. He opened the trunk and placed the first crate inside. Sully placed the second crate next to the first. Mason closed the trunk as they turned and headed back to the cabin. Sully gave Mason a subtle glance as he slowly walked away from the car. Mason returned to his driver's seat wondering what was in the crates. He had a fairly good idea, but he really wanted a look. Unfortunately, the two padlocks told him he would have to wait.

36

MARIE WAS TOLD THAT DINNER should be served. She started preparing the plates as Carolina prepared the sauce to accompany the main dish, once again adding Phillipe's mixture to the thick, rich, lemon butter sauce.

Marie placed the golden-brown Frenched chicken on each plate, along with some Lyonnaise potatoes. *Haricot verts* provided the perfect accompaniment with their green and yellow color. Carolina added the thick creamy sauce, and the plates were as beautiful as they were deadly. The one problem with their plan was that they could not taste anything to see if the sauce was too overpowering so, every time they served a dish, they waited a few minutes to get confirmation that everything was ok. They waited in silence wondering if someone would come barging through the door, or if the evening would simply continue.

Carolina placed three plates on her tray and Marie the other three. They entered the dining area and placed them in front of their guests, First Kliest, then Volmer, Hauptman and the rest. Volmer grabbed Marie around the waist as she walked by and pulled her in close. She mildly resisted and tried to play it off.

"I would like to introduce you to my guests."

Marie looked up at the men around the table, dressed in perfectly fitted and pressed uniforms, buttons and buckles shining. The sight of these terrible men staring back at her made her uneasy. The only saving grace for Marie, if everything went as planned, she would never have to see any of them again. Inside she reveled in that thought. The night she saved Volmer's life, had led to this evening. The resistance had started and grown, she and Sully were together, and they were fighting a secret war against a terrifying enemy. Tonight, would be their first victory in what she hoped would be many.

Volmer's voice brought her back to reality as he told his

guests about her cooking and how she had always taken special care of him. That comment was met with snickering and laughter. Marie was disgusted at the remark and silently said under her breath, "Enjoy your last meal." She broke away from Volmer, "I must return to the kitchen. Gentleman, enjoy. I assure you after you try this meal, you will think you have died and gone to heaven." Before she left, she topped off every glass with a 1933 Chateau Latour.

She entered the kitchen and leaned back against the wall as the door shut.

"Are you ok?" Collette asked coming over.

Marie nodded, "I just can't wait to get out of here. They are vile human beings. I hope Phillipe got it right. I hope each of them suffer. I almost wish I could be there to watch Volmer slowly die in front of my eyes."

They waited as the main course was enjoyed. Knowing the evening was almost over, a quiet calm came over the kitchen as Carolina prepared her chocolate cake for dessert. The icing was a mixture of butter, cacao powder dark chocolate, and poison. The richness of the cake would cover all other tastes. The men were now five bottles of wine and two of champagne into the night. She could probably serve them Phillipe's concoction in a bowl, and they would not notice. Placing a large slice on each plate, Carolina went back into the dining area and served the slices with a scoop of locally made caramel ice cream and homemade whipped cream. The men laughed the entire time at jokes she could not understand.

The one man not laughing was Kliest. He smiled occasionally, but mostly seemed unamused by the amateurish antics of his subordinates. He passed on the cake and rose to announce his departure. Volmer stood and nearly knocked over his chair. All the men stood and in drunken unison yelled, "*Heil* Hitler." Volmer followed his friend to the door. Kliest turned around. "Enjoy your night, Franz. I expect tomorrow you will regain control of your people and your town. If you do not, I will be back to do it myself." Kliest pulled on his gloves and jacket and left.

Sully was stationed at the bottom of the path with another man as Kliest appeared. Mason perked up in his seat and exited the vehicle. Shielding his face, he opened the door to the back of the newly polished Mercedes as Kliest approached. The car was parked under two lights, neither of which were directly above. Shadows covered the car and the ground as bugs flew around the lights. Sully walked behind Kliest accompanying him to his car. Kliest arrived disgusted and removed his coat, he handed it to his driver, "Take me back to Paris."

Mason nodded as Sully passed the car and headed down the gravel road on a patrol. Mason got in the front seat and the car pulled away. Kliest stared out the window as they slowed down near Sully.

"Why are we stopping?" he asked as Sully quickly opened the door and slid in with his gun pointed at Kliest.

Mason sped away as they pulled out of the back lot and onto the main street.

"Who are you? Kliest asked Sully, who said nothing as Mason removed his hat. Mason slowed down and turned around briefly, "Hello Johan, been a long time. You're not going back to Paris; in fact, you will never see Paris ever again." Sully leaned in and with the butt of his gun, knocked Kliest out. His body slumped against the door as they drove off into the night.

WITH VOLMER AND HIS MEN sufficiently stuffed with poisoned food and drink, the night was winding down. Collette and Carolina were cleaning up in the kitchen as Marie cleaned the dining room. Volmer and his men had retired to the main hotel for nightcaps and cigars. Marie was calm and calculated as she cleaned up as quickly as she could; the three of them needed to get out of there. She turned to head back to the kitchen when Volmer appeared with two glasses of champagne. He closed the door and locked it.

"My dear, I wanted to thank you for a wonderful meal."

Volmer's words slurred as he spoke. He was unsteady and sweat glistened on his forehead. He was a disgusting sight.

"You do not need to thank me," Marie replied as she put down the linens she was carrying.

Volmer stumbled toward her, "Have a drink with me. I would like some company."

Marie backed away to the other side of the table, "You're drunk, you should lie down."

"That's exactly what I had in mind, lying down with you."

"That is not going to happen." Marie replied, slightly smirking.

Volmer's voice rose as he followed her around the table. Every time he took two steps, she took two steps. "I gave you the pleasure of cooking for my guests tonight; I expect something in return for my hospitality. I could very easily close your café and you would not be able to cook for anyone. I don't want to do that, but I need you to meet me halfway, preferably on that couch over there." Volmer smiled at his attempt at humor, his teeth red from wine.

"Lieutenant, please, I need to go." Marie headed for the door and Volmer in an instant was between her and the door. He nearly fell into the door, while regaining his balance. He put the two glasses down and slowly walked toward her.

He stumbled forward as he grabbed for her. Marie stepped back and Volmer fell forward again, his two hundred-plus pound frame falling. Volmer landed with a thud, his head hitting the edge of the table. He hit the ground on his right side and began laughing as he rolled over.

"Oops," he said with a drunken smile. Marie ran over to the bookcase and found *The Count of Monte Cristo*. She pulled it open and grabbed the Colt inside. Turning back to Volmer, who was pulling himself off the ground, she pointed it at him. "Don't make me use this."

Volmer stared at her, staggering back and forth. He broke out in a drunken laugh at the sight of the gun. He started to cough as he laughed, grabbing one of the linens from the table. He coughed into it leaving a reddish saliva residue on it. He threw it aside and looked at Marie. She knew the reddish liquid was not wine but blood. Volmer's stomach lining was starting to bleed from the amount of poison he had ingested.

He looked at the linen on the ground and coughed again into his hand. He looked at the blood and then at Marie. "What have you done to me?"

"I have done nothing to you. I think you should sit down; you don't look well."

He held onto the table as he looked at her. The color in his face draining with every second. Marie just stared back at him with a mixture of anger and satisfaction. Anger at the actions of this disgusting man and satisfaction that he was beginning a slow, painful death. She was just sorry she would not be around to see it.

Volmer lost his balance and fell to one knee, eventually rolling over on his back. Marie walked over and stood over him.

"Are you going to save me again? I thought you were my guardian angel?" he whispered, staring up at her.

Marie chuckled slightly. "No, I am the other angel. Goodbye, lieutenant; I suggest you make your peace with God."

She stepped over him, put the Colt back in the book, and reached the door and unlocked it. She took one last look at the man on the floor whose head had fallen to the side. He was still breathing but not for long.

She exited the room and closed the door, locking it with the key which she tossed into the plant in the hallway. Heading back to the kitchen, she met with Collette and Carolina. The three quickly headed back to the truck. Marie was shaken so Carolina drove. The three women had accomplished their plan. The night was not over yet, they were heading to Phillipe's farmhouse where hopefully one German major would be their next victim.

37

MASON NAVIGATED THE DARK STREETS carefully, with one eye on Kliest in the rear-view mirror. Kliest had regained consciousness and had a look of smugness on his face. Sully sat next to him with the major's Luger pointed at him.

Kliest exhaled as if this entire episode were just one large inconvenience. He looked out the window at the passing fields like a small child on a Sunday drive with his parents.

Phillipe's farm was several miles outside of town. They took a roundabout route to avoid checkpoints. After several miles of bumpy driving, Kliest finally spoke up. "So, who are you?" he said turning to Sully.

"Shut up," Sully replied.

"Mason, I see you now have an underling to do your dirty work for you. I imagine that was the only course of action when you realized how incapable you are of coming after me alone."

Mason looked at him in the mirror. "You know, you're still an asshole."

"Why do you always resort to name calling? We are just having a nice conversation."

"Shut up," Sully said again.

"I'm curious," the major said, turning back to Sully. "Is that all you ever say? Shut up?" Kliest mimicked Sully's New York accent. "Has Mason told you how I was able to snatch his precious Collette from right under his nose? Oh, he was so upset with me. Mason, did you tell your friend here, how I disappeared right in front of you? That must have been frustrating for you. I wish I could have seen your face."

"You know what," Mason said as they reached the dirt road leading to Phillipe's farmhouse. "You may have disappeared that night, but I did get Collette back and kept the painting, so I'd say I did pretty well. And being that you are riding in your own car as my prisoner, I would say I have done well again. You're a piece of shit and you always will be. You cannot help it. It is just so natural for you to be subhuman, you and all your Nazi friends. You think you're invincible, but I'm gonna take you down one by one."

Kliest laughed at this notion. "Mason, once again you are too busy celebrating to see the real picture. You are so predictable you make my job easier. I do not expect you or your friend to see that through your hatred for me. Let's just try to get through the night together. Maybe you will begin to see the error of your ways?"

Kliest turned back to the window as the car rumbled up the dirt road.

Mason laughed. Kliest looked back at him, "I'm glad you find me amusing."

"You are not the reason I am laughing," Mason said as he reached the entrance to the farm. "I think it's funny that you actually believe you're going to live through the night."

They pulled into the farmhouse yard and parked around the back of the barn, out of sight from the road. Mason noticed that Collette and the others were not there yet. He had no way of knowing if they succeeded and were on their way or had been detained at headquarters. He had a good feeling that Collette, Marie, and Carolina were in route. He had no reason to think otherwise.

He and Sully exited the vehicle and stood beside it as Phillipe emerged from the barn. Looking like an ironworker in his heavy leather apron and work gloves, Phillipe approached, happy to see them. He removed his glove and the three shook hands. Phillipe leaned over to get a look at Kliest who stared straight ahead.

"Was he any trouble?" he asked looking up to Mason.

"No, he's been fine. He has no idea what is in store for him."

"Any word from the women?" Phillipe said with a touch of concern.

Both Sully and Mason shook their head.

"Is everything ready in there?" Mason said with a nod to the barn.

"Yes, we are all set. The pit is ready for your guest."

The three men heard a sound in the distance and Mason walked slowly to the edge of the barn. He looked out and saw two headlights coming up the dirt road. They shook back and forth, and Mason knew it was the truck. He cautiously walked toward the gate as the truck turned in. He kept one hand on the pistol at his side as the truck approached. It slowed and stopped, and Mason could finally relax. The three women had returned in one piece. Collette jumped out holding *The Count of Monte Cristo* and embraced Mason, saying nothing.

He kissed the top of her head, "You smell like a chef," he said smiling at her. "Did you need to use the book?"

"No...thankfully," she responded, leaning into him. "Volmer collapsed before Marie needed to use it."

Marie and Carolina approached. "It's good to see you both," Mason said as they smiled at him.

The group reunited at Kliest's side door. Everyone took a glance in at their prisoner like children at a zoo getting a closer look at an exotic animal. Kliest sat stoically staring straight ahead, pretending to be oblivious to the growing horde outside his door.

Mason looked at Sully. "You ready?" Sully nodded and Mason went to the side door. He opened it, "Get out," he said coldly.

Kliest sighed and looked at him, "Oh you do know other words," he said sarcastically.

"Shut up," Sully replied with a grin.

Kliest slowly got out and stood up. He wiped some dirt off his sleeves as he stood and looked around. He was standing on the dirt near an entrance to a large barn. A slightly unpleasant odor hung in the air. He stared at his captors one at a time. He recognized Carolina as one of the servers at the dinner and Marie as the apple of Volmer's eye. He immediately knew he had been conned into a dinner celebration and Volmer had clearly underestimated his townspeople as being loyal to the Reich. He looked from Marie to Collette and smiled. "My dearest Collette, how lovely to see you again. "

Collette stared back, emotionless.

"Let's go," Sully said as he pushed the major in the back.

Kliest lurched forward and stumbled a bit but regained his balance. He followed Mason through the doors of the barn and into a large room. A table on the left side was covered with containers of various farming pesticides. Several glass containers and syringes lay next to them. On the right side, a large burlap covered pile of fertilizer was against the far wall. Kliest looked at the far end of the room where an open pit was surrounded by stones. Sully pushed the Major forward again toward the pit. The smell from the pit grew more toxic as Kliest approached. He was doing everything to maintain his composure but with every passing second, he grew more uneasy; his eyes began to itch.

"That's far enough," Sully said. "Turn around."

Kliest turned to face Mason and Sully, his back to the pit.

"Is this your solution, shoot me and dump me in an old well? Seems rather barbaric, even for you Mason."

"Shut up and listen," Sully said. "You have a choice. You can talk and answer the questions we have, or you can die in a rather unsavory way. You sent several people to London to try to kill us; you failed. How many more operatives are in London? It's quite simple; the amount of information we get determines how long you get to continue living. I am prepared to offer you a deal. I have the backing of the parliament of the British empire. You can die here in this old farmhouse in that pit behind you, or you can give me information and be offered asylum as an informant in London for the remainder of the war."

Kliest stared back at Sully and then turned to Mason, "This must be confounding for you. I can feel your hatred for me and your desire to end my life. To find out that I could be an asset to the British empire must eat away at you. I can live out the war in a cushy manor house outside of London, and there is nothing you can do to me." He turned back to Sully. "Why would I betray my country?"

"You've been poisoned." Mason stepped forward. "You're dying right now even though you don't know it yet. Your insides will begin to shut down in the coming days and you will essentially rot from the inside out until your heart gives out. You see this?" Mason held up a small vial of clear liquid. "This is medicine that will counteract the poison. For every answer you give, I will put some aside for you. It won't cure you entirely, but it will help."

"You expect me to believe you are going to save my life?"

"No, I don't; but you don't have much choice, do you?"

"What assurance do I have that you are telling me the truth?"

"None, you're going to have to trust us." Mason said, smiling arrogantly. "First question: What is Totenkopf?"

Kliest smiled at the word.

"Mason, once again we find ourselves in this little cat and mouse game of what is real and what is not. You think you know what is going on but, as usual, you do not. Do you really think I would betray my country without assurances from the British government? Take me back to London and I will give you the information you request but not until I have written confirmation of asylum."

"How many of your people are still in London? Are they going after Churchill?" Mason said impatiently.

"Take me to London; I hear it is lovely this time of year. "

Mason stared as Kliest smiled back. He stepped forward and grabbed the major by the lapels of his uniform. He pushed Kliest back to the edge of the pit, "Totenkopf," Mason said firmly.

"London," Kliest said through his gritted teeth.

Mason pushed him closer to the edge.

"Mason...don't. We need him alive." Sully stepped forward and touched Mason on the shoulder.

"I can't let him live. I do not believe a word that comes out of his mouth. I would not believe any information he would provide. He is going to lead us on a wild goose chase to keep himself alive."

Mason turned to Sully. With his right arm he removed his pistol and pointed it between Kliest's eyes while he held him up with his left arm. Kliest grabbed at Mason's uniform as he moved his hand over Kliest's throat. He began squeezing the major's throat while holding the pistol barrel against his face, "I am going to count to three. One...two...three."

Mason pulled the trigger and the gun clicked.

"No!" Kliest yelled, his eyes wide with fear. "Ok, ok I will talk."

Mason threw him to the ground. Kliest looked up in terror as Mason pointed the gun at him again. Click. Still no shot. Kliest tried to back away on his back pushing the ground with his hands and feet. Mason followed slowly continually pulling the trigger. The group looked on with concern as Mason followed Kliest.

Kliest finally gave up and laid down on his back with his hands up. He closed his eyes and exhaled, lying on the ground a broken man, mentally and physically. He coughed and wiped his mouth. A small mixture of saliva and blood transferred to the back of his hand.

He looked up at Mason who smiled back at him. Kliest coughed again as he tried to regain his breath.

"Your end has begun," Mason shook the vial of medicine in front of Kliest

"You said you would help me if I talked," Kliest said pleading his case.

"Start talking. Give me names of your people," Mason said, staring at his nemesis lying on the dirty barn floor.

"There are no more names, at least I don't know them. I am telling the truth. I created Totenkopf at the behest of Himmler. He wanted assassins who could blend into society and mirror their targets in actions and looks. Men, women, old, young. They are trained to kill or die. If they fail in eliminating their target, they take their own lives. They are people who have truly little in life, so they have given theirs to the Reich in return for great riches for them and their families. I sent some early recruits to London after you, but they didn't succeed."

"But they ultimately kill themselves so there are no riches. I imagine their families never see any of it, those riches end up in your pocket. In fact, I am quite sure those riches are in two trunks in the back of your car," Mason said with disdain as he continued. "How do you live with yourself? Transporting people in cattle cars, stealing everything they have and then killing or enslaving them. There is a special ring in hell awaiting you."

"Spoils of war, Mason. I had a feeling it was you who was poking around the railyards. I am impressed. I am just glad you picked up my trail of breadcrumbs and came back to get me. I was not sure you would connect all the dots. I am glad you took it upon yourself to rescue some very scared women. I underestimated you. Those women had very little to offer, so I will let you have them. There will be plenty more train loads you can't save." He wiped his mouth with the back of his hand. "Mason, if you kill me you will join me down below in that ring of hell. Wrath is a deadly sin, Mason. Choose wisely."

Mason looked at him in disbelief, "How did you know about the train?"

"A little voice told me."

"Who's?"

"A nervous little British one."

Mason knew exactly who he was talking about. Roger Knightsbridge from the War Offices. He was always giving Mason classified information; now Mason realized he had been fed that information.

"I trust you know Roger?" Kliest said, his arrogance reappearing.

"Is that how you got to John Cleary?" Sully said, exasperated.

"And the others." Kliest replied. "Roger was very valuable to me. He was quite forthcoming with information in exchange for some of those riches we talked about. "

Sully was dismayed. "Who killed John Cleary?"

"One of our more beautiful and deadly women. Unfortunately for me, she succeeded against her first target but not her second." He looked at Mason with a smirk.

Mason turned and looked at Sully.

"Get him up." Sully said.

"You really want to take this piece of shit back to London with us?" Mason said with disdain.

"That's the last thing I want to do but my orders are what they are."

Mason dragged Kliest to his feet. Kliest smiled slightly, "Perhaps we can be friends now since we will be travelling together."

Mason turned back to him. "Shut up," he said in unison with Sully.

They pushed him back toward the others and threw him to the ground in front of everyone. Sully explained the plan, much to Collette's chagrin. She looked at Mason and her displeasure was evident all over her face. Mason gave her a "nothing I can do" shrug.

Collette stood for a minute in shock. They had come all the way to France to find this guy, and now were going to drag him all the way back to London with them.

Mason dragged Kliest to his feet and pushed him over to the table. "Stay here."

"Gladly," Kliest said as he smiled. Mason ignored him, not giving him the satisfaction.

He walked back to Sully and they began talking about their plan. Both men hated the idea of taking a prisoner with them, but they saw no other option. Sully had to get word to London about Knightsbridge. He had access to very high-level intelligence and needed to be stopped right away. He would use the radio hidden in the truck to call London immediately. He would also request an emergency extraction for them. Mason, Collette, Sarah, the other women, and himself. London had said they were on their own to get home, but the stakes had changed.

"I hate the idea of this guy living out his years in London." Sully said to Mason as they stood with their backs to the group.

Kliest was standing near the table wiping dirt from his uniform when everyone was startled by the sound of a gunshot. Mason and Sully turned around quickly with their guns drawn. Kliest lay on the ground gasping for breath, blood on his chest. Standing over him holding a book by Alexander Dumas in her left hand and a gun in her right was Collette. She fired one more shot between his eyes and Kliest fell limply to the ground.

Everyone stood there shocked as Collette turned around, "I couldn't let him live, not after what he did to me and those women."

Mason stared back in silence and then turned to Sully, "I guess we don't need to worry about him living out his days in London anymore."

"I was worried the whole time that you were going to kill him." Sully said stunned.

"Me too," Mason replied as they both stood their staring at the dead major.

Sully turned to Mason and then back to Collette, he said nothing. He did not blame Collette; he would have done the same thing.

38

MASON SAT QUIETLY IN THE front seat of Phillipe's car. Sully drove and Marie and Collette sat in the backseat. They were on their way to meet up with Luc for their ride back into free France. Mason replayed the scenario repeatedly in his head. He was ecstatic that Kliest was dead and rotting in a well in Phillipe's barn, but he felt for Collette. He felt guilty for not knowing how much pain she had suffered at the hands of Kliest. If he had known, he never would have let him live. Collette had never spoken about the ordeal and Mason had never asked. She kept telling him she was fine. He wiped a tear away from his eye as he looked out the window. He knew that killing Kliest would not bring her the peace she so badly craved.

Sully and Marie decided to stay in France. Sully felt he could do better behind enemy lines than on the home front and Marie needed help. Retaliation would come from the Nazis and he did not want her to face that alone. They decided to close the café and disappear into Paris for the time being. He had briefed the higher ups in London, and for now, they would stay.

He had fought extremely hard to keep Marie's love for him alive through challenging circumstances, and it was time for them to stay together. It was a complicated existence but one they had to try. If he went back to London without her, he would regret it the rest of his life. They would help Ganoux grow the resistance, and with Mason in London he would have the support back home. He had asked Mason what his thoughts were on him staying. Mason agreed with him. "You can't deny how you feel. I tried for many years and my feelings for Collette were always there. When we reconnected, I vowed not to let her go. Life is too short, and in these days for many people, it's even shorter."

Mason was happy that Ganoux would have the support of

people like Sully, Marie, Phillipe, Carolina, and everyone else who would join up to fight the Nazis in the shadows. Sully would help retrieve the bodies left behind in the sunflower field, and Kliest's driver. They would make them permanently disappear before heading to Paris They decided to leave the body in the mausoleum and Phillipe would make a mixture to prevent the rancid smell of decomposition from drifting too far.

They reached the rendezvous point and Mason turned to Sully, "I guess this is it."

Sully nodded, "Yep, for now. Something tells me our paths will cross again at some point."

The four got out of the car and said their goodbyes. They hoped to meet again in peacetime to celebrate the small victory they had achieved by taking out several high-ranking members of the Nazi command in Lien. And, of course, Kliest a terrible man who had hurt many people and would have hurt many more.

Mason and Sully shook hands and embraced. "Take care, my friend. I am sure we will be in touch," Mason said as he patted him on the back. "Hard to believe this all started with you thinking I killed John Cleary."

Sully chuckled, "Yep, since then we have had quite a time. On my call to London I told them about Roger, and they were going to track him down immediately. Keep me posted on that situation. They will need your help."

"Keep in touch all right? I am only a covert radio call away." Mason smiled as he and Collette turned toward Luc's truck.

"Hey Mason," Sully said as they walked away, "Do you think Kliest was telling the truth about there being no plot against Churchill?"

"I don't know. Like I said, I do not believe a word that man says, and luckily for us we don't have to hear him talk anymore."

Collette got in the front seat of Luc's truck and Mason climbed back into his wine barrel for the ride back across the border. It was early morning and Luc was on his usual run. In approximately twenty minutes they would be back at the winery with Anna's sister and they could all start heading back to London.

Sully had arranged for a plane to arrive tonight in the fields of the winery and take Mason, Collette, Sarah, and the rest of the women to London where they would be offered the chance to stay. The British government was ecstatic over the elimination of the two German commanders, so they offered the women sanctuary as a reward for their service. They also would have the chance to debrief fifteen women captured by the Nazis. They hoped to gain some valuable information from them. It was another small victory for a few victims of the Nazi regime.

As Mason bounced around in his barrel, he thought again about Kliest. He was glad he was dead but also felt like there was unfinished business. Kind of anticlimactic. A plot to assassinate the British Prime Minister, if successful, would end the war immediately and all of Europe would be under German control. A brazen plan but Mason was not sure Kliest would have been given the authority to carry it out. He began to accept the idea that Kliest came after him and Sully as a sort of game, just to let Mason know he could get to him. Mason took a deep breath of dried white wine and pictured Kliest rotting away in the French countryside. He closed his eyes and exhaled. One less piece of shit in the world.

They reached the winery and reunited with Sarah. She was so happy to have Collette back and she thanked Mason again for the great news that they would be heading to London that night. She kept telling Collette how happy she would be to see Anna again. Collette could imagine the scene of the two sisters reuniting. Anna had no idea that this was happening. They made sure to not share any news about the reunion.

Six women decided to stay in Europe and head south to Spain, hoping to eventually find information on their loved ones. That left nine women including Sarah who would be brought to freedom.

The plane arrived and landed quietly on the grass field after dark. With extraordinarily little cargo other than people and two wooden crates filled with stolen valuables, they were back in the air quickly. The route would take them south and then out over the water to turn north again, therefore avoiding the mainland and any German anti-aircraft fire.

Collette slept on Mason's shoulder with Sarah asleep next to her. Mason sat stoically staring straight ahead. Collette's bag sat next to him, *The Count of Monte Cristo* sticking out of the top. He reached for it and opened it. For a few moments he stared at the gun in the cutout inside, the gun that ended Kliest's life. He smiled briefly, slapped the book closed, and then shut his eyes.

The plane landed two hours later at a British airfield outside of London. The cargo was top secret, and the plane was met by Sully's men. All the women would be taken to a hospital nearby for evaluation. Mason would accompany them and eventually take Sarah home. He needed to be debriefed about the entire operation, so as Collette went home and Sarah was at the hospital, he would meet with British SIS and explain why they were missing one high ranking German major on their plane.

Sully had briefed his people and rumor had it, Churchill was less than pleased.

"Be careful," Collette said as she got into the car for the ride into London.

"Are you ever going to stop telling me to be careful?" he said smiling.

"Nope." She replied with a wink."

"I will see you soon. You can tell Anna her sister is coming home today."

Collette's car pulled away as Mason and the others waited for the truck to take them to the hospital.

"As soon as I am done, I will come to the hospital and we will head back so you can see your sister," Mason said as Sarah got ready to get into the truck.

Wiping tears away, she looked at Mason, "I can't believe

it. Thank you. Is it odd that I don't know what to say to her?"

"Start with hi, you'll figure it out from there."

She nodded and climbed into the back of the truck.

Mason was rushed into a hangar on the airfield and he sat outside a small office. A few men stood guard as he waited to be called into his debrief. After a few minutes, the door opened and a man appeared, "Mason, they are ready for you."

He approached the door and walked inside. Two men sat behind a desk and stared at him as he entered.

"Come in, Mason."

Mason did not recognize the first man, but he was inconsequential sitting next to the man puffing on a cigar. Winston Churchill sat at the other table staring at him as Mason sat.

"Good evening Mr. Prime Minister."

"Mason, it is good to see you alive and well. So, tell me why I am missing two especially important men here, Sully and my German prisoner."

The booming voice of the Prime Minister shook Mason a bit as smoke filled the room. Mason began to tell the story and he attempted to explain the crazy ordeal he had just been a part of. Churchill listened intently and only interjected a few times. He seemed fascinated by the plans of a ragtag group of men and women who managed to deal a substantial blow to the Nazis in a way that would hopefully attract more people to their cause. The Prime Minister was especially amazed at the fifteen women Mason had rescued from the train car. Mason told him of their determination that the plot on his life was not a reality.

"That is good to hear, but I am sure there will be others," he said as he exhaled his cigar smoke toward the ceiling.

Churchill expressed interest in meeting the rescued women and welcoming them to London, especially Sarah. He wanted to congratulate her on being reunited with a family member under seemingly insurmountable odds. After the debrief, Mason was escorted along with the Prime Minister in Churchill's private car to the hospital.

Collette arrived back at her flat visibly exhausted and worn. Her father smiled slightly at the sight of her and embraced her for what seemed like a millennium. Her mother welcomed her home similarly. Anna stood in the doorway and waited for her chance. Collette saw her and immediately began crying. Anna ran over and they embraced. Collette's tears dripping on to Anna's head.

"I need to talk to you," she said as Anna looked up at her.

Collette led her into the living room, and they sat down on the couch. Angeline brought in some tea and cookies. Collette took a sip of tea and looked at Anna, who was eagerly awaiting the news from her trip.

In between tears, Collette took a deep breath. "Anna, we were able to find out what happened to your sister Sarah. The group of people I was with rescued a train full of German refugees and your sister was on board."

Anna sat back and the emotions of the words she just heard overcame her.

"Oh my gosh, where is she?" Anna tried to hold back her tears but was unable to. She wiped her face as her nose sniffled. She began shaking as she cried. Collette leaned over and hugged her, "She is coming home tonight. Right now, she is with Mason at the hospital. She is fine; it's just precautionary, and then they will both come here."

Anna cried on Collette's shoulder for a minute and then asked, "How did you know it was her?"

"She looks like you and she was one of the few who spoke English. After talking with her for a few minutes, I knew it was her." Collette smiled as Anna wiped her tears away. Anna sniffled and began to shake her head, "Sarah does not speak English, in fact, she barely speaks at all."

"Anna, she speaks very fine English, maybe she learned it recently."

Anna was still shaking her head slightly, "That's not possible, she has problems—problems learning. She has difficulty with even learning simple tasks. My parents always kept her home from school because she had so much trouble learning. She is extremely sweet but would hardly communicate with strangers, she was always too afraid."

Collette's color drained from her face as she sat back. "Oh my God…what have we done?" she said sitting back.

"What is it? Is it not her?" Anna asked as she saw the immediate concern on the face of Collette.

MASON ARRIVED WITH THE PRIME MINISTER under intense security at the hospital. He followed Churchill into the hospital, Churchill saluting the servicemen with his cane as he walked. Two guards followed behind as they were led into a private wing. They passed several rooms of patients and arrived at the waiting area. Some of the rescued women were sitting in the area drinking tea and coffee and eating some muffins and scones. Their eyes widened as Churchill walked in. One woman's scone fell out of her mouth as her jaw dropped.

"Welcome to London, you are all very brave women. You are safe here and will continue to be. You have my word; I will personally see to it," he said as Mason watched.

Some did not understand what was being said but they did not have to. The famous British Prime Minister was standing in front of them and that was enough.

Churchill turned to Mason, "Where is Sarah? I should like to say hello to her.

They walked down the hospital hallway past the main desk toward Sarah's room. A phone rang in the distance and an orderly answered. The woman placed the receiver on the desk and looked up, "Is there a Mason Wright here?"

Mason stopped, "Yes, that's me."

"You have a phone call. A woman named Collette is on the line. She says it is extremely urgent."

Mason turned to Churchill, "I'm sorry."

"Well go get your phone call, don't keep Collette waiting."

Mason walked over put down his bag and picked up the receiver, "Hello."

"Mason, it's not her. Sarah is not who we think she is."

"What are you talking about?"

"I spoke to Anna and she said it is impossible for that woman to be her sister."

"I don't understand."

"Mason, just go and get her; she is not who she claims to be."

Mason immediately thought of Kliest's words: "Assassins who blend into society. Mirror their targets. Old, young, man, woman."

He dropped the receiver and yelled to Churchill's men to secure him and get him out of the hospital. They immediately scooped him up and disappeared down the hallway toward the entrance. Mason ran to the room where Sarah was being treated.

He looked in and the bed was empty, the sheets pulled back. A nurse lay on the floor, bleeding from her neck. He walked over, removed his bag from his shoulder, and knelt beside her. There was no need to check for a pulse, she was already dead.

As Mason stood back up, he felt a sharp pain in his back as Sarah jammed a surgical scalpel deep into his shoulder, he fell forward over the dead nurse. Sarah closed the door quietly and locked it. Mason writhed as he tried to reach the scalpel in his shoulder blade. He rolled on the floor streaking the white tiles with red blood. Sarah came over and stood looking down at him, "Don't die on me yet, Mason." She kicked him in the ribs. He winced and she smiled, "That was for Kliest."

Mason struggled to speak as he spit some blood out, "You'll never get to Churchill."

"Churchill?" Sarah replied shaking her head "You think I am here to kill him? I am here to kill you."

Mason spit out some more blood, "You'll never make it out of here. "

"Let me worry about that," she said as she kicked him again. Mason rolled over and spit out some more blood. A man's voice could be heard on the other side of the door as he began pounding on it. "Open this door! Mr. Wright? Sir, are you okay?" The pounding continued.

Sarah turned and looked at the door and back at Mason. He lay on the floor in a pool of blood, some his, some from the dead nurse next to him.

"Like I said, you won't get out of here alive," he said as he tried to move. His ribs were broken from the two blows she had delivered to them. He coughed as he looked around for anything he could use to defend himself.

Sarah walked over and stood over him. He tried to reach for her but she kicked him in the face, blood from his mouth sprayed the wall behind him. He rolled over near the legs of the chair next to the bed. He began to lose consciousness when he felt searing pain as Sarah pulled the scalpel from his back.

"Mr. Wright?" the man yelled again from the other side of the door as the pounding continued.

Sarah looked at the door briefly as Mason gathered all his strength. He raised his right leg and swung his foot connecting with the side of Sarah's knee. It buckled as she collapsed to one leg. She fell backwards grabbing her knee and yelled out in pain. Mason was fairly sure he had dislocated her kneecap. He scrambled to get to his bag as Sarah tried to regain her balance, her right knee now bent in a most unorthodox manner. She looked over at Mason as she stood on one leg. She yelled as she dove toward him, the scalpel in her right hand. Mason rolled over and fired one shot into her chest as she landed on his legs. He kicked her off and fired again. Her lifeless body came to rest on the tiled floor with the scalpel rolling out of her hand.

Mason dropped the gun and fell onto his back, his head hitting the floor next to his bag and an old French novel, *The Count of Monte Cristo*.

39

COLLETTE ARRIVED AT THE HOSPITAL with Anna and they immediately were escorted to Mason's room. A hospital nurse met them at the door, "He will be fine; he has two broken ribs and a nasty bruise on his face. His back wound was deep so he will be receiving some medication for that."

"Can we see him?"

"Yes, of course."

The nurse opened the door and Mason lay in the bed on his back.

He looked up as the door opened and saw Collette and Anna followed by the nurse. He managed a slight grin through his bruised mouth.

"Hi, how do you feel?" Collette said as she approached.

"Lousy." Mason replied as he looked at her.

She leaned in and kissed him.

"Ouch," he said as she pressed on his ribs.

They talked for a few minutes and the nurse stepped in, "He needs his rest."

"I understand," Collette said. She kissed him one more time and they left the room.

A man met them in the hallway and explained the current situation. British intelligence had compiled the list of names of the women who had just arrived with them from France. The name Sarah Dressler was on the list and through an interpreter, he had located her, she was resting in a hospital room under heavy guard.

She had been in the train car, just too terrified to speak. She was still extremely afraid and had barely said anything except her name.

The woman they thought was Sarah was dead, but Anna's real sister was still here at the hospital. Anna was confused about the whole situation and so was Collette. She prayed that the woman in the hospital bed was Sarah Dressler, Anna's real sister, or the pain for Anna might not be something she would ever overcome.

Collette led Anna through the hallway to Room 11. "Are you ready?"

Anna nodded and Collette opened the door. Lying in the bed was Sarah Dressler, curled up in a fetal position, asleep. Anna approached her and she awoke, rolling over after hearing someone in the room. Anna stopped short when she saw Sarah's face. She burst into tears and ran to the bedside. Sarah seemed confused. Anna spoke to her in German as they embraced. Sarah was shaking as her younger sister held her tight. Sarah's eyes filled with tears as the two sisters cried together in an embrace. Collette stood at the door, her face was red from emotion. She looked up and Mason appeared in his hospital gown walking with a cane. Collette looked at Mason who was wiping tears away as he watched the emotional reunion.

"You're supposed to be in bed." Collette said in between sniffles.

"I know, don't tell anyone."

"I can't believe we found her."

Mason wiped his face. "Honestly, I can't either. This is all because of you, you know that. From day one last year in Paris, you vowed to take care of Anna and find her family. I am utterly amazed by you." He kissed the top of her head as Anna turned to them.

"Come meet my sister, Sarah," Anna said through a tearful smile.

They walked over and Anna introduced them to her. Sarah looked at both of them and managed two words, "Thank you."

About the Author

Steven Knapp was born in New Jersey. After living overseas for the better part of the first decade of his life in Belgium, Germany, and Brazil, he returned to New Jersey. The experience of living overseas stayed with Steven, as he as always loved to travel.

A graduate of Seton Hall University with a B.A. in Psychology, he has been the owner of Steven Knapp Home Improvements LLC, for over 22 years. He started writing with no experience—just a story to tell. Steven is an avid reader with a special interest in the lesser-known stories of World War II era history. *The Secrets of St. Joanna* is his second novel in The Mason Wright Series. He is currently working on the third book in the series, *The Ruins of St. Vincent* while continuing to run his home improvement business, where he puts his creativity to work to help his clients bring their ideas to life.

Steven resides in New Jersey with his wife of almost 20 years, Lori, and their two cats, Sylvester and Bam. Spending time with family and friends, visiting New York City and listening to live music, and giving talks about his books at wineries, book clubs, and other venues are some of the places you will find them when not at home.

Follow Steven on his website: https://stevenknappwritings.com, on Facebook, and on Amazon. And Look for Book 3 in the Mason Wright Series, coming in 2021:

THE RUINS OF ST. VINCENT

Made in the USA
Middletown, DE
12 December 2020

27414973R00170